CW01625119

and the Lad from the Manor

A story written by an ex-miner, about two young miners from the early seventies and their adventures.

For comments email dj60271@gmail.com

David Jackson

The Author

David Jackson was born into a poor working-class family in April 1956, and he had many fond memories of his childhood. Going to work and exploring seventies life as a young lad was an adventure for him, which taught him the values of respect for other people. He worked on the coal face for seventeen years, before spending the rest of his working life supporting adults with autism.

Email – jakeandsam53@gmail.com

Produced by Biddles Books, King's Lynn, Norfolk PE32 1SF

Preface

We day dream and explore our deepest thoughts of having an adventure, excitement, love and reliving fond memories of our youth, this story is to live and feel the 70s life.

Introduction

The 70s were, rough, tough adventurous times for the working class, there were plenty of jobs, beer was cheap, and the music was good. People would fight and then laughed, there was a culture of violence between rockers and skinheads, and everyone seemed to be a member of a certain group.

As we explore the seventies through the eyes of two young working-class lads, through fiction and nonfiction, it gives the reader chance to reflect and experience the adventures they had, but also to see that because people behave in a certain way, doesn't mean they're all bad. Life always challenges us, and can bring out the best of who we truly are.

To the Reader. While reading the story try playing the songs in the book, it creates an atmosphere to the scene.

All names in this book have been chosen from the internet and all names associated with the characters are a coincidence.

Please Note- This book is more appropriate to the sixteen plus reader, some of the text may appear to be offensive, as it describes working class life and language.

This book is completely the authors own work, free from professionals, proof reading the text and altering the story, which then gives the reader an idea of who the author really is.

Song for the introduction, *Working Class Hero* by John Lennon.

Jake's Childhood

Jake was born in 1956 at the local hospital in Worksop, his dad David and mom Phyllis, had previously got married because she was pregnant, in that day it was said, 'If you make your bed, then you can lay in it', and it was normal to get married in this way. His mom gave birth to his sister Rebecca, who had complications and after three weeks she sadly died.

When Jake's mom told him about Rebecca, he could always remember the look on her face, as she described the way she cared for her daughter, how she was christened in hospital, until the day she died. She said." In those days it was different, your Uncle Alf took your sister away to a lonely funeral", and to this day, Jake does not know where she is buried. Phyllis very rarely talked about Rebecca, but would never have forgot.

They first lived with Jake's Nan Lucy, and Grandad Bob, in an old end terraced house in Worksop. The front door looked straight onto the street, which had two stone steps that were always cleanly rubbed. Under the front window on the path next to the wall, was a grate, which the coal man would lift to pour the coal into the cellar below.

When you walked down the arch shaped brick passage, you entered a small concrete yard which was shared with your neighbour. At the bottom of the yard was the outside toilet next to an open outhouse, in which the tin bath was stored. To the left of the entrance passage was the green wooden back door, which was made from floorboards. As

you walked in, on the right was a small, round, cast iron tub, set in brickwork with a fireplace underneath, this was used to heat the water for washing. Next to this was an old cast iron mangle used to wring out the clothes. In the kitchen was a large coal fire place, with an oven to cook meat and bake pastries, and a stove which heated the water to have a bath.
Jake's nan Lucy, always wore a pinny, she was polite and never swore and preferred to say flipping instead. His grandfather Bob, was short and bold, he liked to have and drink of cider and smoked sixty park drive cigarettes every day.

Bob and Lucy both liked to have a bet on the horses, Bob worked at the local glassworks, and every lunch time he used to take bets to the bookies for his mates, and every street corner seemed to have a bookmaker. Bob used to study horseracing, but Lucy used to just slowly waggle her backside as she stuck a needle into a list of runner's names.
One day, Bob was looking through the newspaper at the horse racing results, and was amazed at what he had read.
"I don't believe that, all five races at Doncaster have been won with a rank outsider".
Lucy picks up her old pink national health service glasses, puts them on, takes her betting slip from out of the draw and starts to read it.

"What's their names again?". Bob starts to slowly read them out. "1.30pm Penny Piece 33-1". Lucy smiles as she checks her betting slip. "I've got that". Bob looks up. "What!". "Next". "2.pm Sugar 20-1". "I've got that, next". Bob started to go red in the face, he was getting angry and jealous. "2.30pm Joiner 25-1". "I've got that, next". Bob started to pace up and down. "3.pm Sugar and Spice 50-1". "I've got that, next". "I don't believe it". Bob was shaking his head as he was looking at the results, thinking, just one more race, the 3.30pm, she can't have this one. "3.30pm Table Top 100-1".

Lucy had a big grin on her face, as she took off her glasses and put them down on the table.
"I've got that one as well, it's my lucky day, how many winners have you got Bob?". Bob starts to shout and swear. "I don't believe it, you know how many fucking winners I've got".
Bob picked up the newspaper, screwed it up, threw it onto the floor, jumped up and down, turned around towards the chimney breast and banged his head on the wall. Lucy laughed, thinking grumpy old sod. "Here you are", and she handed Bob the betting slip. "Take five shillings for collecting my winnings".
Bob took Lucy's betting slip, feeling groggy wishing he hadn't banged his head, and promised himself that he would not do that again. He picked up his horse racing guide, and as he walked out of the front door, he threw it over the fence into the field.

For the first two years of Phyllis's marriage, David was in the forces and she didn't see much of him. When he came out they lived with Bob and Lucy for another year.

Bob and Dave got on well, one evening when they were playing darts together, they heard screaming and shouting from old Mr Taylor's next door. Lucy, Bob, Phyllis and David ran out into the backyard and saw a young girl of about seventeen, scantily dressed, running off up the ginnel. Mr Taylor who was around seventy years old, was stood in his underpants with his hands over his head, while Mrs Taylor, his wife, was hitting him with her old wooden walking stick.

Mr Taylor worked at the local fishing tackle shop, and had been knocking off a female assistant there called Chloe. He had brought her home thinking that his wife would be out for the day, but she came back home early and caught them shagging on the floor. Of course, this did not go down very well with Mrs Taylor and she gave out her own method of justice. She hit Mr Taylor that many times, he eventually fell to the ground, she then collected her clothes and left, and no one ever saw her again. Lucy and Phyllis were disgusted, calling him a dirty old man, but Bob and Dave stood grinning as they watched the show, and this was a talking point for many years to come.

When Jake was three years old, the council rehoused them, and they moved into a prefab. It was like a sectional garage but with rooms. It had a front and back garden, which looked onto an enclosed grassed area, which was shared by fellow neighbours.

As he grew older, he was left to fend for himself, times were safer then. He continually made bonfires, dug deep hole's, and went up to the local woods. If Jake had any toys, he would take them to pieces and leave them on the floor, or burn them on a fire. However, he had a fascination for toy soldiers, comics, and collecting cards about batman.

When he was ten, the council rehoused them, and they went to live in Manton, a large council estate that bordered the local mining village. It was small, brick, semi-detached house, the front looked out onto the main street and the back looked over the local cemetery. For years, Jake was too frightened to look out of the back window into the dark. The gardens were small at the front and large at the back, which was ideal, as many of the neighbours had pigeons and used to race them.
When they were moving to their new house, they carried their furniture round on a wheel barrow, it was only a mile away. Old Charlie, a next-door neighbour helped them, and Jake can always remember his dad and Charlie pushing the settee on the wheelbarrow, chatting merrily as they went.

From the age of eleven to fourteen were adventurous times for Jake, he had a good Jamaican friend called Stephen. One sunny day they were walking through their local woods, which was close to a local private college, it was were young wealthy people went who were not bright enough to go to university.

As Jake and Stephen followed the winding path they heard some lads, they looked behind and saw about ten youths who seemed quite tall running towards them, shouting." Get here you little bastards".

Jake and Steve started to run, but it was difficult running through the brambles. The college lads were quick and so close, they could see their faces and were enjoying the hunt. Jake's friend Steve, knew he could not keep up. "Run Jake, don't wait for me".

Jake ran like a deer, jumping over the bracken, running along the large fallen trees, until he got to a clearing in the woods, which brought him onto the main road. He looked back, and he couldn't see his friend. Jake paused, frightened to go back into the woods, he caught his breath and decided to backtrack slowly to see if he could find him. As he stepped forward to walk into the woods, Steve suddenly walked out crying, blood coming from his nose, his clothes torn, Jake was shocked.

"What have they done to you Steve?".

"They have thrown me into the nettles, kicked and punched me, I played dead, so they became frightened and ran off, they were not bothered if I died". Steve wiped away his tears and they made their way home, they promised never to talk about what had happened that day, and they never did.

Jake used to spend a lot of time on the Chesterfield canal, which is where he first learnt to swim. One day when he was twelve, he was stood next to the canal lock watching his mates swimming. Two girls, Cindy and Kelly, a little bit older than Jake came and stood each side of him. Suddenly, he felt himself being pushed, and heard a laugh as he fell into the canal. It was about six feet deep and he could not swim. Jake panicked, but started to do the doggy paddle, and somehow got to the side, grabbed hold of the edge of the brickwork, and pulled himself up. He stood there soaking wet, everyone was laughing, he was quite shocked because he thought he was going to drown, but also pleased that he had learnt to swim. They played football, cricket, went fishing, there was always something to do.
Jake and Terry had a stick business, they had a small old pram and would go to the local woodyard and purchase sleeper ends, take them back to Jake's, chop them up into sticks, and made them into bundles. Terry and Jake then went door to door selling them to the locals.

Jake learnt to read, write, and make calculations through reading comics such as the Dandy, Beano, fishing magazines and racing papers.

Jake used to study the horse racing form and the different bets you could place. When he found a horse that may win, he would write out the bet on the back of a fag packet and walk down to the local bookies. He would

then stand outside and ask someone to take it in for him, or collect his winnings. Jake first started to bet on the horses at twelve years old, and most of Jake's friends used to bet or smoke.
It was 1971 and the grand national was due, Jake had studied the horse racing form for three weeks. He concluded that Specify would, in his opinion win. He told his parents, all his friends, but no one believed him, Jake put 25p to win on Specify. As Jake and his dad watched the race, it was very close up to the last furlong, Specify moved up from fifth to second place, with just 100 yards to the finish, on the last 50 yards Specify pulled in front and won by half a length. Jake jumped up and down for joy, his dad smiled, Specify had won at 28-1 and Jake had won £4.50.

Jake's school days were both fun and unpleasant, even more so when he went to the Priory, his local secondary school. He was always a small scruffy kid, and was at the bottom of the class for every subject, except for once in maths, where they put him into a higher group. He was feeling so proud of himself, but a week later they realised they had made a mistake, and put him back down. Being able to concentrate always escaped him, and while the teacher was talking, he would sit and daydream. Jake was always jealous of his friends, because they always seemed far more intelligent than him.
Strangely, all the teachers used to enjoy punishing Jake, he could tell, because when they were to deliver the

punishment they would always smile, and walk away looking satisfied, as though they had achieved something special and rewarding. It seemed he would receive the slipper or stick for, not paying attention, playing football, talking in class, the list was endless, but maybe he was also a little cheeky.

One day, Jake and six of his friends were caught playing football in the playground, by Mr Curtis the Deputy Head. (Rule was, that you could only play football on the school field). "Jake", he shouts. Jake looked round, you could not miss, Mr Curtis's deep voice. "What Sir?". Mr Curtis looked as though he had claimed another victim. "Come here, I want you". Jake walked slowly over and stood in front of Mr Curtis. "Are you supposed to be playing football in the playground lad?". Jake looked down at the ground, he knew what was to come. "No sir". Mr Curtis rounded up the lads with a glee in his eye. "All of you, go and stand outside Mr Salmon's office now". There was a small skinny lad, wearing grey school shorts and looked quite pretty, who was hiding behind Jake, he was terrified of Mr Curtis. "I can see you Matthew, you can't hide behind Jake, you know the procedure, go and wait outside my classroom now". All the kids were horrified, Mr Salmon was bad enough, but Mr Curtis was brutal in a different way. He had been a sergeant in the German army, but now he was a teacher. He had a special instrument of torture, a black plimsoll slipper with a swastika carved into it. Only special pupils received this privilege and Matthew was one. Matthew walked from behind Jake, and slowly walked over to Mr Curtis's classroom.

The other kids left the ball and walked in a line through the blue double doors, which led into a long corridor. Mr Salmon's office was at the very bottom, they stood along the corridor wall and lined up silently waiting outside of his door. Mr Salmon was feared for giving out severe physical punishment, even the toughest of the lads in school feared him. He did not use a slipper or ruler, but an old thick cane walking stick. No one messed with Mr Salmon, he was the man, master of punishment, demon of pain.
Jonathan, Jake's friend was frightened. “Let’s run off Jake”. Jake didn't think that was a very good idea.
“No Jonathan, it will mean we will get twice the punishment next time”. Jonathan was really trembling, but agreed. “Ok Jake”. Jake has an idea.” Right lads”. Everyone looks and listens with tension in their face.
“I will go in for the cane first, and when everyone has received their punishment, I will go in again, just to prove we are not scared”. Jake's friends looked away smiling, probably thinking it was a stupid idea, but didn't want to tell Jake and put him off, just so they could see what might happen.
At fourteen, you can be defiant and don't always realise how easy it is to make a stupid decision.
Jake went and stood in front of his six friends, the bell rang, it was end of the break, all the kids in the playground lined up outside the main doors, waiting to be

told when they can walk in. Mr Curtis was stood at the front of the line. “Ok children, in you go”.
The children walked into the school, down the corridor and into their classes. As each child passed Jake and his friends, who were stood outside Mr Salmon's office, they looked at them as though to say, “I'm glad it's not me”.

All the schoolchildren had gone into class, the corridor was quiet, they heard the staff room door open then close, which was at the far end of the corridor. The lads all looked round, it was Mr Salmon and he was walking down towards his office. When he reached them, he stood firm, he was small, had a shiny bald head, grey jacket, white shirt, blue tie, well ironed black trousers and spoke with a stutter.
“Mr Curtis as told m, m, me you were all p, p, playing football in the playground, you know your punishment, b, b, boys”, the lads all answered together. “Yes Sir “.
Jake began to smile at the way Mr Salmon stuttered, his friends all looked down trying not to laugh.
Mr Salmon walked up to Jake. “Are you g, g, grinning lad?”. Jake looked down trying to hide his smile.
“No Sir”. Mr Salmon was getting angry, he doesn't like cheeky school children. “Look at me w, w, when I am t, t, talking to you”. Jake looked up at Mr Salmon who was looking very serious, he started to laugh and could not stop.
Jake's friends were softly tapping their feet on the floor, patting their thighs, gritting their teeth, anything to stop

themselves bursting out into laughter. Mr Salmon was not amused. “Right, i, i, into my office now”.
Mr Salmon was furious, he grabbed hold of the back of Jake's neck with his right hand, opened the door with his left hand and as soon as it was open, threw Jake into his office. Jake went hurdling towards the wall as Mr Salmon slammed the door behind him.

There was a large, old wooden desk in the far-right hand corner of the office, with Mr Salmons old wooden chair with padded grey arms behind it. Jake looked at the desk, he could hear a clicking noise behind him. As he looked round, he saw Mr Salmon picking up the thickest cane walking stick he had ever seen. Jake took a big deep breath, thinking this is not so funny now. Mr Salmon walked over to Jake, with a large cane in his right hand. “Jake, bend over the desk”.
As Jake bent over the old large wooden desk, he felt Mr Salmon grabbing hold of his neck with his left hand, slightly twisted his thumb and index finger, securing the bottom of Jake’s neck and the palm of his hand pushing his head down, squashing his face cheek flat on the desk.

Mr Salmon had perfected the art of caning through many years of experience, and Jake could not move.
There was a pause and the noise of, shoo, shoo, from the cane going through the air.
Mr Salmon was getting warmed up, he had a lot of children to punish that day. Jake heard a sudden thud, followed by an excruciating pain on his backside, he gritted his teeth, another one followed shortly, his body

riddled with the pain, he had never felt anything like it before. Crack, a third blow, this brought tears to Jake's eyes, there was a short pause and Mr Salmon released his hold on Jake. He stood up and looked sadly at Mr Salmon, feeling ill with the pain, Mr Salmon points to the door. "Out Boy".

Jake slowly walked out of the office, but as soon as he saw his friends he stood upright and proud, this was false, he could hardly walk with the pain, all Jake's friends looked anxious.

Mr Salmon came out of his office, the cane held over his right shoulder. "Next". Ralph walked in, and the door slammed behind him. Jake walked to the back of the queue and went and stood with his friend Jonathan. "Are you ok Jake?". Jake gave a little smile. "Fine". Jake was in agony, but he was not going to show it. Jonathan wondered if Jake would keep to his word. "Are you going to go back in the queue, like you said you would Jake?". Rest of his friends were listening. "Yeah let's see what you are made off". Jake had now realised the painful consequences of what he had said. He thought he was being tough, but now he couldn't back down, he would not only lose face, but the ribbing from the lads would be far worse than the pain. "Course I am".

Jake got in the queue behind his mate Jonathan. Jake's friends went into the office one by one, and they all came out with a tear in their eyes, shoulders down as they quietly made their way back to their classrooms.

Mr Salmond stood at his door, there was only Jake and Jonathan left, and his friend was dreading this. "Next". Jonathan slowly walked into Mr Salmon's office. "Hurry up, I haven't got all day". Mr Salmon pushed Johnathan into the office and slammed the door behind him.
Jake stood there on his own, whack, whack, whack he heard from the office in quick succession.
The door quickly opened, and Jonathan came running out, crying, as he ran down the corridor.

Mr Salmon popped his head around the half-opened door, he had a big smile on his face. "Are you last Jake?", Jake stood there feeling very lonely and lost. "Yes Sir". Mr Salmon quietly walked back into his office and Jake followed.
The headmaster stood next to his desk, he looked puzzled as he looked at Jake. Jake, stood looking at Mr Salmon, still feeling the pain from his earlier punishment. "Have you already been punished once today Jake?". Jake doesn't answer the question, he daren't say yes, or no. "I don't know sir".
Jake knows he has blown it, Mr Salmon is too smart for him. He was wondering, how he had managed to get himself into this position. "Go and bend over my desk Jake, you seem to enjoy punishment, so punishment is what you will get".
As Jake leant over the desk, he heard Mr Salmon looking in the corner for another stick.
"Ah, this is a good one". The headmaster had found what he was looking for.

Jake looked round, he saw Mr Salmon holding a long thin riding crop in his hand, as he walked over to Jake he had a happy, but cruel smile on his face. Jake turned back round to look towards the top of the desk, his arms stretched out and he held the edge tightly, knowing of what pain was to come, promising himself that he would never do this again.

Mr Salmon held Jake at the back of the neck, pushing his head down hard on the desk. Whoosh Crack. Whoosh Crack. Whoosh Crack. The pain was tremendous, Jake was feeling sick, a pause at three strikes, Jake thought this was over, but Mr Salmond did not let go of his head. Whoosh Crack. Whoosh Crack. Whoosh Crack, all in quick succession. Jake was in agony, he thought that the punishment would never end, his backside felt like it was being severely burnt and he was going to die.

Mr Salmon let go of Jake's head, and Jake fell onto the floor crying. He walked over to the corner of the office and put his riding crop away with pride, he then walked back over to Jake and looked down at him.

“Get up Jake”, he said in a commanding voice. Jake jumped up straight away in case he got caned again, he stood as straight as he possibly could, considering the pain he was in and looked at Mr Salmon.

“Are you going to be c, c, c, clever again Jake?”. Jake had learnt his lesson. “No Sir. Sorry Sir”. He replied with a tremor in his voice, now holding back the tears.

“Good, now go to your c, c class Jake”.

Mr Salmon went and sat down in his chair, lent back and put both feet up on his desk, thinking, it's been a good day for caning.
Jake went over to the door, slowly turned the round brass door handle and opened it, slowly creeped out, closing it gently behind him. He stood there for a moment, pleased that the punishment was over, and knowing it was worth keeping to his word.

The office door suddenly opened, and Jake stopped smiling, he started to walk away from the office and never looked back as he limped with the pain. His fear of Mr Salmon overcame this, and Jake didn't stop walking until he got to the far end of the corridor. As he turned the corner, he bumped into Jonathan who was waiting for him.
"Are you ok mate?" Jake puts on a brave face. "Of course, mate, the cane doesn't bother me".
Jake stood upright, they went out of the doors and walked across the tarmac playground, towards another two classrooms annexed from the main school, Jake was thinking, that in the future, he would never mess around with the older generation.

Jake and Jonathan walked over to an old brick building that was divided into two, one side for woodwork, the other gardening. As they walked through the entrance, the gardening classroom was on the left, and the door was open. Mr Woodman the gardening teacher was waiting there, he knew why they were late and appeared

to be keen to leave, as he was looking at his watch.
Mr Woodman had arranged for a guest speaker called Derek to come in. He was to give the class a lecture on how to grow roses, you can imagine, a class of fourteen-year old's enthusiasm for this subject. Mr Woodman was pleased they had arrived. “Sit down lads “. The classroom was set up with four long lines of tables, with an isle at either end. Jake and Jonathan sat at the back of the class with the rest of their friends. A middle aged, tall slim man with ginger hair, dressed as a hippy, wearing a red cowboy hat, brown corduroy trousers and flowered shirt was sat down, half way down the front of the class facing the children.
“Ok everyone, we have with us today a gentleman called Derek, a local rose enthusiast who is going to introduce you to growing roses, I will see you all later”.
Mr Woodman walked over to the entrance door, picked up his coat, and quickly walked out.

Derek started to talk about growing roses, his voice was quiet and boring, but he looked very relaxed.
None of the kids were paying attention, Jake had an idea of what they may do. “Let's make up a song”. Jonathan knew of such a song. “I know, let's use the music from my mom's favourite song, this is how it goes. “The minute you walked in the joint”. Jake starts to join in. “Bum “. Jonathan stopped and thought.
“I could see you had a big suspender”. Jake adds another word. “Bum bum”. Jonathan carries on. “A real big

suspender. Big lill's so divine. I wouldn't mind spending a little time in bed, with you". Jake's turn.
"I know what to do, u, u, u". Jonathan and Jake sing together. "Big suspender, spend, a little time with me, bum, bum. Spend, a little time with me".
Jake and Jonathan started laughing and so did their friends around them.

They sang the full song together:

"The minute you walked in the joint.

Bum bum.

I could see you had a big suspender.

Bum bum.

Real big suspender.

Bum bum.

Big lill's so divine.

I wouldn't mind spending a little time, in bed, with you.

Bum bum.

I would know what to do.

Bum bum

Big suspender, spend a little time with me".

As they sang their song, more and more of the kids joined in, shaking from side to side. Derek suddenly had to leave the class. "Ok everyone, I just have to go to the toilet, I won't be long ". And no one noticed he had gone.

After about five minutes, Derek came back into the classroom and sat down. As he looked around, he was oblivious to the classroom chaos, paper airplanes were flying through the air, children were sitting on the tables, and Derek carried on talking about roses as though there was nothing happening. He seemed to be quite happy and in a world of his own. Little did they know at that time, growing roses, wasn't his only talent.

Matthew walked into the classroom, he had a bright red face, in tears and could hardly walk. He went to the back of the class and stood next to Jake. All the other school children looked at him, not feeling sorry for him, but glad it wasn't them. Jake smiles, “What's happened then Matthew?”. Matthew wipes away his tears, other children listen intently, they like a good story.
“Well, when Mr Curtis came over, he took me into his classroom, it was his free session, and no one would be there all afternoon. He went to his cupboard and pulled out a box of plimsolls. Next, he took out a black cape and put it around his shoulders, followed by a square hat with a piece of string hanging down, he had a strange type of joyful grin as he looked at me. He then described to me what he was going to do.
“Right Matthew, you see this black size twelve plimsoll”, and held it under my nose. It had a swastika cut out of the sole, sweaty and stunk, he went on to say. “I'm going to bend you over my desk and give you six of my jolly best “.

He pushed me against his old wooden desk, held me down by the scruff of the neck and spanked me, once on my left arse cheek and once on the right. He repeated this, three times and then let me go. I stood up waiting for him to say something, but he didn't, he just told me to go. I went to the toilet, stood on the sink and looked in the mirror, it's awful what he has done to me". Jake was interested in Mathews injury. "Let's look then Matthew." He looked over at Derek, he wasn't taking any notice, and slowly pulled his short trousers down and bent over. Jonathan and Jake were amazed, and shouted a couple of mates over. "Barney, Steve, come and look at this." They all stood round and couldn't believe their eyes. Matthew had a red shape, of a large plimsoll on each arse cheek, with a white, vivid swastika in the middle, everyone, was well impressed. There was only one thing Barney could say. "Mathew, you're the man".
Mathew carried on with the lesson talking to his friends, but he soon gained the reputation for being the only one in the school, to regularly receive that special, privileged slipper. Where ever he walked, both in the school and out in the street, children would put up their arm and shout, "MATHEW".

It was nearly home time and Mr Woodman rushed into the class, sweat dripping from his forehead, he sees the chaos in the classroom. "STOP".
Everyone quickly stops what they are doing and sits down, Jonathan and Jake were still giggling at the back.

Mr Woodman stood next to Derek at the front of the class, all the children payed attention. “I like to thank Derek for his lecture today on roses”. Mr Woodman started to clap, and the class joined in. “Would you like to say something Derek?”.
Derek looked around, his eyes were half shut, and he began to speak with a slurred voice. “I would like to thank you all for listening so intently to day, and I have really enjoyed it”. Mr Woodman was pleased with the classes response. “Thank you, Derek,”.
Derek took his blue coat from the back of his chair and put it on, he then picked up his brown leather bag, put it over his shoulder and walked out. As the door closed behind him, Mr Woodman spoke to the class, in a stern loud voice. “Right you lot, I have a good mind to report you all to Mr Salmon”. The bell rang for home time. “All of you, get out”.

All the kids ran out of the classroom, tripping over each other as they went, Jonathan and Jake slowly followed. As they walked out, Mr Woodman was sat on his desk, looking out of the window smiling.
Jonathan and Jake walked up to the school gates and there was a crowd of kids gathered around, they peeped through the crowd and could see a police car, it appeared that Derek was sat in the back. Barney was stood just in front of them, he must have been six feet tall and could see everything, Jake pulled the bottom of Barneys Jacket and he looked down. “What’s going on Barney?”. Jake

asked. “It’s Derek, he's been arrested, they have gone through his bag and I think they may have found something, the police don't seem to happy. Derek doesn't look too worried, he’s sat there with a big grin on his face. Karly said, they were waiting outside the school gates for him, and when they stopped him, he put up his two fingers and said, PEACE MAN”.

Derek was the talk of the school, and week later he was on the front page of the local paper.
Headlines, Rose grower hides secret cannabis factory.
Derek’s picture was on the front page, and it appears, he used rose growing as a cover for growing cannabis.
Jake and Jonathan never heard anything about being foolish in class, either from Mr Salmon or Mr Woodman after that, maybe they shouldn't have left Derek teaching unsupervised.

A month had gone by, and one lunch time, Jake and his friends were cross country training. As they were running through their local woods, Jake saw Mr Woodman and Mrs Elliot kneeling behind some bushes.
“Look who’s there Johnathan”. Jonathan stopped and looked, the other lads were behind him. “Jake, lets run past them and pretend we haven't seen them”. Jonathan, Jake and his friends ran over to the bush were Mr Woodman and Mrs Elliot were. As they passed, they both jumped up, Mr Woodman pulling up his trousers and Mrs Elliot pulling down her skirt. All the lads ran passed

smiling and greeted their teachers. “Hullo Mr Woodman, hullo, Mrs Elliott”. A week later, Mr Woodman came to school with two black eyes and a split lip, and they never saw Mrs Elliot again.

It was July 1972 and their last day at school, it was 3pm and they were all stood in the main hall. Mr Salmon was stood on the stage and wished all the school leavers the very best. They walked out for the final time in single file. Jake was pleased his school days were over, and could look forward to the new adventures he would experience. However, as he said goodbye to his friends, some he would never see again, he felt a strange type of sadness, but it was time to start a new life, with new friends. Jonathan, at sixteen years old fell in love with a girl who broke his heart, he overdosed on tablets and sadly died. When Jake heard of his death, he felt a great loss and always remembered his good friend.

Cricket Field

It was a cold February afternoon, Jake and Terry were walking down the road towards the shops, when they saw their friend Steve, he shouts over. "Come on Jake, let's go for a game of football on Manton club field ". Terry and Jake liked to play football, "Ok Steve". Steve kicked his ball over the road to Terry, who stopped it by his feet, and they waited for Steve to walk over and join them. As they walked down the road, a local miner called Bill, who was about sixty plus years old had just finished on his regular day shift. At the same time each day, he cycled his way home, the journey meant he had to travel up Hardwick Road East, which led to where he lived on Manton Crescent. He was very slow at cycling, and always had to make his way through a gauntlet of waiting dogs. Terry, Jake and Steve stood and watched, as all their pet dogs were waiting to chase the old collier.

As Bill slowly pedalled up the road, the dogs started to stand at their gates, waiting for the right moment to begin the chase. As he got fifty yards up the road, Toby, Jake's dog, was the first, barking, as he ran after old Bill. One by one, the dogs ran out of their garden gates, until there were at least a dozen dogs running behind old Bill, nipping his trouser bottoms and barking fiercely.
Bill started to peddle faster and faster, as the dogs got to the top of the street they gave up the chase, as it was on other dog's territory, they would then turn around with their tails wagging, and if possible, would have a smile on their face. Old Bill, knowing once again that it was safe to

get off his bike, would sit on a garden wall, taking deep breaths before biking around the corner to his home. Terry, Steve and Jake, all turned around smiling, Terry as a cruel thought. “I wonder what would have happened if old Bill had fell off his bike”.

It was getting dark, as they got to the bottom of the street, Adam, a 40-year-old man who had a learning disability, was stood on the corner and shouted over. “Do you want a game of football lads?"
Jake liked to play football with Adam, but not today. “Another day Adam “.

Adam was happy that Jake had acknowledged him, and knew from experience that one day he would play football with him. They crossed the road onto the Manton Club Field, Johnny Handsome was sat on a wall smoking a fag, he was sixteen, a year older than the others. Terry wondered what it was like to smoke. “Johnny, give us a drag of your fag”.

Johnny gave Terry the fag, he held it with his finger and thumb, he thought it made you look hard, he put into his mouth and took a deep breath, deeply inhaling the smoke. Terry immediately started to cough and quickly gave Johnny the fag back, he began to feel dizzy, and everyone laughed. Johnny smiles and took another drag of his fag. “Anyone else?”. Jake and Steve didn't want to be ill like their friend Terry. “No thanks mate”.
Johnny had something special in mind. “Ay lads, I've got something to show you, follow me”. Johnny started to

walk over to the big white cricket board on the field, with a seat in the front of it. They all followed closely by, Johnny stopped and stood in front of a small bench.

“Right, stand there lads”. The lads looked on, Steve was bouncing his ball up and down.

“Are you watching lads?”. He pulled his trousers and underpants down and sat on the bench, pulled out his penis and started to slowly masturbate. As they watched, Jake took out some sweets and handed them around, Johnny was getting excited. “Watch this”. Steve smiled and threw his ball at Johnny's head just has he was coming, it bounced back, and Steve caught it, they all cheered, Johnny was coming as Steve had caught the ball. Jake was impressed. “We could do this as a party trick “.

Johnny thought everyone was cheering him, but the lads found bouncing the ball off someone's head and catching it while they were coming, was far more impressive.

It was time for Johnny to finish his scene, he looked at everyone with a cunning grin. “I’ve got something for you”. Johnny wiped his penis with his finger, pulled up his pants and trousers and walked towards Terry with his hand held up, he was going to wipe his sperm on him, the lads all stepped back.

Johnny had a face of mischief, and started to chase them around the field, they were all laughing as they ran off in different directions. Johnny was soon out of breath, maybe because of the fags he smoked and started to walk. They all waited at the entrance for each other, and

saw Johnny wiping his hands on the grass. Steve's enjoyed the chase. "We're ok now lads ". Johnny walked up to them, looking pleased with himself.
"That was a good one, weren't it lads ". They all looked and smiled.

"Sure, was Johnny". They all sat on the Manton club field wall, and for the rest of the evening talked about their previous tricks, while shouting to the young girls as they walked past.

Going for a Job

When a young lad left school, they would usually apply for a job at the pit or the local woodyard. Jake had planned to look for a job the following day and had asked his dad to wake him up. "Jake, come on, it's bleeding time to get up and go for a job".

It was 1972 and Jake was fifteen, he had just left secondary school and was looking for a job that July. He got up, got dressed and as he went out of the back door he did not know where to go, and decided to try the local Manton pit, just down the road.

As Jake walked into the pit yard he saw old Bill, who regularly rode his bike up Jake's street.
"Hey mate, could you tell me where to go for a job?". Bill looked around and noticed Jake. "What's that mate?". Jake repeated his question. "Could you tell me where to go for a job please mate?".
Jake's getting a little frustrated, having to keep repeating himself. Bill walks over to Jake and puts his hand up to his ear, indicating that he has not heard him. "Say again young man". Jake's now getting agitated, he's nervous about going for a job, he leans over to Bill's right ear and shouts. "Could you tell me where to go for a job please mate?". Bill has a big smile on his face, and puts his right hand on Jake's left shoulder. "There's no need to shout son, I heard you the first time. You need to see the training officer, his office his over there, just follow the signs", and Bill pointed to the direction Jake was to take.

The pit yard was dusty and noisy, and Jake eventually found the offices. There were three steps which led up to a double red door. As Jake entered the building he had to walk down a long, narrow corridor, each office had a person's name on, such as manager and deputy manager. At the end of the corridor was a young man stood outside an office who he thought he recognised. When Jake got up to him he realised it was Ian, a young lad he went to school with, who was a year older than him.

"Ae up Ian, what are you doing here?". Ian started to explain what had happened. "I am an apprentice electrician and was working in the pit top electrical shop. A bloke was taking the mickey, so I told him to fuck off, and he reported me to the training officer". Meeting Ian was lucky for Jake, as it had helped him to find the right office.

As Ian and Jake were talking, Brian the training officer came walking down the long corridor towards them. When he got to his office he stopped, looked harshly at Ian, shook his head and walked in and closed the door. Jake waited a minute, looked at Ian and he nodded, Jake knocked on the office door. "Come in"

As Jake walked in, Brian was sat behind his small wooden desk, looking through what appeared to be a file, it could have been Ian's.

Brian stopped, looked up, peering above his reading glasses.

“What's your name son?”. Jake stared straight at Brian. “Jake Jackson sir”. Brian smiled,

“You can cut out the sir, you're not at school now”.

Jake was feeling very nervous, but for the first time, starting to feel grown up and on a level playing field with the adults. “Could I have an application form for a job please?”. “What would you like to be?”
“I don't know, I just want a job”. Brian walks over to the filing cabinet and takes out a form. “Here you are lad, fill in this form and bring it back to me, you will be sent to the local Dinnington college for some tests and a medical, from there we shall offer you a choice of apprenticeships”. Jake was really pleased, his first attempt to find a job and he looks successful. “Ok, thank you Brian “.

Jake walked out of the office, he didn't speak to Ian but just looked and smiled, as he walked away he stopped to fold up his application form and put it in his back pocket, but he was also listening to what Brian was going to say to Ian. Brian walked out of his office, he was furious as he stood looking at Ian.
“You again, get into my office”. Ian walked into the office with an arrogant, I don't give a fuck attitude.
The door slammed, Jake looked to see if there was anyone around, it was clear, and he walked back to Brian's office and put his ear to the door, Brian started shouting at Ian.

“Everyone complains about your fucking attitude Ian, you're lazy, don't go to college and you don't listen to anyone, if this keeps on, you’re going to get the sack, what do you have to say for yourself?”.
Brian bangs his fist on the desk in frustration.

Ian stood up straight, with a small smile on one side of his face and said calmly.
“EXCUSE ME BRIAN, I THINK YOU'RE MISTAKING ME, FOR SOMEONE WHO GIVES A FUCK “.
Brian jumps up out of his chair and screams. “Get out of my office now, you're going down the pit on the haulage “.
Working on the haulage, was were men transported material from the shaft side in mine cars to the coalface, it was very hard, dangerous work.

Jake turned around and quickly ran down the corridor, stopped, and took out his application form and pretended to read it. He heard the door bang and as he looked around, he could see Ian calmly walking away. Ian held up his hand and Jake returned the gesture, as Ian walked past he winked and smiled. Jake looked down towards Brian's office, he was stood in the middle of the corridor, angry, red faced, shouting.
“Don't come back again you little bastard”. Jake was stood looking up at a poster on the wall, pretending that he had not heard anything. Brian stormed back into his office, slamming the door behind him as he went.

Jake went back home and completed his application form, English was not his best subject and other than completing his name and address he struggled. Jake's pet dog Toby, kept scratching Jake's hand with his paw, he wanted Jake to play with him while he was sat on the sofa. Toby kept clawing the form out of Jake's hand until he put the form down and gave his dog a pat. Jake heard a knock at the door, he went into the kitchen, opened the door and Terry his schoolmate was stood there. "Are you coming out Jake for a game of football?". Jake was bored with writing out his application form, but would complete it later in the evening.

"Ok mate". He shouted Toby, who ran out into the garden and as they walked down the street, Toby sat at the gate, it was nearly time for old Bill to go riding past.

Lenny the Wood Yard Man

It was Saturday afternoon and Jake is now employed at the local Steetley colliery, as an apprentice fitter and was due to do his underground training. Jake and Texas were going to their local pub, the White Swan. He and his friends used to drink there every session during the weekend, and the pub was always full. Lenny, a big rough forty-year-old man was always in there. Jake and Texas were only sixteen, but as they walked into the pub, acted like eighteen, maybe that's why they got served. They walked up to the bar and Jake ordered the drinks. “Two pints of bitter please Stan”.

As they got served, Lenny was stood at the far end of the bar. “How are you going on Jake, you scruffy little twat?”. Jake looked at Lenny, he never cared what he said to anyone. “Ok Lenny”. Jake wasn't sure about Lenny, if he had too much to drink, Lenny could turn quite nasty and he was strong as an ox.

Lenny worked in the wood yard, sawing full sleepers into sections, where two men would pick up one sleeper, Lenny easily picked them up on his own and placed them on the saw bench. One day, Lenny and his mate Stewart had a bet, to see who could push a sleeper along the saw bench with their head, to see who could get closest to the two-foot wide saw blade.

Lenny won, leaving him with a slight scar above his head, where the saw blade had cut him.

Texas, Jake and Lenny stood at the bar having a laugh together, Annie and her mate Cilla walked into the pub, both were about thirty years old. Annie was slim, and Cilla was very large, and they never had any money. Annie had her kids took into care because she was always in the pub, and often had sex with different men, it was rumoured that she was once a prostitute.
Annie and Cilla sat at a table directly in front of the bar, it was a good place to get men to buy them a drink, a little flirting went a long way, Annie was always a bit forward when she wanted a drink. "Are you buying us a drink Lenny?".
Lenny looked, then laughed. Jake looked at Lenny, he could see he was up to something.
"What would you like girls?". Texas had forgot about meeting his girlfriend Judith.
"What time is it anyone?". Cilla looked at her watch. "Half past one love". Texas was worried. "Jake, I have got to go, I was supposed to meet Judith at 1pm outside Woolworths". Terry picked up his leather Jacket from off a close by chair. "See you later lads".

Texas walked quickly out of the pub, he knew he was in trouble. Cilla had found and opportunity for free drinks now Texas had gone, two's company, three's a crowd, especially when one has a girlfriend. "Would you two like to join us?". Lenny was pleased. "We will ladies".
Lenny walked straight over and sat next to Annie, Jake was a little nervous and stopped at the bar, he was just

sixteen and new to the world, but Cilla and Annie had sailed the world as far as men were concerned. Lenny laughed at Jake. “Come on Jake, you pussy”. Annie teased Jake. “What's up Jake, you’re not frightened of girls, are you?”.
Jake took a deep drink of his pint, he knew he would have to sit with the girls, or he would never live it down. “Ok ladies”. Jake walked over to the table and sat next to Cilla. As he sat down, Cilla patted him on his leg, Jake looked up at the pub ceiling, the colour drained from his face, wondering what he could be getting himself into.

Lenny, Jake and the two girls sat drinking at the table for the rest of the afternoon, Cilla kept on putting her hand on Jake's leg, while Lenny who was outgoing, had his arm around Annie's shoulder, he knew what to expect. Jake tried to make conversation with Annie as he looked over the table away from Cilla. “Have you been married Annie?”. Annie put her drink down on the table. “I'm still married Jake, my husband's called Ralph, I haven’t seen him for a long time. Jake was inquisitive. “Why is that Annie?”. “Well, me and Ralph was out one night and this bloke Rob, who had a bit of a reputation for being a streetfighter, started flirting around me. Well Ralph, being the very jealous type, asked Rob to leave me alone. Rob suddenly punched Ralph on the nose breaking it instantly. Ralph stepped back, and from nowhere he grabbed Rob around the throat, pulled him down to his waist and dragged him outside of the pub, and then threw him onto the ground. Rob tried to pick himself up, but Ralph repeatedly kicked his arms from underneath him, and then started to kick him in the head. When the onlookers managed to pull Ralph away, Rob was laid motionless, blood streaming from his head. When the ambulance and police arrived, Rob was declared dead, Ralph has a ferocious, jealous temper".

Meanwhile, Lenny was well on his way to being drunk, and did not have a care in the world, even after hearing Annie's story. Jake looked at Cilla. "What about you Cilla, have you got a husband or boyfriend?".
"I've had a few boyfriends in my time, but we never got on, they never really understood me.
Everything could be fine, I would walk up to them to give them a kiss, and suddenly, I would slash them with a razor, or stab them with a knife.
When I was younger, I tied a man called Barry down to a bed, and then blindfolded him. He thought he was in for a good time, but it was not to be. I went into the lounge, picked up the iron and plugged it in. When it was hot I unplugged it, walked over to Barry and placed the hot iron on his chest. You could hear his screams through the gag over his mouth, and how I held the iron onto his chest while he wriggled, I will never know. I only held it on for about a minute, just enough time to enjoy the smell of burning flesh. I took the iron off Barry's chest, and went and put it back in the room to do the ironing the next day.

Barry was really upset with me, I knew this, because as soon as I released him, he dived straight out of the bedroom window to escape. He must have forgot that I lived in a flat which was two stories up. Anyway, I looked out of the window and Barry was laid naked, flat out on the ground. He was lucky, because he had just missed a man walking his dog. An ambulance came and took him to the hospital, I just made myself a cup of tea and had an early night. My friend Jenny came around the following day, she knocked on my door and came in, she told me that the night before, the police and ambulance service had found a naked man outside the flats, with two broken arms and legs from a fall, which they could understand, but what they could not work out is, why he had got a severe burn mark on his chest, in the shape of a clothing iron, and in the middle, it said, Russell Hob.
I never heard anything from the police, so I suppose Barry never told anyone about what had happened that night".

Jake's stuck for words of what to say, he daren't upset Cilla after a story like that, he has an idea.
"I'll get the last drinks in, I've got to go shopping after that". Jake walks up to the bar.
"Lenny, Cilla, Annie, what would you like to drink?". They all look at Jake. "We will have same as you Jake".
Jake shouts to the pub landlord, Stan walks through from the taproom, he's been watching racing on TV. "You've got twenty minutes to drink up it's 2.50pm Jake." Stan

rang the bell for last orders and walked back over to Jake. “Jake, here”. Jake leans over the bar, Stan looks behind him to see if anyone is listening, he had been on two weeks holiday from his job at the pit. “When you see Maureen, tell her I have something for her”. Jake smiled. “Ok Stan”. Mildred the landlady suddenly walked into the bar. Stan changes the conversation. “Yes, Jake what do you want?”. “Four pints of bitter please Stan”. Mildred looked at Stan while he poured out the drinks, and then looked at Jake, she gave him the impression that she knew what they were talking about. “Forty-eight pence please Jake”. Jake gave Stan the money. “Thanks Stan”. Mildred was still stood near Stan, as Jake took the drinks to the table he heard her questioning him.

“Stan, what have you been talking about? You two looked deep in conversation, the way you two were lent over the bar together, gave me the impression you did not want anyone to hear”.

Stan walked over to the taproom side of the bar and Mildred followed him, Stan told Mildred a lie.

“I told Jake to be careful with Cilla and Annie, as he could easily get himself into trouble. Mildred, you know he's only a young lad and is vulnerable”. Mildred half believed him. “Ok Stan, but I'm watching you”. Stan’s quick thinking saved him from a lot of earache.

It’s 3.10pm and Stan rang the final bell for closing time. “Come on ladies and gentlemen, it's time to close “. They

all finished their drinks, stood up and walked out of the pub, Annie wanted an interesting afternoon.
“Lenny, would you and Jake like to come back to my place for a drink?”. Annie lived in a council flat on the local estate, which was traditional and run down, and was just around the corner from the pub. Lenny was pleased with the offer. “Course we will love “(in a slurred voice). Cilla was stood next to Jake and nudged him with her elbow. “What about you Jake?”.
Jake was looking for an excuse, he didn't want an iron shaped burn on his chest with a branded name of Russell Hob, while his mates had crosses and dragons on theirs, he would never be able to sunbathe again. “I’ve got to go shopping Cilla”.
Lenny looks on, he's heard what Jake had said, and he is not too happy about Jake not wanting to go back to Annie's flat, this may mean that they don’t want Lenny to go either.
“Yes, you fucking are Jake”. He says in a firm voice. “You're only going back for a drink, the shops don't close until 5pm”. Cilla wants Jake to go back, she’s just bought a new iron and it’s at Annie’s flat. “Listen to your dad Jake, you will be fine”, she says with a torturing grin.
Jake was torn in two ways. One, if he didn't go back with Cilla, Lenny would be upset, and Jake didn’t know how Lenny would react. Or two, if he did go back, what would Cilla do to him. Jake decided to take the risk.
“Ok Cilla, I'll come back for a drink”. Cilla smiled and grabbed hold off Jake's arm, Jake fell silent, as she walked with him, she felt like a female predator that was

catching a young fish. Annie and Lenny walked next to each other, talking as they went, as though they knew each other well.

As they arrived at the flats, the street was covered in litter and broken bottles, kids were running around with no shoes on, swearing at them as they walked past. They walked down a small ginnel, up to a double fire door, that led onto a short dark corridor and a flight of concrete stairs. Sheffield Wednesday for the cup was sprayed on the wall, which was wrongly spelt as the n and e was missing. They made their way up the open stairs, and walked along the landing. Annie stopped at the green door, number 13, with the broken window. Jake took this as a bad omen, the number and colour is supposed to be unlucky. She pushed open the unlocked door and invited them into the flat. As they walked into the kitchen, there was a bad smell of urine, unwashed pots were in the sink, and everywhere was untidy.
Lenny and Annie went straight towards the bedroom, Lenny walked in first and Annie followed. Annie closed the door behind them, there was a loud thud. Lenny shouted out. “Bastard!”. “What's up Lenny?”. Annie asked. “I’ve tripped over your fucking shoes”. And they both began to laugh.
Jake didn’t know it, but found out later that Annie was on the game, and her and Lenny had been together a few times before.

Jake was stood in the lounge, he looked around the room, the curtains were pulled down, clothes and papers were strewn everywhere, and there were holes in the middle of the lounge carpet. Cilla tried to sweet talk young Jake. "Come with me into the bedroom Jake". She took hold of Jake's hand and led him into the bedroom, they sat on the bed and talked for a while. "You are very young Jake; would you like to take off my clothes?". Suddenly, Lenny burst into the bedroom, laughing. "Come on Jake, it's obvious you don't know how to fuck".

Jake felt relieved that Lenny had saved him from Cilla, and off Jake and Lenny went, out of the flat, and back down the street. Lenny was laughing as he told Jake that Annie had charged him £1 for a fuck, but when she went to the toilet he took £5, out of her purse. They parted at the bottom of the street and Jake went shopping to buy a new shirt, and trousers.

After going shopping, Jake went home and got changed ready for the evening session. He put on his new clothes, looked at himself in the mirror and felt smart.

On the way down to the Swan, Jake called for his mate Jimmy, who never had any money and soft Jake always bought his drinks. As they walked into the pub they noticed Steff sat in the corner, next to the slot machine. Jake shouted over to Steff. "Are you alright Steff? Is it ok if we sit with you in a minute"?

Sometimes, Steff liked to sit on his own. Jake and Jimmy got a drink and sat down with Steff and he started to tell them stories of the fights he had with Duke and the rest of the Worksop skinheads, when he was a hells angel.

As the night went on, Lenny walked into the pub, he looked like he had a lot to drink? Jake walked up to the bar to greet him. "Are you alright Lenny?". Lenny shouted. "Fuck off Jake".
Lenny's speech was slurred and everyone in the pub looked round, he had got everyone's attention.
Lenny shouted out to everyone in the pub. "What do you think to this prick, we went back to Annie's, I had to fuck Cilla her mate as well because Jake couldn't do it".
Jake felt embarrassed and angry, all his mates were laughing, he felt he had to say something to save face.
Jake stood in front of Lenny and looked up at him.
"Lenny, Fuck Off".
Lenny immediately grabbed hold of Jake, which was not difficult, only weighing eight stone and four feet ten inches tall, Lenny weighed about sixteen stone and was built like a brick shithouse. Lenny dragged Jake through the pub, out of the back door and threw him into the small tarmacked courtyard.
Jake picked himself up from the ground and stood ready to fight, Lenny was stood about six feet away, and looking for someone to kill, all the pub had come outside to watch. Jake's mate Jimmy shouts. "KICK HIM IN THE BOLLOCKS JAKE".

Jake was on flight or fight mode, he ran up to Lenny and punched him as hard as he could, hitting Lenny in the face. Lenny put his hand up to his mouth and his top teeth fell out. Jake had broken Lenny's top false teeth into two pieces. Lenny threw his teeth to the ground, ran up to Jake, picked him up and lifted him above his shoulders. Everyone gasped, Lenny slammed Jake down hard onto the ground. Jake knew what was coming next and curled up in a ball, hands over his head and face to protect himself.

Jake was right, Lenny started kick Jake on the head and in the ribs, looking for a spot which was not protected. Jake felt the kicking suddenly stop and heard someone say. "That's enough".

Someone had walked over and pulled Lenny back out of the way, Jake quickly got up and realised it was Steff, who was looking down at Jake. "Are you ok Jake?". Jake rubbed the gravel from his face with both hands. "Fine Steff, thanks for that". Jake was quite proud he had survived the onslaught from Lenny.

They all went back into the pub, and Jake bought Steff a drink, Lenny put his false teeth into his pocket and went up to the bar, he was too drunk to care. Everyone was laughing, that such a little person could break such a hard man's false teeth.

The following day at around 3.30pm, Jake was walking to the fishing tackle shop, Lenny was stood at the bottom of

the hill talking to one of his friends and spotted Jake, trying to walk quietly past.
“Come here you little bastard, you think you're clever don't you”. Lenny started to run across the road towards Jake, however Jake had youth, speed, and of course fear on his side. This time he was not penned in, as Lenny tried to grab Jake, he was able to duck and dive and ran circles around him, before running off down the street, flagging him as he went. Jake could hear Lenny shouting, but could not make out what it was.

Later that night Jake walked into the pub, Lenny was stood at the bar, Jake smiled and walked up to him.
“Lenny, I am sorry punching you in the mouth, and for breaking your false teeth in two places”. Jake held out his right hand. Lenny looked at Jake with a cunning expression. “Thanks Jake, it's ok”.
Lenny held out his right hand and suddenly punched Jake on the nose with his left. Jake felt a sickening blow, the next thing he knew, was that his mates and Lenny were holding him up in a sitting position on the pub floor, and his was face covered in blood, Lenny had broken Jake's nose. He quickly recovered and sat down at a table, Lenny brought him a drink over, it was Lenny’s turn to smile. “Here you are mate, we are quits.” Jake smiled and picked up his pint. “Cheers Lenny”.
Jake’s nose was sore, his ribs ached from the beating the night before, but he was pleased that the riff with Lenny, was now over.

Old Stan, Landlord of the White Swan

Old Stan was the landlord of the White Swan, he also worked at the same nearby colliery as Jake, where he was a coalface miner. Stan's shift started at 10.20 a m and finished at 6 pm, which also gave him time to manage his pub. He was knocking off Maureen, who worked in the pit canteen. At 10 a m each day, Stan had to change into his pit clothes, so he could collect his pit lamp and rescuer for 10.15 a m, so he could go down the coal mine at 10.20 a m sharp.

Stan would arrive in the canteen for about 9.40 a m each day, Maureen would then close the canteen, even though it was not supposed to close until 10 a m, and they would then have a quick cuddle. Everyone knew what was happening and thought it was funny, but Stan and Maureen thought it was a secret.

Stan worked with two other men called Fred and Herbert, who were always playing tricks on their workmates. One day they hatched a plan, they decided to arrive in the canteen at 9.20 a m and leave at 10.10.a m. Fred and Herbert didn't tell their old friend Stan what they were going to do. Maureen, had been on holiday for a week and it was her first Monday back at work. Fred and Herbert both decided to arrive early that morning, they got changed into their pit gear and went and sat in the canteen. As usual, Stan arrived at 9.40 a m, he walked into the canteen with a big grin on his face, he had really missed Maureen, until he suddenly noticed Fred and Herbert sat in the corner having a cup of tea and chatting, as though nothing was going on. Stan, hoping they would soon leave, sat down with them, he couldn't say anything because of Maureen and his secret. They chatted, chatted, and chatted, Stan kept looking at the clock on the wall, it was 10.10 a m and Fred and Herbert decided to go.

“Ok Stan, you’d better get changed”. Stan made an excuse. “I’ve just have to get some chewing tobacco lads, I won't be long”. Fred and Herbert walked out smiling. As the canteen door closed behind them, Maureen rushed over and locked the door, and they both ran behind the counter for a cuddle. Stan then had to rush through the baths, getting changed, and collecting his lamp and rescuer. Fred and Herbert were looking on as they stood at the shaft side, it was 10.20 a m, Gregg the banks man, (The banksman oversees loading and unloading of the cage) rang to the winding engine man for man riding, to let him know that men would be going down the pit. (The winding engine man, operates the winding engine that lowers the cage into the mine shaft). The banksman puts the gates down on the cage. “Ok lads, where’s your mate?”. They looked down the long winding steps, and could see old Stan running up, breathing heavily as he went. They shouted down to old Stan. “Come on you old bastard, what have you been doing until now?”.

Stan got up to the top of the steps, he gave the banksman his tally and walked onto the cage covered in sweat. “Are you ok Stan?”. Fred asked, knowing what was wrong, Herbert had to ask Stan the question.

“Have you been shagging Maureen?”. Herbert gave a cheeky smile. Stan looked, he realised what they had done. “You bastards, you knew all along and you made me wait until the last minute”. Stan’s face was full of exhaustion and anger, Fred had to tell Stan.
“Of course, everyone knows Stan, you just thought they didn’t”. The gate to the cage went down, the banksman rang to the winding engine man, to lower the cage into the shaft. As they went down the shaft, Fred and Herbert started to sing. “She loves you, yeah, yeah, yeah”. Stan started to laugh and they all had a good giggle. Fred and Herbert have had their fun, and promised not to do it again.

However, shortly after, Stan's wife found out about Maureen, one her relatives who worked at the same colliery must have told her, for the next few months Stan's life was a misery. He had to finish his job at the pit, which he loved and had to work behind the bar, where Mildred could keep an eye on him. Stan looked sad, he asked Jake one evening if he had seen anything of Maureen, but Jake said no. He didn't want to tell him that his good friends Herbert and Fred were now seeing her, it would have broken his heart, and Mildred always questioned Jake to see if he knew anything.

The Chase

It was 9pm and Jake had been playing snooker at his local snooker hall, with his friend Tony, and was on his way down to his local pub the White Swan, he called at the fish shop and was enjoying his chips. As he entered the main street, Duke's and his skinhead gang suddenly walked around the corner and nearly bumped into Jake. He stopped and gasped for breath, his leather jacket which was to long for him, was hanging down unzipped. "Ok Duke, ok Wolf, ok Brady". Jake had a big stupid grin on his face covering up his nerves, their Air Wear boots, Levi's jeans, ben Sherman shirts and Crombie coats, looked so smart, yet so frightening. They were all a lot taller than Jake, as they looked down at him their eyes were penetrating and wide, it was time for Jake to go. "See you lads".

Jake turned around and started to walk a different way towards the White Swan, the skinheads slowly followed. Jane, Duke's girlfriend ran up to Jake. "RUN, they are going to beat you up". Jane was slim, small and attractive, Jake couldn't help himself, a daring grin came onto his face. "Thanks, would you like to come out for a drink with me one night".

Jake grabbed hold of Jane and kissed her on the lips, she paused, then pushed him away, smiling. Duke's gang heard and saw what was happening. Duke wasn't too pleased. "Grebo Bastard".

The skinheads slowly started to walk faster, before suddenly bursting into a sprint. Wolf loves a chase.
“We're going to kill you, you Grebo bastard”.
Jake threw his chips into the air and started to run, it's a good job he was light and fast. He heard their battle cry, and the sound of heavy boots running along behind him. “Worksop Skinheads”, Jake knew he was going to die. He ran down the ginnel of a terraced house, across the garden, jumped over a pile of rubbish, ducked under the low washing line and vaulted over the wall into the next garden. He stopped, popped his head up and looked over the wall. He could see Duke running down the garden, where he suddenly tripped over a small bike, Wolf, who was tall, ran into the washing line nearly choking himself and went flying backwards onto the ground, Brady slipped on some mud and went sliding forwards, trying to keep his balance, before hitting the clothes post and falling next to his friend, the others were not far behind.

Jake smiled and couldn't resist shouting. “You wankers”. Coin the phrase, shout now, regret later! They saw Jake looking at them, he dropped down onto the garden and the chase resumed. The skinheads ran down the garden path and they jumped over the wall, Wolf was gasping for breath, Duke was limping and furious, Brady was covered in mud, and they were all were going to make Jake pay. Jake ran out onto the side street, he was closely chased by the skinheads. Jake ran across the swings, onto the canch, into the church yard, and only had 800 metres to go, before he got to the White Swan where he would be safe.

Suddenly, his button broke on the waist of his jeans, leaving him to run while holding them up. Meanwhile, most of the skinheads had fell well behind and had given up the chase, they knew Jake and they would see him again, but Wolf was still in close pursuit and was quickly gaining ground. Jake had only one option, Wolf was running very closely behind him, as he caught him up, Jake, suddenly fell quickly to the ground in a crouching position. Wolf could not stop and ran straight into Jake, sending Wolf flying, hitting the ground with a heavy thud. Jake quickly looked at Wolf, he knew he was in with a chance. He jumped up, grabbed hold of the waist of his jeans with his left hand, and ran to the nearby White Swan.

Jake fell exhausted through the pub doors. Buttony, Texas and Hogger were sat at a small round table, half pissed as they looked at Jake. Hogger looked at Jake through the bottom of his pint pot. “What’s fucking up with you?”. Jake, catches his breath. “I've been chased by Dukes’ gang, they were going to kill me”. Texas wasn't impressed. “Bastards, they're not getting away with that”.

They all jumped up out of their chairs and ran out to look for the Worksop Skinheads. Jake ordered a drink and sat down, feeling safe but knew he had to confront Duke another day, but if his friends did find the skinheads, there was nothing they could do, none of them could fight or run, if they were sober, they wouldn't even want to fight.

Hogger, Texas and Buttony saw Duke and his girlfriend Jane walking through the street. Buttony shouts over the road to Duke. “Hey! we want a word with you”. Duke and his girlfriend stop and wait as Jake’s friends walk over to them. Texas threatens Duke. “What do you think you’re fucking doing, threatening Jake, you wanker”.
They stood in front of Duke, Hogger looked like he had not had a wash for a month, Buttony weighed about six stone and his face was covered in spots, and Texas was wearing an old worn out leather jacket with a fag stuck out the side of his mouth.
Duke and Jane laughed, Jane walked up to Texas, looked at him and suddenly grabbed hold of his bollocks. The fag fell out of Texas’s mouth and his eyes watered, as Jane slowly squeezed, Hogger and Buttony stepped back in fear. As Jane let go, Texas fell to the ground and Duke and Jane calmly walked on their way.
Hogger and Buttony picked Texas up off the ground and helped him back to the Swan, all three were silent, two in shock, one in agony. Jake’s mates walked back into to the pub with smiles on their faces and were going to cover up what had happened. Texas limped up to Jake. “We can't see anyone Jake, I think you’re taking the fucking piss”.

They all jumped onto Jake and held him on the floor, Texas laughed and punched Jake in the stomach and hit him with his knee, on the thigh of Jake's right leg. They then let Jake stand up and they all sat down and had a drink together, another adventure was over for Jake, but as he looked round at his friends, he knew they were not telling the true story.

Silver, Car Park Fight

Sam, Dan and Russ, were running a small fag ring on the Manor Estate, providing a service to the local youngsters, just part of a wider ring which was overseen by Silver, a notorious bare-knuckle fighter who ran all the gangs on the estate. He was well known for beating the British bare-knuckle fighter, Johnny, a local Sheffield gangster six month earlier, who wanted to take over the business. Silver had been drinking in the Manor Social Club, and was stood at the bar having a laugh with his friends. A young well-dressed man called Pecker, walked into the pub and up to the barman. “Who is Silver?”. Keith the barman looked over to a small group of men at the far side of the pub, he pointed then shouted. “Silver, there's a young man wants you”. Silver looked over smiling. “Why?”. The young gangster Pecker, stood there with a cocky attitude, he shouts. “We've got something in the van of interest to you Silver”.
“Who are you?”, Silver asks. “Pecker”, the young gangster replies. Silver picks up his freshly bought pint of Tetley bitter and drinks it in one, he's been here many times before, there may be trouble waiting, just that they don’t know it.

The young gangster walks out of the pub, as he walks down the steps he whistles to his mate, who is sat in a big white transit van. Paddy, a small, stocky, scruffy guy jumps out, walks around the van and stands next to the passenger side back door, Paddy nods to Pecker.

Meanwhile, Silver makes his way out of the tap room, through the green double doors and stands on the steps to the entrance to the pub, he looks over. Pecker, is now stood at the driver's side back door. "Do you want to have a look at this mate?". Silver's naturally cautious, he's been caught out too many times before. "Ok Lads". Silver slowly walks down the pub steps and across the small tarmac car park. As he gets to the white van, Paddy taps on the back door and suddenly both doors fly open. Paddy looks at Silver with a smug face. "Think you are clever Silver? ".

Pecker steps back out of the way, Shane a large rough looking man jumps out of the van, he's a bare-knuckle fighter and hitman from Liverpool, he has tattoos of knives on his face, and a bullet on his forehead. There's a knife scar from his top lip to underneath his left eye, part of his right ear is missing as though it has been bit off in a fight, his chin is square, and his face is expressionless. He rests his fists, which look like seven-pound hammers on the van floor as he climbs out. Silver as instinctively weighed him up as the doors had opened, and had taken a step back. Shane climbs out of the van, not realising that he is defenceless and as left his guard down. As he stands upright, Silver steps in and throws a furious right hand to Shane's jaw. Shane's upper body immediately spins half way around, before collapsing onto the floor in a heap. Paddy steps back in disbelief, Pecker jumps back into the van, Silver smiles, his mates shout to him as they are all now stood at the pub door. "Are you ok mate? ".

Silver looks at Paddy and nods, Paddy puts up his hand as a gesture of its over, and Silver walks away. He hears Shane groaning as he regains consciousness, as he comes around Paddy helps him into the back of the van. Des, one of Silver's friends, thinks he knows who they are.

“I'm sure there Johnny’s friends”. Silver agrees. “There will be a lot more of them next time”.

Youth Club Fight

It was a cold Wednesday afternoon, Silver had seen Sam walking home from work.

"Hey Sam". Sam's tired, he had just finished his day shift at the local Treeton Colliery, and he's not used to getting up at four in the morning. "What's up?".

Sam's hair is still wet from the shower at the pit, and there is coal dust around his eyes from working in the coal preparation plant on the pit top. "I'll meet you and your friends at the youth club at about eight tonight, don't forget".

The pit bus passes Sam as it drops off the day shift miners from the estate. He walks down the street towards the fish shop, great he thinks. In those days, all the fish and chip shops were tasty and cheap. Sam walks into the fish shop, feeling famished. "Fish, chips and peas please". Already tasting them, knowing his mother will have nothing in the house to eat until she comes home from work at 6.pm, after doing some shopping.

Elaine, a young lady is serving behind the counter. "Sorry Sam, we're just closing. Sam's upset, he points. "There's some fish and chips there in the counter". Elaine looks at the fish, "Are you hungry Sam?". Elaine says with a cruel smile. Sam looks at Elaine with a straight face. "I could die for some chips ".

"Sorry, there ordered, you'll have to come back tonight".

Marge, the old lady cleaning the counter grins and says to her friend. "This is the best time of day, they always run in see if there are any chips left". Sam looks down sadly. "Looks like a tin of beans a sausage from the shop then ". The staff giggle, as Sam starts to walk out Elaine shouts. "Ay, we were joking, come here". Elaine picks up a bag, takes two large scoops of chips and puts them in, she then takes a scoop of peas from a large silver pan, and pours them slowly over the chips. Sam's so hungry and so excited, Elaine looks at Sam with the bags of chips and peas in her hand. "Salt and vinegar love?". Sam licks his lips. "Loads please". She then picks up a large fish, puts it on the top of the chips and peas and pours on more salt and vinegar, sticks in a wooden fork, and passes them to Sam, smiling.

Sam walks out of the chip shop, and sits on a small wall where people usually stand their bikes. He began to eat his chips, there are two dogs, called Pedigree and Chum, laid closely by, looking at Sam eating his meal. Dan and Russ come walking past, Sam's close friends, they had both been on a rest day, so they could play snooker. "How's it going Sam?". Sam swallows a chip. "Ok lads, Silver wants to meet us at the youth club tonight, will you come around for me at 7pm".
Russ and Dan pinch a chip. "Ok mate". They then walk off talking about their latest game of snooker.

Sam had finished eating his chips and had saved his fish until last, this is the best bit.

A young lad John, is giving his friend Mark a lift on his pushbike, John is stood up peddling, while Mark is sat on the seat. They ride closely towards Sam, John shouts. ”Ae up Sam”, Sam had just picked up his fish with both hands and is about to take a bite. As John rides towards him, Mark draws back his right hand, and as they pass, Mark slaps Sam on the side of his head. BOOF! Sam’s fish goes flying, he shouts out with surprise, “Bastard”. John and Mark ride off laughing, giving Sam, the wanking sign as they go.

The best part of Sam's meal now lays on the ground, Sam looks around to see if anyone is looking, with intentions of picking it up, the coast is clear. He turns around and with horror sees the two dogs running toward his fish, they have been sat nearby waiting for customers from the fish shop, to either give them their unwanted chips, or eat the ones they drop.
Sam makes a move towards his fish but feels his arm swept away, both dogs have run forward and in half a second it's gone. They sit down and look up at Sam, with fish and grease around their lips. Sam’s not to happy. “You bastards”. Pedigree and Chum walk over to a bowl of water, which had been left outside the fish shop for customers dogs to drink. Sam looks sadly at the floor and all that is left is a bit of chip grease, he looks around and sees the dogs drinking out of the bowl, their tails are wagging as they then walk off down the street to sit

outside the local shop, waiting for kids to give them a sweet, until the fish shop opens later in the evening.

Sam's throws his chip papers onto the floor, he stands up and hears someone call. "You can pick them up lad". It was the local policeman, Bill, a tall slim character that had been in the army in his time, some thought he may have been in the S.A.S as he had no fear of anyone.
Bill, who lived and worked on the estate was well respected. In the 1972 miners' strike he often bought the miners a drink in the welfare. If there was any trouble, Bill would just give you a slap, however, any thieving on the Manor, he would have a word with Silver and he would sort it out. You could do whatever you wanted off the Manor, but not on Bills turf. Sam sadly looked over at Bill. "Ok Bill".

Sam picks up the papers and puts them in the bin. Bills also a boxing coach on the Manor, he shouts over. "Don't forget boxing training tomorrow night lad". Sam smiles, he likes training. "Ok Bill". Sam starts to walk down the road, his dog Rover sees him and runs up to him excitedly, and they began to wrestle. He runs down the street and into his yard as Rover chases him.

Sam opens the door and walks into the house, which is always untidy and cold, Rover goes over to his silver metal dog bowl and picks it up with his teeth. Sam looks admiringly down at his dog, "Ok Rover". Sam goes to the cupboard, takes out Rovers tin of chappie dog food,

opens the tin and scrapes it into the bowl. Rover can't wait to eat it, within one second it had gone, Rover then walks into the lounge. Sam makes himself a cup of tea, he's tired from the early shift and decides to lay on the sofa and have a sleep. As he walks into the lounge Sam sees Rover comfortably asleep on the sofa. "Come on off there ". Sam shouts in a deep voice. Rover pays no attention, he never as, maybe it's the mongrel in him.
It's half past three and Sam is feeling tired, he makes a fire and decides to lay on the floor, he takes a pillow, wraps himself up in a coat and lays down on the carpet, he feels so comfortable as he looks at the flames coming from the coal fire and he quickly falls to sleep.

It's six o'clock and Sam's mom Linda, walks in from work, she puts the carrier bag of shopping on the top of the twin tub washing machine, Rovers wakes up and runs in to greet her with his tail wagging, he thinks he may have a treat. She fusses Rover. "Good boy, I've a treat for you." Rover sits down, ears pricking up, Linda goes over to a bag and takes out a bone she has got from the local butchers. "Here you are Rover". She opens the back door and throws it outside, Rover runs out, picks up the bone and takes it into the dry broken down shed at the bottom of the garden, it's his favourite hideout where he can eat his bone in peace.

Linda leaves the door open and walks into the front room, she sees Sam soundly asleep on the floor, she picks up

the hairy grey dog blanket from the corner of the room, and puts it over Sam, he's is so tired he doesn't notice. Linda lights a fag, picks up a magazine and goes upstairs to have a nice bath. As she relaxed she looks at the clock and its 6.50 pm, it's nearly time for Emmerdale Farm (started 1972). She jumps out of the bath, puts on her dressing gown, a towel round her hair and goes running down stairs. As Linda walks into the room, she trips over Sam and then turns on the light and TV. She picks up a fag from the table and lights it, thinking she's just in time for her favourite programme. She then walks over to the sofa, but Rover had come back into the house and was laid there. “Move Rover”.
Rover doesn't move, he's sound asleep after enjoying his bone, she takes a big puff of her fag, then stubs it on Rovers backside. Rover yelps, he jumps up and runs into the kitchen, Linda looks, shakes her head,
“Stupid dog, he never learns”.

As Linda sits down, Emmerdale begins, there's a knock at the door, she sighs, “Come in”.
Dan and Russ walk through the door and into the lounge, Dan looks around for Sam, he's supposed to be ready to go out.
“Where's Sam?”, Linda points at a dog blanket on the floor. “He's laid there and won't move”.
Dan smiles, “I'll show you how to get him up”. Dan takes out a sweet from his coat pocket, puts it in his mouth and gives it a good suck. He shouts Sam's dog. “Rover”.

Rover warily walks into the room and steers clear of Linda, Dan gives him a lick of his sweet. “Sit”.
Russ and Linda smile, Rover sits down, tail wagging, “Watch this”. Dan puts the sticky sweet on Sam's face cheek. “Ok Rover “. Rover runs over to Sam, and starts to lick the sweet from his face.
Sam suddenly sits up, his dog is still jumping up at him, his hair is all ruffled, eyes black from the coal dust, and is still half asleep. He wipes his eyes, he remembers they must meet Silver tonight. “Come on, we've got to get the youth club for eight”. Dan’s pleased his trick as worked. “We know that Sam, we are waiting for you”. Sam jumps up, runs upstairs has a quick wash and puts on his jeans, T- shirt, suit jacket and winkle picker boots. He quickly combs his hair and runs down stairs, at sixteen you have the energy to do that. “Alright lads let's go, see you mom”. Dan and Russ shout as they go out of the back door, “See you Linda”.

As they walk up the garden path, they jump over an old silver rusty dustbin that as blown over in the wind, and they walk along the street chatting, Sam stops, Dan and Russ look on.
“Dan, come here and close your eyes, I have something special for you”. Dan stands in front of Sam.
Sam suddenly slaps Dan with cupped hands on both ears at the same time, dropping him to the floor.

Russ laughs, Dan gets up staggering. “What's that for?” Sam smiles. “For putting the sweet on my face”, they all laugh, it's quits.

It’s Wednesday night, it will be quite at the youth club, table tennis finishes at 7.45pm, and then old Ted usually gives the hall a good sweep, in between nipping out for a bottle whisky from the beer off, and having a fag, which usually takes about an hour.
Sam, Dan and Russ walk along the road, until they take a short right at the bus stop, which leads to an old stone drill hall, which was once used for training the dad's army in the second world war, but for many years now it had been used for a youth club, and down stairs there is an amateur boxing club.
As they get to the bottom of the steps, they meet a young lad who nods, they have not seen him before and does not appear to be local, Dan’s suspicious. “I don't like him lads, he maybe a grass for other gangs outside of the Manor”. Dan’s asks him a question, he needs to know who he is. “What's your name mate”. The young lad appears uncomfortable. “Ryan mate, I'm just waiting for a friend “. Silver just walks from around the corner of the street and shouts. “Hey lads “. They are distracted, Sam, Dan and Russ turn around, looking down the street from off the steps. “Ok Silver” they shout excitedly.
Young Ryan smiles, unknowing to the gang, they nearly broke his cover.

Silver runs up the road and jumps the eight steps, two at a time. He smiles, “You are a scruffy lot”. They all laugh.

They walk through the wide green, heavy double doors that lead into the youth club. It’s 8.pm and the caretaker Ted is putting his brush away. “Ok Ted” they all shout. Ted turns around in the broom cupboard and bangs his head on the low door frame, knocking his cap over his glasses.
“Wait lads, do me a favour, just watch the club for me, while I fetch a drink from the off licence”. “Ok” Silver says, the others nod. Ted puts on his old black donkey jacket, straightens his cap and walks out of the youth club, he is on a mission to buy his half bottle of whisky.

As Ted walks out, Ryan is sat on a small wall outside, with an unlit fag in his mouth. He sees Ted approaching. “Have you got a light mate?”. Old Ted stops, takes out a box of matches, strikes a match and cups it in his hands so the wind doesn't blow it out. Ryan puts his cigarette in the flame and inhales, until the cigarette is glowing red. “Thanks Mate”. Old Ted smiles, “Ok young man”.
Ryan makes prying conversation. “Are you finished for the night”. Old Ted looks at Ryan. “No, I'm only nipping out for an hour, Silvers in there if you need anything”. Ryan nods, “Thanks mate”.

Little does Ted know, that he has innocently given Ryan’s friends time to finish their business with Silver. Ryan

waits until Ted is out of sight, he then runs around the corner to the red telephone box. He phones Johnny at his local pub, the Old Crown Inn near the centre of Sheffield. The phone rings and the barman picks it up. “It’s Chris”. “Hullo, Its Ryan, is Johnny there.” Chris shouts. “Johnny the phone “.
Johnny sends over one of his gang. Paddy walks over to the bar and Chris passes him the phone. “What's up”, he says in a deep arrogant voice. “It’s Ryan, tell Johnny that Silvers in the Manor youth club with three young lads, they are on their own and the caretaker will not be back for an hour”.
Paddy puts the phone down, walks over to Johnny and whispers in his ear the message Ryan had given him. Johnny puts a plan into action, it's time to put things straight.
“Paddy, go and phone Soul, tell him to meet us at the Manor youth club straight away.” As Paddy goes to the phone it's noisy, the gang members are gambling or having a laugh.
Johnny had quickly worked out that it would take fifteen minutes to travel to the youth club, thirty minutes for business, which would leave them fifteen minutes spare. If they set off now they will have plenty of time. Johnny stands up, he's at the far end of the pub, there are about twenty gang members loyal to Johnny. “Quite lads.” Everyone stops what they are doing and listens. “We've got business”, he walks out of the pub and they all follow.

As they walk into the car park, there are four transit vans and one pickup. Two lads jump into the pickup and the others climb into the vans.

Johnny leads the way from the Crown Pub, they drive slowly as they don't want to get pulled up for speeding. As they make their way along the road up to the youth club, they see Ryan stood next to a small van, talking to Soul who had just arrived, he waves Johnny down. “Johnny, Silver and three off his young friends are in the hall, you'll see the double doors when you walk in, just go through them”.
Johnny tells Ryan to go keep watch outside the youth club. The vans and pickup rolled into the carpark and park in line as not to cause suspicion. They all get out of their vans, some carrying pickaxe handles, some chains, but there is one person stands out called SOUL. He’s, about six feet, broad, unshaven, dark long black curly hair and walks with a limp, he has no expression and he carries a joiner’s bag for his special tools. He is well known around Sheffield for carrying out punishment and torture. No one speaks to Soul, unless they must, as his behaviour is to unpredictable.

Johnny leads the way, they slowly walk in through the entrance to the youth club, past a juke box near the double doors leading to the hall. Johnny whispers to a young lad called Josh, who’s new to this kind of work. “When we've gone into the hall, you keep watch and put some music on for Soul", and gave him a handful of coins. All the gang stand quietly behind Johnny, Soul leans over the jukebox with both hands looking for his favourite song, when he finds it, he waves Josh over. Josh quickly walks over to Soul, he points to the name of the song, Run-around Sue. Josh nods, puts the money in the juke box and selects the song to play six times.

Meanwhile, Silver, Dan, Russ and Sam are at the far end of the hall, sat on a bench used for gymnastics.
Silver talks about his latest business deal. "I've got some cheap beer in lads, so I need you to help me deliver it around the estate". There's a loud BANG!
Johnny kicks open the door and the gangsters all walk in, Silver, Sam, Russ and Dan look down the hall and quickly stand up, they know there's trouble. The gangsters make a line across the hall, two large, rough looking gangsters stand in front of the doors to make sure no one runs out, and up to now, no one ever as.
Silver steps in front of his young friends, but they quickly line up beside him. Silver smiles, thinking nice one lads. Dan wonders whether they are a football firm. "I bet these are Sheffield Wednesday supporters". (Everyone from the Manor supports Sheffield United, and there is bitter conflict between the fans). Sam and Russ agree, nodding their heads.
Silver is quiet, he knows what this is about. Johnny shouts, his voice echoes around the hall. "Silver, you knew I could not let this go, it's my turn now". Russ looks

and smiles, they still think they are Wednesday fans. "Fuck this, I hate Wednesday fans", and they all start to sing their Sheffield United song"

Oh, when the blades, oh when the blades,

Go Marching in, go marching in,

Oh, when the blades go marching in,

We want to be, in that number,

When the blades go marching in.

The Manor Lads are now all hyped up, looking forward to the battle.

Silver laughs and says to Sam Dan and Russ. "We are the Manor Lads, and we only step forward, we never step back, no matter what happens, we show no fear ". The Manor Lads start to walk forward towards the gangsters, they have practiced this many times before at football matches, no matter what happens, they will stay together. But the gangsters are well organised and tooled up, some with pick axe handles, others with chains or knives, they begin to walk towards Silver, Dan, Russ and Sam. The gangsters suddenly charge forward, splitting up the Manor Lads with the sheer weight of the gang, they are like a roman legion.

Silver suddenly finds himself surrounded, one gang member Paddy steps in and swings his pick axe handle, Silver ducks and it goes flying past his head. He quickly steps forward hitting Paddy with a left jab on the nose, sending him falling to the ground, with his nose bleeding. Silver feels an excruciating pain to the back of his head, he has been hit from behind by Mike, splitting his head above his left ear. He drops down and is knelt up on one leg. Digger is stood in the front of Silver and brings his pickaxe handle down hard, on Silver's right knee. Sam sees Silver go down, even though they are surrounded, from nowhere he quickly steps forward, hurling himself through the air, headbutting the skinny gangster Brody in the front of him. With a kind of a twist and jump, Sam finds himself putting his hand on Silver's shoulder.

Dan, Russ and the gangsters look on, wondering how Sam had managed to do that. Mike, draws back the pick axe handle to hit Sam. Sam instinctively steps forward, kicking him in the groin, Mike cries out in pain, and goes down. Dan and Russ's spirits are very high, they charge head first through the gangsters standing in front of them, their youth, lack of fear and adrenaline now kicks in. Their priority is to protect one of their own, Silver.
Dan steps forward to Silvers rights side, Joe hits Dan with a pickaxe handle on his left shoulder, he feels a sickening pain, his shoulder drops, but he stands by Silver. Joe takes another swing, Dan ducks, he is slow due to his injury, it catches the top of his head, leaving him with a large gash. Dan instinctively steps to his right, punching Joe in the ribs with his right fist, followed by a right to his nose, Joe goes down, there are no prisoners or surrender

today, all four of the Manor Lads are fighting for their lives.
Russ steps in front of Silver protecting him from the front, Barron hits him with a chain across the front of his forehead, splitting it open above his right eye. Russ grabs Baron by his shirt and headbutts him on the nose, he staggers back, covered in blood and dazed. Russ smiles, as he starts to sing another united song, Sam and Dan join in.

"Take my hand,

Take my whole life to,

But I can't help,

Falling in love with you"

They repeat the song, and clap the best they can.

"Take my hand,

Take my whole life to,

But I can't help,

Falling in love with you".

Silver shakes his head with a smile, and thinks if he is to die this day, there can't be a more painful, prouder way to go.

The Manor Lads shout, "Manor Lads united, will never be defeated". All the gangsters have stopped for a second, they look at Sam Dan and Russ, all covered in blood, stood next to Silver, who is now badly injured on the floor.

The atmosphere that is created, is one of whatever was to happen that day, the Manor Lads would be back.

All the gangsters form a small circle around the Manor Lads, there is nowhere to go, the Manor Lads look round at each other and smile, as they stand around Silver. Silver, even though he knows what is to come, feels a great sense of pride, that these young Manor Lads are protecting him against overwhelming odds.
The gangsters step forward and rain down a barrage of blows, knocking Dan, Russ and Sam to the floor, they are hit all over their bodies as they curl up to protect themselves.

Johnny Shouts! “STOP!” All the gangsters stand back, Silver is laid on the floor unable to stand up with his shattered knee, his face and head are covered in bruises and blood. Sam, Dan and Russ are covered in grazes and cuts. Johnny orders the gang what to do. “Pin them down”. Paddy lifts Silver up, he is sat upright and feels dazed, his shattered right knee is bent back, his right arm is broken and hanging down by his side. Six of the gangsters, three on Dan, three on Russ drag them over to the benches they had been sat on earlier, and they are both pinned down longways. Sam stands up, a gangster takes hold of each arm, Joe stands behind him with a knife to his throat. Sam’s feeling angry, but any move now may mean further injury to his friends.

“Rights lads”, Johnny says, in a clear, triumphant voice. “I'm going to teach you a lesson that you don't fuck with Johnny, or his gang, if you do, you will be given a present you will never forget”.

Johnny hears arguing outside, suddenly, a young girl called Jan comes running into the hall, she's been looking for her friends and thought something was wrong. Josh follows Jan, he's looking worried and knows he will get a slap from Johnny for this. Jan’s shocked, when she sees the state of the Manor Lad’s. Johnny’s annoyed. “Take her out”.

Josh grabs Jan by her long hair, she screams as he drags her out of the hall, he wants to put her somewhere safe or she will also get hurt. He drags her towards the caretaker’s broom cupboard, Jan struggles, her Irish fight is in her. Josh pulls open the unlocked broom cupboard door, and throws Jan in. As soon as Josh releases Jan's hair, she spins around towards him, and with both hands, attacks him, leaving deep scratches on both sides of his face. Josh pushes Jan very hard with both hands on her chest, she goes tumbling back, tripping over the buckets and mops in the cupboard. He closes the door and puts on the padlock. The cupboard is now locked from the outside. Jan keeps kicking the door and Josh needs to keep her quiet. Sam’s been watching out of the corner of his eye, but there is nothing he can do.

Soul's been standing quietly outside of the hall, reading his car magazine and listening to the jukebox music, he had not taken any notice of what was happening, but is irritated with Jan's screaming. Soul walks over and stands next to the broom cupboard door." If you don't shut up you bitch I'm going to slash your face, if you say anything to anyone, I will find you, so keep quiet". Jan decides to stay quiet, it's not the time or the place to do anything and decides to sit and wait. Johnny shouts. "Soul". Soul rolls up his Elvis music magazine and puts it in his double buttoned, charcoal coloured , herringbone striped coat pocket, he picks up his tool bag and walks into the hall, he looks over at the four Manner Lads, Johnny points at Silver. "Put this one out of action so he can no longer fight, just scar the other three".
Silver, for the first time in his life is feeling helpless, not for himself, but for his brave young friends. Silver knows the gangsters are about to finish his fighting career.

Soul walks over to the coat pegs on the far side of the hall, takes off his coat and hangs it up, he then rolls up his black shirt sleeves. On his right forearm, he has the name of his old girlfriend, who he once loved, who was called Sue, on his left arm a tattoo of her face. He picks up his bag and walks over to Silver, and puts it down beside him. He puts his hand out and Paddy gives him the pick axe handle, Soul walks behind Silver, signs to the gangsters to step back, Silvers not going anywhere. Coldly and swiftly Soul brings the pick axe handle down on Silver's right shoulder, causing it to shatter. Silver cries out, then falls back onto the floor, the right-hand side of his body his now paralyzed.

Soul gently gives the pick axe handle back to Paddy, Sam is looking on in anger, Dan and Russ are still laid out on the benches, wondering what's going to happen to them next.
Soul goes to his bag, puts in his hand and takes out a short, wide flat ended screwdriver. He walks over to Silver, kneels over him, grabs his face and slowly gouges out Silvers right eye, leaving it laying on the floor next to him. Silver screams out and falls unconscious with the pain, everyone is quiet with the brutality. Soul calmly walks back over to his bag, takes out a cloth, wipes his screwdriver and then puts it back in the bag, Soul then stands waiting patiently for his next task. Johnny's smiling, he walks over to Sam, the gangsters spin him around towards Johnny, he grabs hold of Sam's chin, with his large right hand. Sam and Johnny look each other in the eyes, like two boxers about to do battle. "I think you're a pretty boy, I'll save you while last, you can watch your mates suffer first".

Johnny points to Dan and Russ, both held down on the benches. Soul takes out an old paraffin blow lamp and a box of matches. He puts the lamp on the floor and pumps it with the small brass handle. He then takes out a match and opens the screwed valve, the paraffin gas hisses as it comes out. Soul lights a match, puts it to the nozzle of the lamp, and with a big whoosh, the fuel is ignited, which gives out a hot blue flame. He picks up the lamp and walks over to Dan who starts to struggle, but is firmly held down by the gangsters. Soul puts the hot flame to Dan's left face cheek and holds it there for a second, just long enough to slightly burn him, Dan screams, and he then pulls the blow lamp away.

Soul then walks over to Russ, but Russ doesn't struggle, that's a mistake, it gives Soul the impression that he is not frightened. The gangsters hold Russ tightly down on the bench, Soul puts the burning flame onto Russ's left neck just below his ear. Russ starts to scream and struggle, Soul smiles, and holds it there for about five seconds, just long enough to smell the flesh burning, and moves the blow lamp away. For Russ this was an eternity, he is in agony, his ear and neck are badly burnt, Russ no longer struggles and looks frightened. Soul looks, he knows he has broken the young lad.

Soul returns to Dan who thought he had got off lightly, but not today. Soul turns off the blow lamp, the brass end is glowing red, he smiles, the gangsters hold Dan tight, he struggles and shouts. "You Bastard". Sam looks on, unable to do anything other than collect the hatred he is experiencing, he can take revenge another day. Soul mechanically puts the red-hot brass end of the blowtorch under Dan's right eye, his skin sizzles with the heat, Dan

goes into shock and is unable to scream. Soul then slowly pulls the hot metal end of the blowtorch along Dan's face, until it's level with his nose, leaving a three-inch-long black burn.
Soul takes away the blow lamp, rests it down on the floor next to his bag, leaving it to cool. Dan has tears running down his face from the agony he has endured. Soul puts his hand in his bag, takes out a Stanley knife and opens it up. Sam looks, he has no fear, that's his last weapon of defiance. Dan and Russ are both looking over, even though they are in pain, they also fear for what is going to happen to their friend.

,

Johnny stands in the front of Sam, Soul's watching closely. "You are a pretty boy, and every time you look in the mirror, you will remember how I made you smile ". Sam stares, Johnny steps back, Soul walks over to Sam, puts the knife inside Sam's top left-hand lip, and slowly cuts Sam's face cheek until it reaches under his left eye, blood shoots everywhere. Sam stares deep into Soul's eyes. Soul puts the knife into Sam's right lip and repeats the procedure with clinical precision. Sam's eyes water, not with just his pain, but also for the pain his friends have gone through, and he is also worried, of what may have happened to Jan.
Soul takes away the knife, he has finished his work, Sam looks straight in front, both denying pain and defeat. Johnny decides it's time to go. "Ok, that's enough, let's go, we've done here." The gangsters release their hold on the Manor Lads. Dan and Russ fall off the bench and lay

on the floor, Sam just stands looking at the gangsters as the gang walk away, staring into their eyes as they walk past, determined to remember their faces. The gangsters grin, Paddy shouts to Sam. "Are you ok smiler?".

Silver lays motionless in a pool of blood, Sam is still stood up, looking distantly towards his friend Silver, blood running down his face, he may have been going into shock. Russ and Dan slowly stand up, even though injured, they walk over to Silver. As they crouch over him, Dan gently touches Silver's shoulder, Silver cries out, Russ gently pulls Dan's hand away, a reassuring hand is putting Silver through a lot of pain. They hear a thud, and they both look around towards their friend, Sam was now kneeling, head crouched, with a large pool of blood on the floor. Dan shouts to his friend. "Sam". They run over to Sam fearing the worse, they kneel beside their friend, Dan asks Sam if he is ok. Sam nods yes, he can't speak, Dan puts his hand under Sam's chin and lifts his head, they are horrified to see the wounds on Sam's face.

Jan has heard the gangsters leave and starts to kick the broom cupboard door. Ted the caretaker comes walking back towards the youth club, it seems unusually quiet and he becomes suspicious. He gathers pace and walks quickly up the steps into the entrance to the club. He hears a banging noise coming from his broom cupboard,

he walks over and shouts. "Who is it?" Jan recognises old Ted's voice. "It's Jan"
Stan recognises the voice and as he unlocks the padlock with his keys, the door bursts open and Jan goes rushing past Ted. "Quick" she says. Jan runs into the hall, Ted follows, they see what has happened. Ted, knows what to do. "I'm phoning for the ambulance and police", and rushes to the phone. Jan runs over to Sam, she asks him if he is alright, Sam is looking down, he is unable to speak, she shouts out, "Ted's phoning for an ambulance, helps on the way", but Dan and Russ are more concerned about Silver. "See to Silver Jan'.
Jan walks over to Silver, he's is unconscious, she kneels beside him, Jan cannot do anything, he needs a paramedic, she just stares into space as she is shocked with the sight of her friend's injuries.

Two ambulances and a policeman arrive, they are met by Ted, he takes them quickly through the entrance and up to the double doors of the hall, the paramedic pushes the door open and walks quickly in, the policeman closely follows. Sam is now stood facing the wall, propped up with his arms, Russ and Dan are now laid on the floor, bleeding, and in pain from their burns.
The paramedics, Mark, Hafeez, Rashid, Jessica and a policeman Paul, goes over to assess the casualties. Jan walks over to Mark, as Mark taps Sam on the shoulder. "My friends name his Sam". Sam turns around and Mark is shocked at the injuries to Sam's face, but doesn't show

it, he doesn't want to worry Sam. “Sam, don't speak, I'm going to bandage your wounds, you're going to be ok”. Sam stands upright as Mark secures a large bandage tightly around Sam's injury. He puts his arm around Sam's shoulders and starts to lead him away. Sam stops, looks around at his friends, cruelly injured, he feels nothing for himself, but has an overpowering feeling of revenge for what the gangsters have done. Dan and Russ both have their injuries tended by Hafeez, and can stand up without the aid of a paramedic. Hafeez and the lads walk out of the youth club and up to the waiting ambulance, Sam and Mark walk in front. Dan and Russ look down as they climb slowly into the ambulance and sit on two of the single seats, while Sam is gently laid on the stretcher.

Paramedics, Rashida and Jessica supported by Paul a policeman kneel next to Silver, reassuring him that assistance had arrived. They thanked Jan for supporting Silver, she walked over to wait with Ted who was stood next to the doors at the far end of the hall, ready to open them when required.
Blood was seeping through Silvers left hand as it covered his eye. Rashid the paramedic prepared a bandage. “Silver, I need to look at your eye”, Silver moved his hand and his eyelid was closed, covering his missing eye. Rashid applied a dressing and covered Silvers eye with a head bandage, his right shoulder was badly bleeding, Jessica passed Paul a bandage and told him to firmly

hold it onto the wound on Silver's shoulder, to slow the bleeding. Paul was a young constable and had never seen anything like this before, he felt sick. He took the bandage and put it over Silvers wound, it immediately soaked up the blood.
Jessica spoke in a very calm reassuring voice, “It’s ok, just keep applying the pressure”.

It was time to prepare Silver for splints to be placed on his legs, to support his knees. The paramedics explained to him, what they needed to do.
“Silver we are going to have to lay you down and put splints on your legs before we can put you on the stretcher. We don't want to give you any morphine unless we have too, because of your head injury. Silver just wanted to go to hospital. “Let's get on with it”. They laid Silver out flat, put his legs straight and applied the splints. Silver was in pain, but was now feeling more comfortable. He was picked up by the two paramedics and the policeman and slowly laid on a stretcher. He falls unconscious again, the paramedics check his breathing and pulse, he is fine and is quickly rushed to hospital.

When Dan and Russ arrive at the hospital, they are taken into A and E to have their injuries tended, and are released home. Sam is taken straight into theatre and receives special surgery.
When he regains consciousness, he is in the intensive care ward, his face is stinging and is covered with a tight

bandage. Gareth a mature experienced nurse comes over, he explains to Sam that he has had surgery and he should not try to speak. Sam takes a deep breath, he is feeling groggy, he hears a voice, and looks to his left-hand side, and sees his mom Linda. “Sam, what have they done to you?”. She starts to cry, Sam holds out his hand and she squeezes it.

For the next few days, only Sam's close family can visit, and he enjoys laying comfortably in bed, it makes a change to have clean bedding, and a mattress with no springs sticking out, but he is haunted with the experience he has just had. Meanwhile, Dan and Russ have been out on the Manor, everyone stops to ask them what had happened. They're all shocked to hear that Silver has been beaten up, and their friends have been so badly injured, everyone wants to take revenge. Russ tells everyone that they all need to wait to see what Sam would like to do, when he comes out of hospital, they all agree.
Silver is in intensive care, and has lost his right eye, the muscles in his right arm are so badly damaged he will never be able to use it again, both knees are so badly broken, that he will always need a stick to walk.

After a week, Sam is given therapy to prepare him for when he sees his scars. It's Friday afternoon, and Sam is due to have his bandages removed. He is so bored he doesn't care what his face looks like, all he wants to do, is get back to the Manor with his friends. Linda and Neil are sat next to Sam's bed. Susan a young nurse walks in, "Afternoon Sam, the doctor will be coming in about five minutes to remove your bandages".

The nurse tidies round, there's a knock on the door, the doctor then walks in, he's tall, Asian, very polite, with a big smile on his face. "Hullo Sam, I am Dr Singh, can you remember me talking to you, just shortly after your operation". Sam shakes his head, he can't remember, it may be the shock of his injuries.

"Well, I was the doctor who carried out the operation and it went very well, today we are going to remove your bandages". Sam sits up right, it's all quiet, the doctor puts on his plastic gloves and the nurse stands next to him, holding a tray for the scissors and bandages. The doctor cuts the tape and slowly removes the bandages, Sam's face is slowly revealed, Linda and Neil look over intensely. When the bandages are removed, Sam's face is slightly swollen from the injury, but he has a very thin red line from both sides of his lips. The doctor smiles, he is pleased with his work, Linda and Neil are relieved, it's not as bad as they thought. Dr Singh gives Sam advice on what he must do.

"Sam, you must talk very slowly and exercise your face muscles, would you like to go to the toilet and look for yourself?". Sam goes to the toilet, locks the door behind him and looks in the mirror. He sees the scars along his face, remembering what Johnny had said, he will always have a smile on his face.

Everything comes back to Sam, he punches the mirror breaking it into small pieces, and falls onto the floor crying. Gareth, a male nurse passing by hears the crash and kicks open the door, he is aware of Sam's injuries as he has helped nurse him. He goes over to Sam and puts his hand on his shoulder.

"Sam, Sam,". Sam looks up at the nurse. "What". "Your right to be upset, but your scars are only looking worse because they are swelled and new, you're young and they will quickly heal. Dr Singh has done a fantastic job, and they will soon disappear. Remember, you're a Manor Lad, you never go down, come on, stand up". Sam stands up and composes himself, looks at Gareth and gently smiles, he slowly walks back to his room. As he walks in he goes over to his mom and dad and gives them a big hug, Dr Singh smiles." Come here Sam, let me take another look". The doctor gets Sam to say a few words as he looks at his face.

"Ok Sam, this is what we have got, the operation as taken very well, and because of your age the scars will quickly disappear, however you will be left with a very small smile on your right cheek, not to worry though, it will be a cheeky smile". These words would later ring true, not only enhancing Sam's look and character with his friends, but also, upsetting his enemies, in time of conflict.

Sam likes the thought of his new look, and shakes the hand of the doctor, thanking him. Dr Singh says goodbye. "Ok Sam, just take your time with your speech, and if you have any problems come back to the hospital". Sam's looking forward to going home. “Doctor Sing, can I go now?”. He says very gently. “Yes, of course, but I have other patients to see now, good luck Sam”.

Sam quickly picks up the clean clothes his mom and dad have brought him, and they leave the room while he gets dressed. As he walks out of the room, Sam is smiling, his chest is stood out and he stands proud. “Ok mom, dad, let's go”, in a delicate voice. As they walk down the corridor, Gareth and Susan are stood together looking through a patient's record, Sam stops. “Ae”. Gareth and Susan look round, they see Sam with a slight smile on his face, he talks very slowly. “I'd like to thank you both”. Gareth and Susan are pleased.
“Ok Sam, good luck”. Sam goes on his way, and they have other patients to see, but Sam will never forget the special care he has be given, in the Sheffield Hospital.

Linda, Neal and Sam go down in the lift which takes them across from the main entrance door, as Sam walks out of the hospital he takes a deep breath of fresh air, a feeling of being free again. They get into a nearby Taxi, Linda tells the taxi driver their destination. “Manor Estate please love”. The taxi driver, Raj, doesn't like going to the Manor. “Ok love, but you have to pay me first, I’ve have taken people there before, and they have run off without paying”. Sam smiles, he knows a few mates that have done that. Linda gives the taxi driver a fiver, and they set off on their journey. As they travel through Sheffield city centre, along the side of the River Don, they pass the Old Crown Inn, Sam knows it's where Johnny drinks. He peers over, he can see the pickups and people moving around, Sam nods, his day his to come.

The taxi enters the estate, Sam feels happy to be home, he soon arrives back at his house and as he climbs out of the taxi, he hears someone shout. “Sam”. He looks around and sees Dan and Russ, Sam puts up his arm and they come running across, grab him by the waste and pick him up, they all cheer, Dan and Russ are still covered in bandages, they are pleased to be together again.

Disco

The weeks pass, and Sam's injuries have healed, and only leave a small scar which leaves him with a small cheeky smile on the right-hand side of his face. It's Thursday night, and it's Sam's first time back to the youth club since the fight, Dan and Russ have come to call for him. As they walk through the streets, their jumping on walls, kicking cans, teasing dogs so they chase them, they are happy again and having fun.

When they arrive at the youth club, Sam walks in followed by his friends, there's music coming from the main hall, as it was disco night, *Low Rider* was being played. Sam pushes open the door and it is full of young people. As they walk in, people stop and stare at Sam and his friends. Brett the DJ stopped playing the music, someone starts to sing, *Holding Out for a Hero.* The atmosphere is electric, everyone joins in, Sam holds Dan and Russ's hand in the air. As their friend's finish singing, Sam, Russ and Dan start to sing one of their football songs?

"For ever and ever,
We'll follow our team,
Were Sheffield United,
We rule supreme
We'll never be mastered,
By no Wednesday bastards,
We'll keep the red flag flying high."

Everyone cheers, and the disco music begins to play.

As they stand at the front of the disco, Sam thought that his wound would turn the girls away, but in truth it was the opposite. There was one young fifteen-year-old girl called Jan, who Sam knew, she was slim and attractive. Sam had a distant crush on her, but whenever he looked her way she always ignored him. She was stood in the right-hand corner of the hall with her two friends, Clare and Sue. Jan had been glimpsing at Sam, wondering what his face, now looked like. Sam was surrounded by three young girls dancing around him, trying to take his hand and talking to him, but Sam was looking over at Jan. There was an immediate attraction, the youth club experience had changed the way Jan felt about Sam. Jan suddenly stood up, walked in between the girls who were flirting with Sam, she looked into Sam's eyes, held out her hand and smiled. Sam, took Jan's hand and they both felt a great sense of warmth and young love. Sam led the way and they walked out of the disco into the carpark. It's cold and Sam takes off his coat, the one which Rover had been laid on earlier, and he puts it around Jan's shoulders, she sniffs it, there's a doggy smell, but she just smiles, it is the thought that counts. Sam put his arm around Jan's shoulder and they huddled together to keep warm, Jan looks at Sam's face. "Sam, your injuries have left you with a short cheeky smile, but it also makes you look dangerous, rough and sexy. You will always have women chasing you now, more than before". Sam's confidence was back, it was time for Jan to go home. "Can I walk you home please Jan?". Jan gave a shy smile, "That would be nice, thanks Sam".

Sam puts his arm around Jan's shoulders and she puts hers around his waist, and they walk closely together towards Jan's home, two young lads ride past and give a whistle. Just down the street from Jan's home there is a bus shelter, Jan looks at her watch. "It's only 9pm, I don't have to be in until 9.30pm, let's stand in the bus shelter". They walk in and Sam is soaking wet, they huddle together under Sam's coat, behind them written on the walls are graffiti poems about their teachers from school. As they stand in the corner, Sam puts his hands around Jan's waist, she puts her hands around Sam's shoulders. They look deeply into one another's eyes, not feeling the cold, there is no meaning to time, just the feeling of love and desire for the first time. Sam and Jan are now deeply in love, and they wish this moment could last for ever, they hear an Irish man's voice calling.

"Jan! Jan!" Jan recognises the voice. "That's my dad, he's looking for me". Sam's concerned, he doesn't want to get Jan into trouble. "What's your dad's name?". "Patrick, why Sam?". "Come on Jan". Jan doesn't want Sam to go. "No Sam". Sam takes Jan's hand and pulls her out of the bus shelter. As they looked up the street they could see a tall man, wearing a raincoat and carrying an umbrella. "It's my dad, he's walking towards us". Sam shouts over to Jan's dad. "Patrick, Jan's here". Patrick looks, he waves, and they walk towards each other. "Patrick, I have walked Jan home because it may not be safe since we had all the trouble at the youth club." Patrick smiles, he holds out

his hand and they shake hands. “What’s your name son?”. Sam looks into Patrick's eyes, he appears honest and strong. “Sam “.
“Ok Sam, are you one of the lads that got injured in the fight at the youth club?”. Sam wonders why he is asking that question. “Yes Sir”. “Rumour has it that you were a brave lad, I admire that, come on Jan let's go home, you’ll see Sam another day”.
Jan kisses Sam on his lips, then walks over to her dad and they walk home together. Sam stands and watches as it rains, his hair and clothes and wet. As Jan reaches her gate she looks down the street and sees Sam standing there, she waves, Sam puts up his hand and she walks into her garden. Sam’s in love, the pleasure this brings takes away the memory of the recent past, which has now gone.

Jan's Revenge

The next day, Jan is due to go to her local catholic school, she has been awake all-night thinking about Sam, her first childhood crush. It's 7.30 a m and it's time to get dressed, Mary, Jan's mom calls in a soft gentle voice. "Your breakfast is ready Jan". Jan looks out of her bedroom window, it is raining and cold, she sees the milkman running quickly from house to house holding his hat, there's a twelve-year-old paperboy, Paul, who is soaked, as he is only wearing his maroon school jacket, but walks as though he doesn't have a care in the world, he looks up and waves to Jan with a cheeky smile, she waves back and closes the curtains. Jan starts to think of Sam and the way he held her tight the night before, she smiles and feels warm from the thought.

Jan quickly gets dressed, runs downstairs and has her breakfast, her mom is ironing in the lounge and dad is at work at the local steelworks in Sheffield. She has a slice of toast and a quick drink of tea, before putting on her coat and picking up her black leather school satchel. She's just about to leave and remembers her mom and runs into the lounge. "Mom, I'm going to school now ", she gives her mom a kiss on the cheek. "Have a good day Jan", "I will ".

As Jan walks out of the door she can't wait to get to the bus stop to tell her friends, but her excitement maybe short lived. As she waits for her bus, Jan sees her two

school friends walking up the road. Sue who is short and tubby, and Clare, who is a little taller than Jan, with long blonde hair, slim, pretty, quite outgoing and jolly. As they arrived at the bus stop, Jan couldn't wait to tell them about Sam, she was so excited.
"Sue, Clare, guess what happened at the youth club last night?". Sue and Claire like a bit of gossip.

"Well you know Sam came into the youth club, you know about the trouble and all the girls were after him, and he turned them down, well he asked if he could walk me home. While we were at the bus stop we kissed, he feels so strong and sexy, he asked if he could meet me again. Sue was impressed. "Wow"
Claire looked down at the ground and went quiet. Clare and Jan were very close friends and wouldn't dream of hurting each other, she now becomes worried. "Jan, there is something I need to tell you". Jan looks at Clare, wondering what it could be, she was feeling so happy. Clare looked straight at Jan, Jan knew it had to be serious, her friend never usually looks at her like that. "A few weeks ago, before Sam had that fight, we were stood talking outside the youth club and he suddenly kissed me. I haven't heard anything about him kissing anyone else, but he might have a bad reputation, I'm so sorry Jan". Jan was heartbroken and burst into tears, the young man she had fell in love with, might have turned out to be a user. She would not see Sam again until the following week at the youth club. Clare put her arms around Jan, and gave her a big hug, and she stopped crying. Sue had

been listening intently and was enjoying the gossip. The bus turned up for school, and as they got onto the bus they had a laugh with their friends, but for Jan, Sam was still at the back of her mind.

The days felt like months, until Thursday evening came around. It was 5pm and Sue and Claire went to call for Jan. They stood at the door and knocked, Jan was making herself look nice, she stopped, ran downstairs and opened the door, she was pleased to see her friends. "One minute", Jan grabbed her coat off the coat hook on the door and shouted to her mom and dad, "I'm going to the youth club now". Mary was reading, and Patrick was watching the news on TV. "Ok be careful".

The girls made their way to the youth club, both Jan and Claire were a little nervous about Sam, and what they may feel when they see him, but Sue was also looking forward to the drama. When they arrive at the youth club there is a large que, young people are giggling and playing around.

Old Ted opens the double doors, and everyone rushes in, they run along the corridor and into the main hall to get the best seats. Jan Clare and Sue laugh as they are pushed and pulled along with the crowd.

Graham, who brags about how he is always wearing the poshest clothes, is running in front and thinks he can get the best seat near the stage, but he trips as he gets close to the hall door. As he falls down people run over the top of him, purposely dropping their ice cream and sticky sweets, and stamping on all parts of his body, laughing as they do so. Jan and her friends find a seat in the far-right hand corner near the stage, Jan as a plan. "Listen girls this is what I am going to do, when Sam comes over to talk to me, I'll go and ask Brett to put on my favourite song?". Sue is finding the plot intriguing, Clare's worried about her friend.

Everyone is dancing, Jan keeps looking up at the clock and glancing over at the entrance doors, waiting for Sam to walk in. BANG, the hall doors fly open, Sam, Dan and Russ fall into the hall and onto the floor laughing, everyone looks around. They stand up and walk towards the front of the disco, Sam looks for Jan, she smiles and shouts. "Sam". He hears Jan and as he looks over he sees her in the far corner, he puts up his hand and smiles, he walks over to see her, Jan can see he is pleased. She stands up, her friends watch wondering what is going to happen, she kisses Sam on the cheek. "Sam, I have a surprise for you, go and stand on the dance floor". Jan walks up onto the stage and asks the DJ to put on a specific song, she takes the microphone and slowly walks down the steps and starts to sing, *These Boots Were Made for Walking,* people start to point with interest at Jan. She stands in the front of Sam as she sings, puts her right index finger on his lips and smiles. Sam stands looking at Jan, wondering what to expect. As Jan sings, she starts to dance, the crowd

stands in a circle around them. As she gets to the end of the song, she stands close to Sam, looks deep into his eyes, he looks into hers, he loves her so much. She puts her hands on his shoulders and moves slowly forward to kiss him. Sam moves towards Jan's lips with his, he closes his eyes and waits with anticipation. She sings the final words to the song. "And one of these days, these boots are going to, walk, all over you".
Sam feels an excruciating pain between his legs and falls helpless onto the floor. Jan's kneed him straight in the bollocks, the crowd groan, Dan and Russ laugh, they walk over and wait to pick him up. As Sam opens his eyes he is shocked and sees Jan stood over him, glaring fiercely. "You'd better not kiss anyone now you're with me ".
Jan walks back over to her friends who are stood up, they have seen everything that has happened, they clap and hug Jan. She picks up her long slim clear glass, takes a drink of her ice filled coke and sits quietly down, feeling proud of what she has just done, but worried that she may have hurt Sam. She stands up and quickly walks back over to him, he is still stood bow legged on the dance floor, holding onto Dan's shoulder as the pain doesn't allow him to stand upright.

He sees Jan and flinches, he covers up his balls with both hands.

Jan looks at Sam and could see he is in a lot of pain. "I'm sorry Sam". She puts both arms around him and gives

him a big hug. Sam smiles, as the pain brings tears to his eyes.
Jan takes Sam's hand and leads him limping through the young people dancing, out of the hall, along the corridor and very slowly down the steps to the car park, they stand there on their own.
"Sam let's have a slow walk home, Sam puts his arm around Jan, so she can support him.

It's windy and lightly raining, as they walk slowly through the housing estate and along the road towards Jan's house. People are sat on their low brick garden walls talking to their neighbours, young kids are playing football in the street, Sam and Jan say hullo to their friends as they casually walk past. Pete, one of Sam's friends is stood up on the seat of his motorbike as he rides along the street, he's just seen what's happened at the youth club and shouts. "Watch your bags there's a knacker snatcher about", he waves as he rides off, Jan and Sam laugh, "That's Pete for you"

A young man slowly walks towards them, who's new to the village, he is tall, has long auburn hair, slim, with a leather jacket, jeans and steel capped boots, he as a fag in the left-hand side of his mouth and a bottle of Guinness in his right hand. His dad Tam, is from Northern Ireland and has come to work at the local steel works. As Jan walks by they look at each other and smile, at the same time they both say, "Ae up", as though they know each other well. Sam suddenly feels angry and jealous, he suddenly stops walking, takes his arm from around Jan's shoulder and shouts. "WHO'S THAT!".

Jan's pleased with Sam's response, this is an opportunity to make him jealous. "It's A J, his dad, is one of my dad's friends". Sam suddenly has a lot of different fears going through his head. "Have you kissed him?". Jan looks at Sam, pauses, gives a sly smile. "I have only kissed him once, it was just over a year ago, at A J's house, we were in the lounge together and my dad and his friend Tam where in the garden, talking business and having a beer". Sam didn't want to hear this, but he needed to know the answer to the question. "We looked at each other, A J came over to me and smiled, he then kissed me on the lips ".

It's not the answer Sam wanted to hear. "Did you enjoy it?". Jan nods, with a small grin. "Yes, but my dad came back in and we stopped and acted as though nothing had happened". Sam takes a deep breath. "Did you meet him again?". "No, A J told me he had a girlfriend, he gave me the impression he was a lady's man". Jan grabbed hold of Sam's hand, he stood there looking stern, Jan was thinking that it was Sam's turn to feel jealous.

As they walk back together, Jan's sees her dog, a large black Labrador stood outside her garden gate, waiting for her to come home. "Max, come on ", he starts to run towards Jan, Sam bends over and pats his knees. "Come

on Max", trying to make it look like Max would sooner greet Sam than Jan. As Max gets closer he picks up speed, Jan keeps quiet and steps back, she knows what is coming next. Sam shouts again. "Come on Max", Max weighs sixteen stone and is now hurtling excitedly towards Sam. As he gets close, Max is unable to stop and runs straight into Sam's legs.
Sam cries out, "OOOOOF" and is knocked flying through the air, before landing flat on his back on the wet muddy pavement, Max yelps and come's to a quick stop on his belly. Jan giggles, she knows what Sam is feeling as it had happened to her before. She runs over to Max, rubs the back of his ear (it's a magic rub for dogs,) and he quickly gets up. Sam is still laid on the floor, mainly for sympathy from Jan than the pain from the injury, Max is still excited. Sam should have got up from the ground when he could, Max runs over to Sam, puts his sludgy paws on Sam's chest and licks his face, Sam laughs as he pushes Max away. He aches all over as he slowly stands up, Jan looks at her dog fussing Sam, it's time to walk home. "Come on Max". Max starts to run home as Jan brushes the sludge from the back of Sam's jacket but makes it worse.

As they walk the last few yards arm in arm, they get to Jan's old wooden green, well-kept gate. She puts her arms around Sam's shoulders and gives him a big kiss. "Good night Sam, I'll see you next week at the youth club".

Sam's pleased, "Ok Jan". She turns around and walks down the concrete path and stops at the back door, she turns around and sees that Sam has been looking at her as she walked away. Jan blows Sam a kiss, he gives her a loving smile and blows her one back. She walks through the door, runs upstairs to her bedroom and pulls the white net curtains to one side. As she looks through the small Georgian flat paned windows, she watches Sam slowly walking down the street, he is in a world of his own, has he thinks about his girlfriend Jan.

Paul the paper lad skids on his bike and stops directly in front of Sam, he is startled. "Fucking hell Paul, you frightened me to death, why don't you get some lights on?". Paul laughs. "It's a good trick Sam, it always frightens everyone". Sam looks down at Paul's bike and sees what appears to be something gruesome." Fucking hell Paul, what's on your handlebars?". Paul looks down with pride as he points to them ". On my right handlebar is my grans false teeth and on the left, is my grandads, they left them to me when they died, so I would have something to remember them by, great aren't they?". Sam screws up his face in disgust. "Couldn't you have had a watch, or candlestick or something Paul?". "NOOOOO Sam, I tried them, but they don't light up, I like these best, see you". As Paul rides down the street, two of the street lights have gone out and you can hear young girls scream, as they see two pair of false teeth flying towards them in the dark.

Sam walks in through his front door, there's a welcoming smell of chips his mom is frying. Linda hears him come in. "Is that you Sam?". Sam kicks off his shoes and leaves them in the hallway and throws his coat onto the bottom step of the stairs. "Yes mom, I'm starving". As he walks into the kitchen, dirty pots are in the sink and the cooker top is covered in grease. Linda passes Sam his chips on an old cracked white round plate, as Sam stands there, she butters two slices of bread and throws them onto the top of his chips. He walks into the front room, the black and white tv is switched on loud. Neil, Sam's dad is laid in his arm chair fast asleep, with half a bottle of beer on the floor and a fag between the fingers of his left hand, lucky for him it had gone out. Sam sits on the sofa, one of the arms was broken, where Sam used to play fight with his dad and the springs had sprung up through the cushion, so he sank uncomfortably deep into them. As Sam eats his chips from the plate on his knee, is dad snores, but all Sam can think about is Jan and what had happened that evening.

He finishes his chips, as he walks into the kitchen he throws his plate into the sink, the back door is open, his mom his talking over the spiked wooden fence to her next-door neighbour. "Night mom". Linda looks round, "Night Sam", and carried on talking. Sam walks up the bare wooden stairs and into his small undecorated bedroom, white paint is flaking off the door and paper his hanging off the walls. His single bed as two checked woollen blankets and a pink tea stained sheet were his mother had spilt her cup of tea, there was a small black striped feather pillow with feathers coming through, and his Beano and Dandy comics were scattered at the side of his bed. He takes off his clothes and throws them onto the floor for the next day. Sam turns off the light and climbs into the cold bed. As he cuddles up into the sheets, all he can think about is Jan, kissing A J, and how much further it could or may have gone. This cuts him deep inside, the emotional pain is greater than the injuries he had experienced from the youth club, which is now mixed with the pain and pleasure from his first teenage crush. All that night, Sam tosses and turns, thinking about Jan, until he drops off to sleep.

It's Saturday morning, his mom shouts, “Come on Sam”, it's 7.30 a m. Linda works at the local hosiery factory making clothes, she is working a short shift today. He falls back to sleep for another couple of hours, he's feeling confused. He hears a knock on the door and looks out of the window, it's his friends Russ and Dan. He puts his clothes on from the night before, and goes to the bathroom and as a quick wash in cold water before going down stairs, he walks over to the to the back door and opens it. His friends are stood their smiling, Russ looks at Sam who's half asleep. “Sam, you look knackered, how did you and Jan get on the other night?” Sam rubs his eyes. “Come on in lads “. They all walk into the lounge followed by Rover, they all stand looking at each other,

Sam's painfully in love and his friends are eager to know what had happened. Dan asks Sam, he can't wait any longer. "Come on then, how did you and Jan get on?". Sam tries to think of a song which describes the way he feels, it comes to him.
"Well lads, it goes like this". Sam starts to sing**,** *I'm Into Something Good.* "I woke up this morning and I was feeling fine, I've got something, on my mind". Russ and Dan stand behind Sam clapping and dancing, Rover stands beside them, one front leg repeatedly crosses the other, and his tail wags to the rhythm of the music.

Sam finishes the song and they all laugh, Rover jumps up at Sam for a fuss. Russ walks over to Sam and pats him on the left shoulder. "So, you had a good night then". Sam goes quiet and suddenly looks sad.
Russ's concerned about his friend." Sam, what's up mate? why don't you sit down and tell us what's bothering you". Sam sits on the chair and his friends sit on the sofa, they wait for Sam to explain what is wrong. Sam looks at his friends with tears in his eyes, as he describes what happened a few nights before with A J . Russ puts his arms around his friend Sam. "Well mate, hang in there, it will all come right, get cleaned up we'll go out and have a laugh". Even the company of Sam's friends, doesn't take away his thoughts of Jan, he will have to see what time brings.

Sam and Jan had arranged to meet the following week at the youth club, all Sam could think about was Jan kissing A J, he had not slept all week and was making himself ill. Wednesday night came and one of Jan's friends put a note through Sam's door, asking him to call for Jan on Thursday evening, so they could walk to the youth club together.

It was Thursday, it had been a long week for Sam, both working a day shift and thinking about Jan.
He got off the pit bus after the day shift, and quietly walked home, his stomach was churning from the mixed up young feelings of both being in love, and jealousy of A J. As he walked into the house, he made a coal fire to heat the hot water, and prepared his clothes early for that evening, making sure everything was right, so he could look smart for Jan. He decided to have a bath, even though it was Thursday (Sam only as a bath on Friday) and has he got dressed he made sure he was neat and tidy. He looked in the mirror and put up his thumbs, there was something missing. “I know what I need “. Sam ran into his parents' bedroom, on the windowsill was a bottle of his dad's brut deodorant, he took off the top and poured it over his shirt. “OH NO”. It wasn't brut in the bottle, it was a secret supply of whiskey his dad had hid from his mom, so she didn't know how much he drank. Sam rushed to the bathroom, picked up a towel and tried to wipe off the whisky, but the smell wasn't going to go away. He gave a big sigh. “Oh well, it's just another

typical day", he brushed himself down, put on his checked jacket and walked out of the back door.

As Sam walked up the road to Jan's, he didn't notice people talking to him, because he was wondering why she wanted to see him. He came to Jan's house, as he walked down the garden path he felt so nervous and sick, thinking it could only be bad news. He paused as he stood at Jan's back door and then knocked. Jan's mom opened the door. "Hullo Sam ". She was pleased to see him", Jan's stood directly behind her. "Do you want to come in?". Sam steps forward, but Jan wants to leave. "It's ok mom, I'm going to walk to the youth club with Sam", Jan pushes past her mom, her mom smiles. "Come on Sam we need to talk", in serious tone, Sam's even more worried now, things go from bad to worse.

Jan silently leads the way, as they walk down the road until they reach a bench at the junction, which all their friends use. She stops, looks at Sam with a straight face as though she has something important to say to him. "Let's sit down Sam". As they sit side by side Jan takes hold of Sam's hand, they look directly into one another's eyes, Sam now thinks Jan is going to finish with him, so she can go out with A J.
Jan breaks the silence. "Sam, I have something to tell you". Sam takes a deep breath, the moment he feared is here. "Well you know A J". "Yes". "Well you know when I said I kissed him". Sam was sure this was it. "Yes".

"Well", Jan pauses, "Well ", Jan pauses again. Sam can't stand the pain. "Jan please tell me, I know you are going to finish with me, so you can go out with A J". Jan looked at Sam, he was starting to cry, his heart was breaking, she had to tell him. "No, of course not, you're a stupid boy, I was just telling you a small lie, I wanted you to know how I felt about you kissing another girl". She then leant over and kissed him on the cheek. Sam jumps up in the air and cheered with delight. "YES".
He starts to do handstands on the bench, Jan starts to giggle, Sam grabs hold of her with both arms and squeezes her tight, he is so happy, but Jan's got a warning for Sam. "Let this be a lesson for you Sam, you'd better be faithful to me ".

They hold hands as they walk to the youth club together, when they arrive they both walk up to the far corner of the stage, where their friends are sat. Clare gives a consenting smile to Jan. "It's nice to see you two together", Jan and Sam kiss each other, Sam needs to express the way he feels. "Wait here everybody". Sam goes onto the stage, talks to the DJ, makes a request and picks up the microphone. All his friends are watching, he starts to sing, *Love Hurts.* The audience slowly dance and hold hands, Jan's touched by his choice of song. As Sam finishes singing his song, Jan runs up onto the stage and hugs him, everyone cheers. It's Jan's turn for a song, she makes her request and stands with anticipation. it's quiet, Sam is stood next to her. She starts to sing, *Seven*

Day Fool. Her friends start to click their fingers and dance to the steady beat. Jan finishes her song and they walk off the stage hand in hand, and for the rest of the evening they dance close together, it feels as though there is no one else is there.

The disco ends, its 10pm, Sam slowly walks Jan home and they hold each other tight. They reach Jan's gate, Mary looks through the window and watches them kiss, she smiles as she can see that they love each other, which reminds her of when she was young, and in love with a hero. They walk to Jan's back door, as she opens it, Sam as to say what he deeply feels. "Jan". Jan looks at Sam. "I Love You".
Another tear comes into his eye, Jan gives him a loving smile and wipes it away with her finger.
"I love you too Sam". She puts her arms tightly around his shoulders and kisses him lovingly on the lips.
"I've got to go now Sam, bye", and she walks into the house. Sam is so happy, he runs down the street singing and dancing, all the pain and anger as now gone, it's now time to enjoy being in love.

Jake Meets Sam

It's 7.30 a m, Jake is sat on a wall at the bottom of his street waiting for the 85 bus to Sheffield, the roads are busy with people going to work, men and woman walk or ride past as they make their way to the local factories. He is about to undertake his underground training at Orgreave Colliery, with other lads from the South Yorkshire Area, where they were trained to work underground at their local colliery's. The bus arrives, he picks up his large string sack bag, which holds his, boots, overalls, belt and helmet. As Jake travels on the bus, he watches people come and go, some going to work, others shopping. He looks out onto the open grass fields, admiring their colour and calmness. As the bus reaches Swallow Nest, near Sheffield, he knows he is near because of the instructions his work mate Ted has given him. The bus passes some factories, a man behind him presses the button which rings a bell, indicating to the driver that a passenger needs the next stop. The bus pulls up, Jake looks out of the bus window and sees the sign for Fence Workshops, National Coal Board.

Two men make their way down the aisle, Jake picks up his bag and follows, he gets off the bus, and as it pulls away, Jake looks around, wondering which way to go. He walks over the road and a bus pulls up on its way to Worksop. Jake thinks that's lucky as he now knows where to catch a bus home. A young lad gets off the bus,

carrying the same kind of bag as Jake, and comes walking towards him.
“Ae up mate, you don't know where Orgreave Pit is do you?”. Sam smiles, “Yes mate, it's up near Treeton Training Centre, are you going there?”.
Jakes relieved he's found the way. “Yes mate, I remember now, when I did my training there we never made the planned visit to the colliery. What's your name mate?”. “I’m Sam, I’m from the Manor Estate just down the road”. Jake smiles, “I've never heard of that place, mind you, I'm from Worksop, it's a small town in the countryside”. Sam laughs. “Is it true, you country lads have sex with chickens”. Jake laughs, “No, only dogs”. Sam likes Jake’s sense of humour. “Come on mate, I'll show you the way”.

It's a two mile walk along a winding path that passes an old pit tip, before going through some open grass fields which leads to Orgreave Colliery. As the five training weeks go by, Sam and Jake become good friends. It's the last day of training, Jake and Sam walk down the winding path to catch the bus home, it may be the last time they see each other. Sam decides to ask Jake if he would like to go out for a drink.
“Jake, do you want to come over tomorrow, (Saturday), you can stop the night at my house, you'll enjoy it on the Manor”. Jake likes the idea.
“That’s great mate, I'll let my mates know tonight, where shall I meet you?”. “Catch the Sheffield train to Darnall, I’ll

be waiting at the station at about 10 a m". "That's great Sam, I'll see you tomorrow." As they get to the end of the path, Jake sees his bus coming, and starts to run to the bus stop, he shouts, "See you tomorrow Sam ". The bus pulls up and he jumps on, Jake's looking forward to going out with Sam, not only as he become a good friend, but the new place is unknown to him, therefore exciting.

When Jake arrives home he has a bath, it is 7pm and time to meet his friends at the local White Swan. As he walks in all the lads are sat in a corner chatting. Jake walks up to the bar, Ken who doesn't know Jake is serving. "Ae up mate, can I have a pint of bitter please?" Ken doesn't think Jake is old enough to drink. "How old are you?". Jake's confident with the way he answers. "Eighteen mate". Ken looks sheepish at Jake. "Alright, bitter it is." Jake picks up his drink, walks over to his friends and sits down. Texas as some news for Jake. "Jake, I've got some bad news for you". Texas pauses, Jake starts to wonder what it could be. "Old Stan has died of a heart attack today". Jake looks down, shakes his head, everyone stops and looks. "Fucking hell Texas, he still owes me a fiver." Everyone starts to laugh, Jimmy giggles. "Stan would have loved to have heard that".

Jake decides to tell his friends where he is going the following evening. The Manton lads are a bit of a click and like their friends to stay together, they may not like Jake going out with someone else, especially Sheffield way. “I've got something to tell you lads”. Hogger looks on. “Your pregnant Jake”. Jake smiles, they all laugh. “No, just that I'm going to stop with my mate on the Manor Estate tomorrow “. Texas is surprised. “That's a rough place Jake”. Jimmy doesn't seem to happy. “You traitor Jake”. Texas, Hogger, Jimmy and Foxy all suddenly jump onto Jake and pull him down onto the pub floor, pinning his arms and legs apart. Steff his sat in the corner with his girlfriend Ruby, there watching with interest of what is happening. Foxy shouts, “Steff come over here and give Jake some fist, he's going out with someone else tomorrow”. “Certainly”, Steff walks over to Jake, he as an evil grin on his face. “Where do you want me to hit him lads?”. Texas decides where to hit Jake. “Just his arms and legs mate, we don't want Jake to be able to use them tomorrow, do we”.

Steff kneels at the right-hand side of Jake, Jake can't stop laughing. He draws back his fist, Jake watches out of the corner of his eye, Steff punches Jake, first on the right arm and then on the right thigh. Jake groans in pain but still can't stop laughing, his mates all have a big smile, rest of the pub as gathered round and are enjoying the display, Jim doesn't think Jake as had enough punishment.

“Give him some more Steff”. Steff steps over Jake and kneels at his left-hand side, he punches Jake first on the thigh and then on the arm, his mates are smiling, Jake’s in agony, but he still has a cheeky grin. Steff stops hitting Jake.

"Have you had enough Jake?". Jake tries not to smile, "Yes Steff". Steff wants to know that Jake as given in, "Who's the daddy Jake?". Jake starts to laugh. "I'm the daddy". Steff punches Jake on the left leg again, Jake groans with the pain. "You're the daddy Steff". Jake's friends release their hold and return to the table for their drinks, Jake is still laid on the floor. As he slowly gets up his arms and legs feel weak and hurt, he staggers over to join his friends. "Are we straight lads?". Texas puts his pint down.

"We were anyway Jake, we just enjoy hitting you". The lads have a good laugh together, and Jake feels good that his friends are ok with him.

On the way home Jake goes to the chippy, a local bully also a woodyard man walks past with a bag of chips. Jake speaks to him, he's just being friendly. "How are you going on Billy, give us a chip". Billy suddenly drops his chips and punches Jake on the nose, it starts to bleed, Jake looks at Billy. "I'll take that as a no then Billy". Jake slowly walks off, Billy's known for suddenly hitting people when he has had a drink, but when he is sober, he is a completely different man.

Jake calls at the fish shop and buys some chips, as he walks home alone the streets are deserted, one of the Worksop Skinheads is walking towards him, Jake's not afraid, there's only one of them. When he draws closer he

recognises him, it's Lez, he's staggering, maybe with too much to drink.
Lez see's Jake. "Jake, you bastard, I want to go to jail with my mate Stuart, I'm going to kill you".
Jake is not feeling too good from the beatings earlier in the evening, but he knows Lez means business.
Lez throws a punch with his right to Jake's head, Jake ducks, steps quickly round the back of Lez, and with both hands pushes him against the fence. Lez spins round but Jake starts to throw a barrage of punches, Lez covers his face with both arms, two men are walking down the street towards them and one shouts. "Ae, what are you doing, leave him alone". Jake shouts back. "He started it". Jake walks off and Lez goes on his way, he's more upset about his friend being locked up than worrying about Jake.

Jake makes his way home, when he gets in everyone's in bed. His dad shouts. "Lock the door Jake, have you had a good night?". Jake sighs. "Great dad, I've lost three fights". His dad his pleased with him. "Well done Jake, I'm proud of you". Jake as a wash and looks in the mirror, his nose his swelled and both eyes are going black. It's 1pm and Jake crawls into bed, looking forward to meeting his friend that day, and the excitement this may bring.

Its Saturday and it's 8am, Jake gets up and has a quick bath, puts on his shirt, trousers, tie and shoes. He goes down stairs and his mom his doing the washing in the old

twin tub. “I’m stopping at my mate’s tonight mam, I will see you tomorrow”. His mom doesn't look up and carries on doing the washing. “Alright duck, your dinner will be in the oven when you come in”.
Jake makes his way to the train station, it's 9.05 a m, and he aches from the night before, but knows he will be fine, just as long has he stays out of any more trouble.

The train arrives at Worksop train station at 9.30 a m, the doors open, the carriage is half full, he climbs on and he sits halfway down the first of the two carriages. The conductor checks to see if everyone is on board, he blows his whistle, the driver peeps his hooter. The trains about to set off as Jake looks out of the window, his nose his hurting but is looking forward to going out with Sam, he hears someone shout. “Come on lads”. Jake looks to his left and out of the window he sees the Worksop skinheads running for the train, he looks back and then forwards, there's no escape. They burst onto the train just as the doors are going to close.

Brady, Duke, Wolf and their friends are pushing and shoving as they walk down the aisle, there on their way to the Wednesday match. Jake slides down in his seat and looks down at the floor, the Worksop skinheads push and shove past Jake, as they go down the aisle looking for a seat. Wolf chooses somewhere to sit. “Let's go to the back lads.” They take up the back four seats of the first carriage, Jake’s gone unnoticed, maybe it's because he is

wearing a shirt, trousers and jacket instead of his usual leather jacket and jeans. He sits and listens to the Worksop skinheads singing Wednesday songs, while he figures out how to get off the train at Darnell without being noticed. The stations pass, Shireoaks, Kiveton Bridge, Kiveton, Woodhouse. Next is Darnell, the stop where Jake is to get off.
The train pulls up at the station, passengers get off and on the train, Jake waits, sitting low in his seat, the conductor blows his whistle, Jake then makes a dash for the door, but Wolf happens to be looking down the aisle. "That's Jake, the cheeky bastard ". Wolf immediately jumps up and gives chase, but Jake is in full motion, he hears the Worksop Skinheads shouting. "Jake, you little bastard." Brady shouts "I'm going to kill you, you wanker". Jake just manages to jump through the train door as the conductor closes it, just in the front of Wolf, the others have followed and have their faces up against the window, looking very angry and bright red.

Sam's stood on the platform and as seen Jake as he jumped off the train, he walks over to meet him.
"Jake, are you ok mate?". Sam has a puzzled look on his face, Jake's out of breath, more through nerves than being unfit. He looks around at the train and see's the Worksop skinheads jumping up and down, he gives them a wanking sign and they start to wave their fists. As the train pulls away they walk backwards down the aisle,

keeping in line with Jake, Sam looks on as the train pulls away from the station.
“What’s up with them Jake?” Jake wipes the sweat from his forehead and smiles. “It's just a few mates having a laugh”. Sam looks down the track as the train slowly leaves the station and builds up speed. “Well, they didn't look to happy to me Jake”. Sam looks at Jake’s face. “How come yours eyes are black, and your nose is swelled Jake? “. Jake grins from the left-hand side of his face. “I have a cheeky smile, men want to hit me, and girls want to kiss me, the two don't match”. Sam likes the answer, it's a good start to the weekend. “Come on, I'll introduce you to the Manor”.

As they walk through the streets it reminds Jake of his own council estate, the houses and roads all appear to be the same, with dogs running around and kids playing football. Sam decides to go for something to eat. “Let's call for a bag of chips Jake”. They walk into the fish shop. Elaine, a middle aged, pretty, slim, blond haired lady, that as her hair tied in a ponytail is serving, and Marge, a mature, small, well rounded lady who moves her false teeth continually from side to side in her mouth, is frying.

“Hullo Sam, what would you like love?”. She looks at Jake and smiles, but Jake's looking around the fish shop, there are two dogs stood at the door. “Who’s your friend Sam, he's a good-looking guy?”.

Jake turns around and smiles at Elaine, and looks into her eyes, he knows he is good looking and likes to flirt. Elaine looks back holding Sam's scoop of chips, before putting them into a bag, as she pours them out half of them miss and go all over the counter, Sam's been looking forward to his big bag of chips. "What are you doing with my chips?". Elaine is more interested in Jake. "Sorry love". Elaine asks Jake a question. "What's your name love, where do you come from?". Jakes calm and playing hard to get. "I'm Jake, I've just come over for the day". Elaine wants to know a bit more about Jake, she's quite attracted to him. "Are you courting love?". Jake smiles and flutters his eyes. "No". Sam's stood waiting. "Can I have my chips now?". Elaine passes Sam his half bag of chips, which aren't even wrapped in paper. "Ten pence please Sam". Sam's been looking forward to his chips. "Where's the other half of my chips?". Sam passes Elaine twenty pence, but she doesn't give him any change, she is so engrossed in Jake she hasn't heard Sam speak. Sam shakes his head, it's Jake's turn to be served.

"What's your name young lady?" Elaine smiles. "Why, do you want to take me out?". Jake puts his hands on the counter. "Maybe, but I'm just out with Sam for today". Elaine thought she might have been in for a date. "Ok Jake, I'll see you around." Elaine takes Jake's order. "What would you like Jake?". "Bag of chips please Elaine". Elaine picks up a large bag for Jake's chips and

she pours them in, one, two, three scoops of chips. Sam looks at his half bag of chips and then looks at Jake's great bag full. Elaine tries to put in a forth scoop, there falling out the top of the bag. “Salt and vinegar Jake?”, and she smiles. “Yes, please Elaine “.
She puts newspaper around Jake's bag of chips and passes them to him. The bag of chips is that large, he must hold them with both hands. “How much is that Elaine?”. “It's on the house love, I'll see you again”. It's Jake's chance to put his flirting into action. “Come here Elaine “. Elaine leans over the counter and Jake kisses her on the cheek. Elaine blushes. “You're a bit forward Jake, I like that”. Jake winks through his black right eye. “See you love”. Elaine looks at Jake s tight backside as he walks out of the fish shop. “Dead right you will love”.

Sam and Jake stand outside the fish shop, Sam's holding his half bag of chips with his left hand and Jake holds his with both hands. “Let's sit on the wall over there Jake”. As they sit and eat their chips, two dogs come over and sit at their side, Jake throws them a couple of chips and they eat them straight away, Pete, one of Sam's friends passes by. “Ae up Sam, who's your friend? he looks like a warm lad with the two black eyes “. Sam laughs, “Its Jake from Worksop.” “Well you know Sam, Jake's going to get some flack off some of the Manor Lads, he will have to stand his ground and earn their respect”. “I know that Pete, we'll see how it goes”.

Pete looks cautiously at Jake. “Jake, are you ok mate, have you heard what I have just said”. Jake gives half a grin, he’s not worried, he's tough, fast and fearless and enjoys the excitement of trouble, but the Manor Lads don't know this. Jake will have his chance later that evening to earn their respect.

Jake looks at the dogs looking up at Sam's chips and has an idea. As Sam is talking to Pete, Jake takes one of his chips and shows it to the dogs, they sit down, Pete looks at what the dogs are doing while he carries on talking to Sam. Jake picks up a chip and puts it on Sam's knee, both dogs suddenly jump up onto Sam, grabbing the chip and knocking his bag of chips out of his hand, Pete laughs, Sam’s upset. “Fucking dogs, they're always taking my chips, but they don't usually take them out of my hand”. Sam had not noticed the chip Jake had put on his knee. Jake looks down at the dogs eating Sam’s chips.
“Never mind Sam, you can have my chips”. He passes Sam the bag, Sam's happy now, and carries on talking to Pete. “Could you get me some salt please Jake”. Jake goes into the fish shop. “Elaine can I borrow the salt please?”. Elaine is pleased to see Jake again. “I thought you had come to ask me out Jake”. Elaine passes Jake the salt pot. As Jake walks out he loosens the lid and he walks over to Sam, trying not to smile. “Here you are Sam”

Sam starts to sprinkle salt onto his chips, and the lid come's off, his chips are now thick with salt. "Bastard", Pete laughs. "You're going to be alright on the Manor Jake, I like your sense of humour". Sam looks at Jake and smiles, he now realises what Jake as done and he throws his chips to the dogs. "Come on Jake, let's go to mine".

They make their way through the housing estate to Sam's house, as they walk in Sam shouts.
"Mom, Jakes here." Linda, Sam's mom is watching TV. "Bring him in love, I don't bite ". Jake follows Sam through the untidy house which makes him feel at home. Linda's sat on the sofa, she looks Jake up and down. "My, you're a good-looking lad, you're stopping tonight aren't you Jake?". Linda makes Jake feel at home. "Yes Linda, thanks". "That's ok love, anytime". Sam smiles, his mom is making Jake welcome, but they have other things to do now. "Were going around to Jan's now mom, see you later". Jake puts up his hand to say good bye. "See you later Linda." "Ok lads, see you tonight in the welfare". As Jake walks out of the room, Linda admires his tight young backside and licks her lips, Sam wants to be on his way. "Come on Jake, I'm going to introduce you to my girlfriend, Jan".

They walk up the street and come to a house with a well-kept garden, they walk down the path and come up to a

blue door. Sam knocks on the door, Jan's mom Mary answers with a greeting smile.
“Hullo Sam, who’s your friend?”. “He’s my mate Jake, he’s stopping for the night, were going to the welfare later”. Mary invites them in. “Go and sit in the lounge lads, Jan’s upstairs with her friend playing some music”. Mary shouts upstairs. “Jan, Sam and his friend are here”. Jan looks at Clare, they wonder who Sam’s friend could be and run downstairs. They walk into the lounge, Jan walks over to Sam and kisses him on the cheek, Jan and Claire look at Jake sat in the lounge chair, all comfortable.
“Who's your friend Sam?”, Jan asks. Clare’s smiles at Jake, he’s playing at looking all innocent, but not appearing to be with the bruises on his face. “He’s Jake from Worksop, he’s stopping at mine tonight”.
Jake stands up, walks over to Clare, says hullo, and gives her a kiss on the cheek, he makes conversation. “What have you been doing?”.
She finds Jake attractive. “Just singing some songs”.
“Great, can we have a go.” Jan thinks that's a good idea, “Of course you can, Sam, help me carry the acoustic guitars down stairs”.
Jan and Sam go upstairs to collect the guitars as Jake and Clare start to chat. “Have you and Jan been friends long Claire?”. “For years, our parents have always been good friends, can you play the guitar Jake?”. “A little bit, but I don’t know if I'm any good at singing”. Jan and Sam walk into the room with the guitars. “Here you are Clare, your guitar”. Sam pulls out two chairs, Clare and Jan pick up their guitars and sit down. “What would you like us to

play Jake?", Claire asks. Jake thinks what would be fun. "*In the Summertime* ok ". The girls begin to sing, Jake calls to Sam, "Come on Sam, stand up and hold my arm". Sam and Jake start to dance while the girls play.

When they have finished singing a few songs they put their guitars down, they need a drink. It's the lads turn to sing. "Come on Jake, you and Sam can sing us a song". Sam picks up the guitar, starts to sing and play *Hang on Snoopy*. As Sam leads, the girls start to dance, clap and they join in the chorus. Jake just stands still feeling a bit out of place. Jan encourages Jake to join in. "Come on Jake". Jake needs something to play. "Have you got a tambourine?". Jan passes Jake a tambourine which is laid next to the sofa. Sam looks at Jake, he wants to play another song. "What song would you like me to play Jake?". "Can you play *Tambourine Man?"* "In a way Jake." "Ok Sam". Jake starts to sing, and play the tambourine, he slowly moves with the music, they all join in and start to dance, and when Jake has finished they all clap. Jake's really pleased, it's the first time he's ever had the courage to sing in the front of anyone. For the rest of the afternoon, they sing, dance and laugh, Clare has an idea. "You should come to the singing competition Jake". Jake's not sure. "We will see".

It's 6pm and the afternoon as quickly gone by, Sam and Jake must get ready to go to the local welfare.

“Mary, can me and Jake have a wash here?”. Mary smiles, “Of course you can Sam, there's some deodorant in the bathroom cupboard”. Sam’s pleased with his friends. “Thanks girls for a great afternoon and for making Jake welcome.” Sam kisses Jan, Jake and Clare smile at each other. Sam and Jake go upstairs to have a wash. “What's it like in the welfare?” Jake asks. “It’s just another welfare, but there's a good group on tonight and they start at 8pm. Jake straightens his tie and jacket, and combs his hair, as he looks in the mirror he feels good, Sam’s waiting to go. “Are you ready Jake?”. Jake takes one final look in the mirror, his face is bruised but he looks smart, “Come on mate, let’s go”.
As they make their way out of the house Sam shouts. “See you Mary, thanks Jan, we'll see you and Clare later”. Jake’s happy about the afternoon. “Thanks ladies”. They all shout. “See you lads”.

As they walk to the welfare, Jake is wondering how Sam had got the scar on his face. “How did you get that scar on your face mate?”. Sam doesn't usually like talking about this experience, but Jake makes him feel both comfortable and strong. “We had a fight with a group of gangsters from Sheffield, one is called Johnny, they originate from the Moody Gang and are brutal. He put our best fighter Silver out of business, and now he's the cock of the Manor. It was one of his gangster members, Soul, who slashed my face, but my time will come “. Jake takes another look at Sam’s scar. “I want a scar like that, it makes you look dead tough". Sam shakes his head. "I think you've got enough with the two black eyes and swelled nose Jake". Sam then smiles, everyone likes his scar.

It's 7pm, and as they arrive at the welfare, they look through the pub windows and it's busy, Cranberry, a young man who is an apprentice with Sam, is stood outside the entrance and shouts. "How are you going on Sam?". He runs over and slaps Sam on the top of his head, and laughs.

They walk through the double doors, on the left of the entrance is a large desk, where an old man called Paul, is sat with a pint of bitter, he is collecting the entrance fee for non-members. "Are you alright Sam, who's your friend?". "It's Jake Paul, he's from Worksop". "Ok, sign him in, here's the book".

Sam writes Jake's name in an old thick large black hardbacked book, which looked like it had been in the club for ever, Jake puts 20 pence in the small wooden collection box for the entrance fee. They then walk to their right and go through another double door, which is half wood half glass, so you can see people on the other side. As they walk into the hall it's packed with people. Jake likes the way it is busy, it reminds him of the Worksop Welfare on a Friday night. "This looks great Sam".

Shane, one of Sam's friends see them, he starts to wave and shouts. "Sam, come down here".

They look down the hall and see Shane waving, as they walk down they see Clare, Jan, Linda and Neil sat round a table. “Sam, you go and see your friends, I’ll get the drinks in”, Jake walks back to the bar. Sam’s pleased, he likes to go rounds. “Nice one mate, I'll get the next round in”. The hall is set in three long lines of oblong tables, one row of tables on each side of the room, and a double row of tables down the middle. In the front of the stage there is a large dance floor. Jake takes the drinks to his friends who are sat in the bottom corner near the stage. “Ae up everybody”. Everyone smiles, Shane wonders who Jake is. “Are you Sam's mate?”. “Yes mate, they call me Jake”. “Can you dance Jake?”, Shane asks. “Yeah mate”.

The Saxons Band arrives, Graham, Biff and Dobby set up their musical instruments. A mature man called Craig walks up onto the stage and introduces the groups, he picks up the microphone. “Order, order.” It all goes quiet, Linda looks up, “I wonder what Craig is going to say”.
I am sorry to say, that the lead singer for tonight's show will not be here because he has flu. I know we have some singers in the club tonight, and I wonder if you would like to help the band out, they would appreciate it.
Jan and Claire shout out. “Yea, we will sing for you Craig”. Craig looks down and nods. “Thank you, ladies”.
The group put up their thumbs and start to talk to one another, as they check that their instruments are in tune.
The mood is one of buzzing with excitement, as the local singers now have a chance to show off their talent.

It's 8.pm, Jan's ready to go onto the stage, "Come on Clare, and you Sue." They walk up onto the stage, Jake and Sam are knocking the beer back and starting to get tipsy. As the girls are stood on the stage, they smile, people are shouting, "Come on girls". Jan turns around to one of the members of the band and tells him what they want them to play, she picks up the microphone and the audience goes silent.

"Ladies and gentlemen, let me introduce to you tonight, The Pink Ladies, on my right Clare, on the left Sue and myself Jan. We will sing the following songs, *Shout and Whiter Shade of Pale*". The audience gives an applause, the lights go down, the band begins to play.

The Pink Ladies begin to sing their song, *Shout by the Shangri Girls,* everyone starts to rock to the music.

Jake's foot is tapping, "Come on Sam let's dance". "A few more drinks first mate." "I'm going for it." Jake walks onto the dance floor and begins to dance to the rhythm of the music, Shane likes Jake's style. "Hey Sam, your mates got some bottle. "Yeah, he's my mate, fuck this I'm joining him".

Sam puts his pint down and walks onto the dance floor, all Sam's friends stand up and join him, they are followed by other members of the audience.

The girls finish singing, and the audience gives an applause, and go for a drink, Sam is pleased with his mate Jake. "Jake you're a warm fucker." Shane pats Jake on the shoulder. "You're dead right mate". Linda's been

watching Jake dance. “You can dance Jake, let's see what you’ve got next”.
Three young black girls walk from the back of the hall, up onto the stage and stand in a line, Maria introduces her fellow singers. “Hullo everyone, we have Anna, Kim and myself Maria and we are called the Silhouettes, we are going to sing, *Do Run Run and The Locomotion”.* The girls begin to sing, people get up and dance, Linda is dancing with Jake, Clare looks and feels jealous, she puts down her drink, walks over to Jake and taps him on the shoulder, Jake looks around and smiles. “Can I have the next dance?” Jake’s pleased, “I'll dance with you now”, and they start to dance together. Jake looks fondly at Clare, “You look great Clare, but you know we are only friends”, “I know Jake, were just having fun”.

The Silhouettes finish their song, the audience cheer, at the bottom of the steps to the stage stood waiting to go up, are three young men dressed as Teddy Boys. As the Silhouettes walk past they smile at them, who then, in return, salute for respect and walk up onto the stage. Ron picks up the microphone, they've turned up their shirt collars.
“Ok ladies and gentlemen, were the three R’s, well known as, Ron, Rick and Rupert. Does anyone out there love Elvis?”. The audience are excited, “Yea, come on lads, bring it on”. Ron looks out into the packed audience. “Ok, we're going to sing for you tonight, *Blue Suede Shoes, Hound Dog and Return to Sender”.* Ron shouts out.

“Come on everybody”. He begins to sing, backed by Rick and Rupert, people are rocking and clicking their fingers in the isles and on the dance floor, even outside the main entrance while they are walking in.

Two hours quickly go by, everyone is laughing and getting drunk, It's the turn of the Four Jacks and they start to sing, *Girls Just Want to Have Fun.*
Half way through the song, Karly stops singing, everyone stops dancing, it goes quiet and people start whispering. The Four Jacks start to sing, *Nutbush, by the City Limits,* Shane nudges Sam and whispers to him. “It’s Johnny, Pecker, Paddy and Johnny's girlfriend Jane”. As Johnny and his gang walk down the aisle towards the stage, they rock to the music, everyone moves to one side, they know how dangerous these people can be. Johnny stops at the last table next to the dance floor were four youths are sat, as Johnny stands over them they look away. “Fuck off and find somewhere else to sit.” They pick up their drinks and hurry away, the gang laugh.

They sit at the table and Johnny puts his hand in his pocket and pulls out fifty quid in tenner’s, he throws Paddy the money, which lands on the table in the front of him. “Here you are Paddy, fetch three double whiskies and a double vodka and coke for Jane”. Jane’s about seventeen years old, small, slim, with long black curly hair, she's dressed in all black trousers, polo necked top and black boots. Everyone has been looking at what is happening, Sam's angry. "Look at that clever bastard", Jake doesn't know who they are. "Who's his girlfriend Sam?". Sam looks at Jake and shakes his head, he doesn't know what Johnny is capable of. "Don't push it Jake, Johnny will kill you". Jake smiles, he will not be able to resist the danger.

There's a big queue at the bar and Paddy walks straight to the front, he throws fifty pounds onto the counter, the young small slim barmaid looks nervously up at Paddy. "Three double whiskies and a double vodka and coke, keep the change as a tab and bring the same drinks over every twenty minutes".
No one says anything to Paddy about jumping the queue, the barmaid serves Paddy, takes his money and doesn't speak. Paddy has a cocky look about him, he picks up the drinks and walks back to his gang.
He puts the drinks down on the table and they all reach over and pick them up, Paddy shouts out in a loud voice, people are still quite and look on. "A toast to Johnny, Cock of the Manor".

People sigh, the dancing and singing as now stopped, there's a sombre mood in the club.
Silver is sat in the corner looking down, his crutches by his side, Sam and his friends look at him, he was once the Manor's hero, and now he is a casualty. Johnny stands up and shouts, "How are you going on Silver, how's your mate smiler?". Sam puts a step forward

towards Johnny's table, but Neil pulls him back. "This is not the time son". Sam's angry, his right fist is clenched, but this is Jake's opportunity.
"It's time for some fun Sam, you're going to sing some songs and I'll dance, trust me Sam, there are many ways to beat this man". Sam likes the idea and leads his friends onto the stage. "Come on lads, it's time to sing".
Dan, Russ, Shane and Sam walk onto the stage and take the band's guitars, Sam looks over at Johnny, who's laughing with his friends.
Jake has put on his jacket, he loosens his tie and ruffles his hair. He's about 5ft tall, weighs 8 stone, but tonight, as he stands on the dance floor, he looks like a giant.
Sam starts to sing, *Whole Lotta Shaking Going On.* Jake starts to dance to the rhythm of the music. Johnny's girlfriend Jane looks and admires this young man having such a good time. She starts to clap to the beat of the music, Jakes watching through the corner of his eye, as he dances. Girlfriends of gangsters are usually too scared to dance, and they miss the fun.

The song ends and a singer out of the audience called Steve, who follows the Saxon's walks onto the stage, picks up one of the guitars from the band and walks up to Sam. He winks to the audience and takes the microphone. "Here's one of the all-time favourites of rock and roll, *Johnny Be Good"*. Steve starts to sing, Jake rocks and rolls to the music, the audience start to clap, Johnny watches, Paddy's impressed." He can dance

Johnny". Johnny doesn't think so. "He's a knob". He says with a sarcastic voice.
Janes, clapping with everyone else and stands up and starts to dance in the front of Johnny, she daren't do anything else. Jake noticed, that Jane has been watching him and gets the impression she would love to dance with him.

Jake now has everyone's attention, but they are scared to go up onto the dance floor where Johnny and his gangsters are sat, they wonder what Jake is going to do. Steve steps down and passes the microphone back to Sam, who starts to sing another song. Jake goes for another drink and Jane downs another double vodka, she's really enjoying the music. Jake's been watching, that's her third double vodka and she will be merry. As Jake has his drink, Sam makes an announcement. "Ok ladies and gentlemen, this is my last song for the evening, before my friend takes the microphone and sings us a few final songs". Sam starts to sing, *I'm a Believer.*

Jake sups up his drink, he walks onto the dance floor and shouts up to Sam, "Sam, pass me the microphone, ask Russ to play *Resurrection Shuffle*". Sam passes Jake the microphone. Jake looks out into the audience and then looks straight at Jane, the music begins to play, and Jake begins to sing. Jane looks at him and starts to dance. Jake slowly moves closely to her, Johnny looks. "What's this twat playing at?". Jane dances towards Jake, they are just a few feet apart on the dance floor, Silvers sat in the corner and smiles, he knows Jake is winding Johnny up. Johnny's not too pleased. "Who's this cheeky fucker?". Paddy's likes the way Jake is dancing. "They dance well together Johnny". Johnny's upset, it's not what he wants to hear, he picks up his drink and throws it into Paddy's face. "Fuck off Paddy". Paddy looks down as he wipes the whiskey from his face, he knows Johnny is getting upset and will thump anyone.

People are looking at Johnny, he puts his right hand into his inside jacket pocket, pulls out a MAC 1950 Semi-Automatic Pistol used by the French Army, and places it in the middle of the table, he looks around making sure that it is a warning to everyone.

Sam sees what has happened and puts up his hand to stop the band playing, he is worried about his friend. Johnny stands up, walks over to Jane and grabs her by the arm, then slaps her in the face, she starts to cry. "Sit down you fucking tart". Johnny points at Jake, with anger in his face. "You little bastard, fuckoff, before I do to you what I did to your friends". Johnny drags Jane back to her seat and carries on drinking as though nothing has happened. Jane has her hands over her face sobbing and feeling helpless. Jake takes a deep breath and steps up onto the stage.
"Ok everyone, I'm going to sing, *For What It's Worth"*. As Jake sings, Johnny knows he is taking the piss, but it's

nearly closing time and he wants another couple of drinks.

Bell rings for last orders and Clare brings Jake a drink, he quickly drinks it, Sam goes over to the dimmer switch and turns the lights down. Jake walks off the stage and onto the dance floor. “Pass me the microphone again Sam”. “Here's the microphone Jake, but you're going to have to be careful with Johnny, your pushing him too far”. “I know mate, great in it.” Sam smiles, he likes the way Jake is winding Johnny up.
Jake makes an announcement to the audience, Johnny and his gang look on, their drunk and have serious faces. Jake brushes his hair back with his hand, tidies his shirt and straightens his loose tie, he's relaxed, looks casual, and he's going to do, what he does best, which is taking the piss.

Ladies and gentlemen, just two more songs for you this evening. Jake starts to sing the *Letter by the Box Tops*. Sam and his friends join in, as they sing they walk slowly down the steps and join Jake on the dance floor, their defiant in a musical way. “My last song for the evening is, *Please Don’t Let Me Be Misunderstood”*. Jake starts to sing and walks over to Johnny; Johnny’s friends look surprised at Jake standing behind him. Johnny looks around and stands up, he towers over Jake, but he carries on singing and moves around Johnny, the audience start to shout. “Come on Jake”, his name as quickly spread.

As the song ends, Johnny stands in front of Jake, the lights come on and there's silence in the hall.
“Now you little bastard, I'm going to kill you.” Jake stands there calmly, with that usual cheeky smile, everyone looks for Jake's response. “Ok mate, let's go into the car park”.
Jake quickly runs over to the fire exit doors next to the stage and pushes them open, he looks out, it's a large open carpark and there’s plenty of space, it's not the same as the small courtyard at the back of the Swan, where he fought Lenny. Jake walked out into the middle of the carpark, it was lit up with street lights. As he stands there he takes a deep breath, thinking, wherever he goes, people want to hit him.

Johnny walks out followed by Paddy, Pecker and Jane. He stands next to the fire exit, looks over at Jake and smiles. He takes off his jacket and passes it to Paddy, as he walks over to Jake he rolls up his shirt sleeves. All the pub has come out to watch, some through the fire exit, others through the main doors, Silver pushes through the crowd to see what is happening, Sam runs over to Jake all concerned.
“What are you doing Jake?”. Jake looks over at Johnny, “It's like this wherever I go Sam, just do me one favour.” “What's that mate?”. “Every time Johnny knocks me to

the ground, just pick me up, but watch closely how he stands and throws punches". Johnny's standing there waiting, letting them have their fun. Jake starts the hard talk and just makes matters worse. "Ok Johnny, or do they call you rubber Johnny. It's time to kill me".

Paddy giggles, Sam and his friends laugh, Silver grins, he like's Jakes confidence and the way he has no fear. Johnny shouts. "I'll show you, who's a rubber Johnny ". All the crowd now start to join in the laughter. Johnny walks straight forward towards Jake, who stands there with his guard down. He steps forward with his left leg straight, Johnny pulls back his right fist and punches Jake cleanly on the nose. Jake's nose bursts open, blood pours out as he is knocked back, then falls to the ground. Someone shouts. "Come on Johnny, leave him alone". Johnny is in for the kill. "Fuck off, or you will get some fist as well".

The old caretaker Ted had been watching closely and moves closer to the fight. Jake gets up and stands in the front of Johnny, he then hits Jake with a quick left jab, followed by a right hook, hitting Jake above the left and right eye, causing a deep but small wound, Jake falls to the ground and Sam runs over.
"Jake, stay down mate." Jake doesn't give in for any one. "Just pick me up mate, I think he's getting tired, just remember his fighting style for when I fight him again". Sam lifts Jake up onto his feet, his face is covered in

blood, both of his eyes are badly swelled and nearly shut. Jake stands defiant, bruised and hurt. Johnny moves in to finish Jake. He steps forward with his left leg leading, throwing two left jabs, hitting Jake under the right and left eye again, followed with a right to his ribs.

Jake falls to his knees, he can hardly see through the swelling of his eyes, but has a feeling that Johnny will follow through with a knee to his face. Jake pulls up both arms in the front of his face and body. He was right, Johnny steps forward and brings his right knee up towards Jake's head, hitting his arms which are covering his face. Jake his knocked back onto the ground and is laid flat on his back. Ted the caretaker steps in, puts his left hand on Johnny's right shoulder and sweeps Johnny's right leg with his left.

Johnny goes straight down onto the ground, he jumps up and pulls his fist back to hit Ted, who steps back, and Sam jumps in between them. Paddy steps next to Johnny, he's seen something. "Johnny there's a police car patrolling round". Johnny looks over across the car park and sees a police car which as stopped, two policemen are looking at what is going off. Johnny decides that it is time to go and looks at Sam. "That's enough for one-night smiler, tell your friend if I ever see him again I will kill him".

Sam runs over to Jake and sits him up, he wipes the blood from his face with his shirt sleeve. Johnny and his gang walk off, they're going to the fish shop before getting the taxi home, they don't want any trouble with the police, especially while Johnny is carrying a gun. Jake spits blood from his mouth as he looks at Johnny walking away, he shouts. “Goodnight Johnny, I'll see you again”. Sam's friends walk over as he lifts Jake up off the ground, is face is swollen and bloody, “Was it worth it mate, look at you”.

Jake looks around at everyone and smiles through his swollen face, Clare comes over takes out a tissue and gently wipes the blood from his lips. “You were so brave Jake”, she puts her arms around him. People start to talk about how they admire Jake, him being so young and small, battling a gangster like Johnny. Shane goes over and lifts Jake’s right arm in the air. “This is the man who as stood for the Manor and as proved his worth”.

People cheer and clap, Jake’s feeling hungry. “Is the chippy still open lads?” they all smile. Sam puts his arm around his friend. “Come on mate”. Sam and Jake slowly walk down to the local fish shop, and sit on the wall talking while eating their chips, two dogs sit either side of Jake, tonight Jake as made many new friends.

Sam and Jake walk to Sam's house, Jake goes up to the bathroom to wash the blood from his face. Sam passes him a pair of tracksuit bottoms and a t-shirt to wear, he puts them on and they laugh, as they are too long and baggy. Linda shouts to Sam, “Sam I'll put Jake's clothes in the wash”. Sam’s proud of Jake. “Listen mate, you've

got a lot of bottle, the Manor will be talking about this for months".
Jakes exhausted, "Thanks Sam, but I'll have to go to bed, I'me knackered". Jake goes into the spare bedroom, he sees Sam's dog laying on the bed, he is too tired to ask him to move and lays next to him, where they fall asleep together.

It's 9am, Jake rolls over and falls out of bed, Sam's dog had been laid on half of the bed all night, while Jake's been laid on the edge. As he lays there, he feels his injuries from the night before and smiles, another adventure to talk about with his friends. Sam's heard Jake falling out of bed and he opens Jake's bedroom door. "Come on Jake, it's time for your train".
He slowly stands up and stretches out his arms, he puts on the clothes Sam as lent him. He goes down stairs and Linda is washing the pots. "Are you ok Linda, are my clothes washed?". "Yes Jake, there on the clothes horse". "Thanks Linda", he goes over to the clothes horse and as he picks them up they are still wet. He stands and looks at them wondering where they could dry, but there isn't the time, he must catch his train. "Thanks Linda".

Jake goes upstairs to the spare bedroom and puts on his wet clothes, as he stands and looks at himself in the mirror, his face is swollen and bruised, he feels a severe stabbing pain in his right ribs, his clothes are wet and creased, but at least they are clean. He goes back down

stairs and Linda is making the drinks, “Would you like a drink of tea Jake “. “Thank you, Linda, thanks for washing my clothes “. “That's ok Jake, but it would have been a good idea to dry them on the washing line before you put them on”. “It's ok Linda, they will dry as I walk, I have to catch the 10.30 a m train, I'm supposed to be playing football this afternoon for my local pub.
Jake quickly has his drink and picks up his jacket from the chair. It's a nice warm sunny morning, and now he looks forward to playing football with his mates. “Are you ready Sam?”. Sam quickly drinks his tea. “Yes mate, let’s go”.

They walk along the street and discuss Johnny’s fighting technique, as they pass the locals they are shouting. “Ae up Jake, well done Jake”. Sam thinks Jake will not want to come down to the Manor again. “Are you coming down again mate, I know it was a bit rough, but we had a good time”.
Jake looks at Sam through his swollen black eyes and smiles, “Yes I will Sam, I'm looking forward to it “.
As they walk past the shops, old Ted is stood outside reading his paper. Jake recognises him and walks over. “Ted, thanks for stepping in last night”. Ted looks up, “That's ok Jake, but Johnny will come looking for you”. “I know, Sam's told me, but what can I do?”. Ted puts his right hand on Jake’s left shoulder, Jake feels strangely safe. “Well, first you should join your local boxing club, then you and Sam should come down every Saturday to the youth club, I will show you a few moves one of my

apache friends as taught me, when we were prisoners of war together in Burma." Jake now feels part of the Manor. "Thanks Ted, I'll take you up on that one day".

Sam and Jake arrive at the train station just as the train arrives, as it pulls up the conductor opens the door. Jake steps on and walks to the front of the first carriage and sits down, the train appears to be empty. The door closes and Sam waves, Jake puts up his arm and smiles. As the train pulls away, he hears someone singing Wednesday songs, Jake looks down the carriage, at the far end he can see the Worksop Skinheads. They must have stayed overnight at Sheffield and visited the night clubs. Jake never dreamt they would be on the Sunday morning train, he has an idea. If he got off at Shireoaks train station, he could walk the last two miles into town, they wouldn't notice him leaving the front of the train until it was too late.

The stations went past until the train was about to arrive at Shireoaks, Jake got up from his seat and stood next to the door, there was a small dividing wall that he could stand behind, where he would not be seen, Jake thought he had outsmarted the Worksop skinheads, but Duke had noticed him.
"Hey Wolf, I'm sure that's Jake down there", they all looked down the aisle, Brady's not sure. "Come on, let's walk down and see who it is".

The train arrives at Shireoaks but doesn't stop there on a Sunday, Jake didn't know this when he hatched his plan. Jake closes his eyes and sighs thinking of what he could do now. The skinheads have walked quietly up to the first carriage, they see Jake looking out of the window of the train door. Duke smiles.

“Hullo Jake, we just thought we would keep you company”. Jake's heart feels like it had stopped, he looks around and sees himself surrounded by the Worksop Skinheads, in their full Sheffield Wednesday glory.

Jake with a nervous voice tries to make conversation, maybe he can talk his way out of trouble.

“Ae up Duke, how did Sheffield Wednesday go on”.

Thinking if they had won the skinheads might be in a good mood and let him go.

Brady replies with an upset face. “They fucking lost to Sheffield United 3-0”.

Duke is about to make things even between Jake and the Worksop Skinheads. “Well Jake, you've been a bit of a cheeky fucker, so when we get off the train, you’ll find out what we are going to do”.

Duke smiles as he looks at the bruising and swelling on Jake's face. “Anyway, what’s happened to you?”. Jake looks up at Duke, he is worn out with the beatings. “I got beat up by Johnny who runs one of the Sheffield gangs”.

Duke gives half a grin, “Good, if I ever meet him I'll buy him a pint”.

Kenny and Lez stand either side of Jake and grab his arms tightly, Brady wants to make sure Jake doesn't get away. "Hold him lads, come on B O let's take Jake's clothes off". The Skinheads pull off Jake's shirt, trousers, shoes and socks, and he his stood there in only his underpants. Jake tries to work out a plan, but knows this is checkmate, and it's their day today, he will have to take what is coming.
Brady is quite pleased with himself, as he looks at Jake stood only in his underwear, other train passengers look at Jake and laugh. "Well Jake, when we get off the train were going to have to decide what we are going to do with you".

The skinheads are all smiling as the train pulls up at Worksop train station, the doors open, Duke and Brady get off first and stand in the front of Jake, and he is escorted off the train by Lez and Kenny. Duke as an idea were to take Jake. "Let's take him to the end of the station car park lads".
As they walk along the platform, people point, stare and giggle at Jake, when they reach the end of the platform he's taken through an old wooden white gate, Jake is surrounded by the skinheads and there is no escape. They turn left and walk along the isolated carpark until the come to an old piece of wasteland, partitioned by a large wooden brown fence. Kenny and Lez throw Jake face first against the fence, he hits it hard with his right shoulder, he turns around, he is stood in just his

underpants and has bruises all over his body. He looks at the skinheads as they stand around him, in a half circle.
“What shall we do to him Duke?” asks Kenny. Duke thinks but Wolf has an idea.
“Tell you what lads, let’s get some nettles and if Jake can walk through a gauntlet smiling, while we thrash him, we will call it quits and the chase will be over”.
Everyone agrees, Lez collects a bunch of nettles and hands them out to each member of the gang.
Jake's stood there in his underpants, he’s heard what they have said, it's a chance to redeem himself. Duke happily informs Jake of his fate. “Right Jake, here’s the deal, if you can walk the gauntlet singing, there is only one Worksop Skinhead with a smile on your face, while being thrashed with nettles, the chase is over. If you fail, we will just thrash you anyway”. Jake as to agree, he knows this is going to hurt, but there’s no other way out.

Jake stands at the end of the two lines, the skinheads hold their nettles ready to strike him as he walks by, he takes a deep breath, stands straight and starts to sing.
“There's only one Worksop Skinhead”, with a smile on his face, Jake walks along the gauntlet, as the nettles rain down on his body they leave a nasty painful sting, the skinheads laugh as they give out the well-deserved punishment and shout. “You’re not so clever now”. “This is for kissing my girlfriend”.
The words become a blur, Jake must focus on his singing, smiling, and getting to the end of the gauntlet. As he reaches the end he stops. The skinheads hold their

nettles in the air and give a triumphant cheer, they have got even with Jake, Duke's pleased that Jake is in a lot of pain.
"Well Jake, I've got to admit it, you've got some bottle, were straight now". Jakes relieved it's all over.
"Ok Duke, I'll stand down, no more taking the piss", and holds out his hand. Duke shakes Jake's hand and nods his head. "Just one more thing Jake, oy lads".
They all run over to Jake and rub his body all over with their hands, making the nettle stings, hurt even more. Jake wriggles with the pain but also laughs, it's the kind of trick he would have played on his friends.
Brady's ready for a pint. "Ok lads, that's enough, let's go down to the Vine". The skinheads walk off happy in their revenge, and the way they have taken it.

Jake looks over at the old large train station clock, which he can just see over the fence, it's 12.05 pm, he wonders how he can get home dressed in just his underpants, but decides there no other way but to walk.
As he walks through the street people laugh and point, Jake just looks down at the footpath trying to ignore everyone. An old man with a raincoat, grey cap and glasses comes riding past on his pushbike, and stops in the front of Jake, he is well known as **Click**, the local pervert. He climbs off his bike and smiles as he looks Jake up and down. "My young man, I've seen ways of getting a man's attention, but I've never seen anything like this before". Jake looks around and makes sure no

one is looking. Wilko, Jake's mate from the pit just happens to be walking past on the opposite side of the road, he shouts. “Hey Jake, have you got a new boyfriend?”. Jake puts his face in his hands, this is a nightmare for him, everyone at the pit will know and he will never live it down, Jake’s starting to get angry. “Look Click, I'm going through a rough patch, just leave me alone”. Click takes no notice, he’s not interested in the way Jake feels. “It looks that way son, but I have to admire your blue underpants, it’s my favourite colour”.
A motorbike pulls up, someone shouts. “Jake”, he looks behind and sees his friend Buttony on his pink, Honda 50 cc. Jake walks over to his friend, Buttony’s laughing at him. “Jake, what's happened to you?”. Jake rubs his head, “It's a long story, can you give me a lift home?”. Buttony nods his head. “Jump on the back mate”. Click looks on, feeling disappointed but thinking to himself, how lucky Jake is to be picked up by a biker. Jake gets on the back of the bike and carries on his journey.

As they ride along people wave and laugh, cars pull alongside pipping their horns at Jake with his underpants on, while riding on the back of the bike.
They reach Jake’s house and Buttony pulls up, Jake climbs slowly off the bike, “Thanks Buttony, I'll buy you a drink in the Swan the next time I see you, can you let the lads know I won't be playing football today”. Buttony’s laughing, “Of course I will Jake, I think you had better hurry up and put some clothes on”.

Jake likes Buttony's bike. "The bikes great Buttony, do you want to sell it?". Buttony's pleased he has found someone to buy it, it's always breaking down. "Yes, I do Jake, I'm after a new one, we'll talk another time.

Jake's dog Toby runs out of the garden and jumps up to greet him, Jake gives him a pat on the head, as he walks into his house he is greeted by his mother, Phyllis. He stands there in his underpants, covered in nettle stings, his face black and blue through fighting.
"Hullo Mom". Phyllis turns around looks at Jake, in a firm you've got to pay voice she says, "Where's the rent Jake", and doesn't notice his injuries, Jakes just glad to be home. "I'll get it for you now mom". Jake goes to the bathroom and as a bath, he recalls his adventures from the weekend wondering how he can keep out of trouble. He gets dried and dressed, picks up the rent from out of his bedroom windowsill and takes it to his mom. "Here you are mom". Phyllis is washing the pots and turns around. "Tar, and don't be late again, your dinners on the room table". Jake goes and sits down at the table and looks down at his fish fingers and chips, all dried up and stuck to the plate. "Mom, what's happened to my dinner?". Phyllis shouts to Jake. "You didn't come home for your tea yesterday, so I thought I would warm it up for you today".
Jake just covers his meal in brown HP sauce, when he as finished eating goes and lays on his bed. It's 4pm and he must be up for the day shift the next day, and as an early

night. His body aches, but he has made many new friends, and if he can stop being cheeky, the Worksop Skinheads will leave him alone.

Millwall Match

The alarm bell rings, it's Saturday 8 am, Duke (Paul) as been awake for the last hour, relaxing ready for the day ahead. He hasn't had a drink the night before, as he will have to have his wits about him today.

The Worksop Skinheads were going to watch Sheffield Wednesday play Millwall at home, this was an important game, if Wednesday win, they will be third from the top of the first division.
The Millwall fans have a well-known reputation for thuggery, well organised violence and are experienced in the art of street fighting, which has been passed on from generation to generation, but more importantly, work as a well-trained unit and enjoy confrontation. It was rumoured, that if you put a member of the Millwall Firm onto the ground, they will always seek revenge, no matter where, or whom it may be.

Paul quickly gets out of bed and turns off the alarm on his clock, goes to the bathroom, as a wash and then returns to his bedroom to get dressed.
He had prepared his clothes the night before, and had hung his t-shirt, Levi jeans and denim jacket on coat hangers which are suspended from his bedroom door.
Getting dressed for the match had to be carried out with precision.
He sits on the bed, first puts on his pants and socks, then his jeans, as he stands up, pulls them tight, ensuring they

are tidy and straight. The t-shirt is carefully taken from the coat hanger and neatly laid on the bed.
He admires the blue and white stripes, before picking up the t-shirt and pulling it over his head, putting in his left arm and then the right, he pulls it straight from the bottom, ensuring there are no creases.

At the entrance to the bedroom, on the bottom wall, there is a full-length mirror which Paul uses for checking the detail of his dress. As he stands there, he looks up and down at his reflection, all his clothes are tidy and in place, next, the finishing touch for any skinhead is the braces. As he picks them up, he holds them in the air and looks to ensure they are straight. He first fastens them onto the back of his jeans and lets them hang down, he then pulls one strap over his left shoulder and the other over the right, ensuring the straps are straight, then clips them onto the front of his Levi Jeans. He checks again in front of the mirror, turning around as he does so, such dress detail, can only be compared to a British soldier.

To finish, Paul stands upright, one last proud check, he reads what is written on his blue and white t-shirt, on the front, Duke and on the back, Worksop Skins. This is a symbol and prowess of expressing that you are a loyal member of the Worksop Skinheads, and you have no fear.
Very few had the courage to wear these t-shirts at a match, because everyone knew who you were, both

friend and foe. However, in the heat of battle with other football firms, your friends were easily recognised if they needed assistance.
All Paul's clothes are to standard, he then walks over to the far corner of his bedroom, under the window on the floor are a pair of black, well-polished Dr Marten Air Wair Boots. He bends down and picks them up with pride, they don't only represent the true skinhead, but are light to run, and strong in a fight, a useful tool.

Phil (Wolf) arrives at Paul's house. Knock, knock, knock. Phil, turns around and looks over the balcony and watches the kids play football, while waiting for Paul to open the door. Paul hears a knock, slowly opens the bedroom curtains and peeps through, he must be careful, sometimes callers are not always your friends. He sees Phil standing outside his back door, he opens the bedroom window, "I won't be a minute mate, the doors locked". Paul walks out of his bedroom through the lounge, where there is a small black and white tv in the corner, a small brown settee is under the window, and he puts his boots next to it, he then walks into the small kitchen and opens the door. Phil's stood smiling waiting to come in. "Are you ok mate".
"Come in Phil and make us a cup of tea while I go to the toilet".

Phil walks in, picks up the kettle, fills it with water and puts it on the gas cooker, he looks for the matches, to his right, is a small double leaf table with one wooden chair, and he finds them on the top. He walks over to the old cooker, turns on the front right-hand gas ring, lights the gas and puts on the kettle. While the kettle boils, he collects two cups from the silver draining board and puts them on the table. “Paul, where's the tea and sugar mate?”. “In the cupboard Phil“. There was one double cupboard with blue doors over the kitchen sink, Phil walked over and opened the door, on the bottom shelf he found the tea and sugar, the rest of the cupboard was bare.

While Phil made the drinks, Paul was sat on the settee slowly putting on his boots, first the left then the right, then it was time to tie the laces. He pulled each lace tight, working from the bottom to the top, when they were equal tied the knot, making sure each loop on both boots was the same length.
He then checked both laces for perfection, Paul stood up and stamped his feet making sure his boots were tight. “How do I look Phil?”. Phil, looked up and down at Paul. “Paul, your bootlace is undone”.
Paul quickly looks down, he was so sure that everything was perfect, Phil laughed, “Only joking”. Paul glared at Phil, his dress code was important to him. “You bastard”. Paul smiled, he should have known better.
There's a knock on the door, Paul’s cautious. “Who is it”, he hears the voice of two children. “Uncle Paul, it's us, we've brought you some buns”. Early every Saturday or Sunday morning they like to bake Paul some buns and bring them around. Paul smiles, he walks over to the door

and unlocks it, two children burst in and throw their arms around his legs. He bends down and fondly holds them, Val walks in behind." Here you are Paul, some buns and scones me and the kids have made for you". She then puts them on the worktop. "Ok Ross, Kirsty, it's time to go, Pauls going out, see you later Paul ". The kids run out laughing, they shout. "See you Uncle Paul", and they slam the door behind them. Paul's happy he's seen his neighbours ". Do you know Phil, if I wasn't seeing someone, I would ask Val out for a drink, they're a lovely family, she's been on her own for two years now"? Phil's not taking any notice, they have a match to go to. "Paul, we have to be at the train station for 12 noon, the train leaves at 12.10 pm, we are meeting the lads at the Vine as usual".

It was a warm day and they decided not to take their denim jackets with them. "Ok Phil, let's go."
Off they went, they walked out of Paul's flat, past St. John's Church, followed the car park through the Worksop miner's welfare, until they come out next to the Regal Cinema, 50 yards up from the Vine where the Worksop Skinheads always met before going to a match. As they got to the Vine's brown varnished double doors, Duke and Wolf heard the sound of heavy boots, suddenly someone jumps in between them and grabs Duke and Wolf's shoulder. It was their friend Kenny, with a big smile on his face. "How are you going on lads?", they smile, "Ok Kenny". As they walked into the pub it was full of

Wednesday fans, Duke, Wolf and Kenny walked over into the left-hand corner, it was 11.05 a m, Wolf buys the drinks. “Ok lads, three lagers”, “Ok mate”, the fans in the pub started to sing. “For ever and ever. We'll follow our team. Were Sheffield Wednesday. We'll rule supreme. We'll never be mastered. By the Millwall bastards. We'll keep the blue flag flying high”.

As Wolf walked over to his friends he was singing, spilling the drinks as he carried them. They started to chat about the match and the pub doors suddenly burst open, Brady, B O, Lez and Ian burst in laughing and pushing each other. There were all dressed the same as Duke, with their individual names on their t-shirts.
They walked up to the bar and purchased their drinks, and went and sat down with Duke and their friends.
As they sat round the table there was a silence as they savoured their beer, this was the prelude for the plan for the match. They always sat together and had their first pint at the same time, they would make three toasts to the day. Kenny stood up, “God bless Wednesday”, Worksop Skinheads all shout, “God bless Wednesday” and then he sat down. Wolf's turn, and he stands up, “May the Worksop Skinheads never surrender”, the Worksop skinheads hold up their pint pots and drink to the toast. Its Dukes turn, he starts to sing, they all stand up. “There's only one Worksop Skinhead. One Worksop Skinhead. One Worksop Skinhead. There's only one Worksop Skinhead. One Worksop Skinhead”.

When they all finish singing they sit down and drink their beer. Brady's keen to organise the day. "Right lads let's make a plan", Duke decides what he wants to do. "If we have any trouble with the Millwall firm, I'll go for the leader, you all keep the others off me". The Worksop Skinheads agree, Wolf looked at his watch. "Ok lads, time to go, the train leaves at 12.10 pm".

They all drank up and made their way out of the pub, as they walked along the footpath towards the train station, they were all quite distinctive, dressed in the same t- shirt, jeans, boots and braces, making their statement, that they are the Worksop Skinheads.

As they got close to the train station they had to walk along a narrow path, where they walked side by side. Jake was walking past on the opposite side of the road, and was eating a toffee apple he had just purchased from the shop. He was always being chased by the Worksop Skinheads, but they had only caught him once. He had promised never to wined them up again, but his cheekiness was getting the better of him, and knew they were on their way to the match and did not have time to chase him today.
Jake shouts with a smile on his face. "Hey! Worksop gay boys, can you catch?". He threw his toffee apple high into the air towards the Worksop Skinheads, hitting Brady on the chest, covering his blue and white t-shirt with red sticky toffee, Brady was fuming, "Jake! you bastard, I'm going to kill you".

Jake runs off laughing, he knows that one day they will catch him again, and give him some more fist, but he feels that it is worth it.

Old Tom, carrying a shopping bag and wearing a flat cap, had spent his entire life as a coal miner and was going shopping in Worksop town centre. As he walked along the footpath, he had seen people having to walk onto the road to get past the skinheads. As the gang reached Tom they did not split, as they liked people to walk around them? Brady covered in toffee and Duke were at the front, Wolf whispered to the rest of the gang. "Ian watch Brady, he will send this old man flying", the rest of the Worksop skinheads were giggling. However, Tom did not stop and started to walk straight towards them, their shoulders met, Brady was confident, thinking he could push this old man out of the way, wanting to appear strong in the front of his friends. But Tom was sixty years old, he had been working down the coal mine from being fourteen. His body was hardened through rough hard work, and he had an attitude of respect for others, he could see that the Worksop skinheads did not have this quality, therefore, Tom could not give way.
"Excuse me lads", Tom said, in a deep rough voice, as he shoved Brady and Duke to either side.
Toms days of pushing mine cars and carrying heavy mining materials had turned his body into a ball of steel, it rolls, and everything moves. They were all surprised, and as Tom carried on walking through the middle of the

gang, they all moved to one side, thinking, it's better to be polite than being shown up by an old man. Duke looked at Brady, “I didn't expect that “, Brady rubs his shoulder and agrees. “Yes Duke, he's a real strong guy, I admire him, he should be in the Worksop skinheads”. Old Tom carries on his journey as though nothing has happened, he’s seen too many of his friends get killed or injured during his days as a coal miner, Duke’s gang meant nothing to him.

The Worksop Skinheads entered the old Worksop train station, with old stone buildings and Victorian steelwork, there was a large stone archway where they purchased their tickets. They payed the stationmaster, as they walked onto the platform it was busy with other Sheffield Wednesday supporters, the gang were chatting and laughing, Wolf starts to sing.

“Never felt more like singing the blues”, all the fans join in. “When Wednesday win, and Millwall lose. Oh Wednesday, you've got me singing the blues”, the atmosphere is electric.

Its 12.10 pm, there's the sound of the train’s horn as it arrives on time, Wednesday fans from Retford and Lincoln are hanging out of the train windows as it pulls into the station, the doors open, and everyone charges on, pushing and laughing at the same time. The Worksop Skinheads climb on and they find a seat at the back of the train. As they sit down together, Kenny wrestles with Lez, B O is reading a football magazine, Brady and Ian talk about Sheffield Wednesday, but Duke looks out through the train window watching the world go by, admiring how everything is so calm. Little does he know, that what happens today, will lead to a change in the rest of his life.

The train pulls up at Sheffield train station and everyone is singing and chanting, Duke notices some Millwall fans on the opposite platform and shouts, "Look lads, on the other platform". Everyone looks through the train window. The Millwall fans have got off the London train which as about ten carriages. As it pulls away it as left around three hundred Millwall supporters.
Most looked very ordinary, wearing caps, jeans and trousers, but there were about six youths, who were wearing white Millwall t-shirts, jeans, boots and they all had short well styled hair, one looked like he was carrying a woman's shoulder bag. They were all about 6ft tall, slim and looked very fit, they seemed to stand out from the rest of the Millwall fans.
They were known to the police as the Millwall Firm, Polly, Cracker, Merit, Coop, Dean and Jean who is a transvestite. The Millwall fans saw the Wednesday fans arriving on the train, they started to chant and point.

The police were waiting for the Millwall fans and they were ushered through the entrance of the railway station, where police on horseback and dog handlers were there to escort them to the football ground. As the Millwall fans walked to the Wednesday ground, they were heckled by Wednesday fans, who were walking to the match. The Millwall firm did not take any notice, but just walked silently, knowing that there was a time and place, and now was not the time.

As they walked along the road the firm were looking for a place to ambush the Wednesday fans, as they walked back from the match. They walked past some old buildings and came up to an old pub, Polly thought this may be a perfect place for an ambush. “Hey Dean, look there, the Shakespeare pub”.
There was a six-foot-high wall all the way around the pub, which had old, heavy, double metal gates. These were pushed back and did not seem to have been closed for a long time as weeds were growing in the front of them. The window shutters in the pub were down, and the newly painted blue door was closed, the landlord had probably closed the pub until the match was over. Dean agreed with Polly, “We'll slip in there on the way back from the match”. The Millwall firm liked to identify certain gangs that were fighting with their fellow Millwall fans, and ambush them outside of the stadium. There was no honour in confronting fans who did not have their own firm. They all weighed up the pub as they walked past, where they may hide and where they could escape. They all agreed, but don't make it obvious that they have

chosen the Shakespeare pub, as the police are watching them, they don't want to make them suspicious.

After walking for about an hour the Millwall fans reach the Wednesday ground, they stand outside the visitor's entrance and are bottled in by the police. The visitors entrance opens, they pay for their ticket, then walk through the turnstile. Inside, there are two policemen with dogs and two carrying out a quick search. Not all fans are stopped, but the fans that look suspicious, or who are recognised by photo are searched and removed from the ground. Stewart, a tall stocky man of about thirty with tattoos on his face, was just being escorted back through the turnstiles, swearing as he went, the Millwall firm expect this and do not carry any weapons.

The firm pay for their tickets, as they walk into the stadium they are stopped by a policeman, while two other policemen with dogs barking look on. John, a young, tall, handsome, slim policeman, stopped the Millwall Firm. "Ok lads, walk over here with me and stand in a line. They stand against a high brick wall that partitions the main street from the football ground. The policeman holds up some photographs and looks at each person in turn. He then starts to walk from one end of the line to the other, standing in front of each person, matching each member with their photograph, he looks into their eyes. Each member of the firm is polite and answer the policeman's questions, none of them want to be arrested and split up from the gang. The policeman stands in front of the final member, Jean, who is wearing tight Marks and Spencer jeans, Millwall t-shirt and carries a small female shoulder bag. The policeman looks at the photograph and smiles. “So, your Jean, the photograph doesn't do you justice, you look far prettier with your lipstick and eyeshadow on”. Jean smiles and blows the policeman a kiss, he’s seen this before and believes the officer is attracted to him. “Thank you officer, you look so handsome and brave”. Jean then wriggled his shoulders. The Policeman winks at Jean, writes him a quick note, looks around to see if anyone is looking and gives it to Jean, and doesn't even check his handbag, a sure sign of attraction, he's concentrating on how Jean looks rather than doing his job, the policeman is happy with the firm. “Ok lads, let's have no trouble from you, off you go”. The firm walk into the middle of the stands, if there's any trouble it will be from the Wednesday fans.

The match kicks off, after ten minutes Wednesday score a goal from just past the halfway line. Wednesday fans start to roar, Millwall fans start to swear. Millwall kicks off, Neil Ardley makes a run and scores from just outside the box. The Millwall fans cheer, but the linesman puts up his flag, the referee gives off side. The Millwall fans are furious, they storm the pitch and run over to the Wednesday fans, some fans start to fight and are quickly arrested. The firm stands calmly, while all the other fans are shouting and swearing, the whistle goes for full time, Wednesday have won 1-0.

The Millwall fans start to leave the stands, Polly takes the lead. “Right lads let's change T-shirts”.
The firm have had a black T shirt underneath their Millwall one, as they swap over, they will not be recognised, or stand out from the crowd.
The Wednesday fans are held back while the Millwall fans are bottled together outside the stadium, and along the road which has been closed. Police with dogs and horses are on all sides, a police officer gives the order to start the fans walking to the train station. The mood is sombre as Millwall have lost, and the heavy policing means they cannot break free to fight with the Wednesday fans.

Millwall fans have walked half a mile down the road towards the train station, an officer radios to his colleague to let the Wednesday fans out of the stadium. As they spill out onto the road, a group of about one hundred Wednesday fans, local to Sheffield who have just been involved in skirmishes, know the route the Millwall fans are to travel. Two Wednesday fans called Trev and Mike lead the way, Trev shouts. “Come on lads”. Mike spurs the fans on, “Let's stone the bastards”. Mike and Trev start to run, and a crowd of Wednesday fans follow. Trev knows all the shortcuts and if they hurry they can find a place to ambush the Millwall fans as they walk past. Trev knows a place where there is a banking covered in trees, it's perfect for an ambush, it looks down over the road the Millwall fans will take, as they pass, they will be able to stone them.

Trev leads the fans as they sprint down back alleys, alongside streets until they reach a grass banking.
Mike and Trev stop, the others all gather round puffing and out of breath, Trev knows this spot well.
"This is it lads". The Wednesday fans make their way up to the top of the banking which is covered in rubbish.
Mike looks for something to throw. "Come on lads, let's get some ammunition".
The Wednesday fans scurried around and collected bottles and bricks from in between the nettles and blackberry bushes, everything was so overgrown. Mike stops, he can hear something. "Listen lads the Millwall fans are coming down the road".
As they grow closer they can hear the fans singing.

"Fuck them all. Fuck them all. Fuck them all. Wednesday, West Ham and Liverpool. Because we are Millwall. And we are the best. We are Millwall so fuck all the rest. Fuck them all, fuck them all, Fuck them all".

The Millwall fans were walking down Shake Moore Road, and had unknowingly drawn level with the Wednesday fans, who were hiding in the trees at the top of the banking. Trev stood up and threw a brick into the middle of the Millwall fans, hitting one on the head knocking him straight down onto the ground. The rest of the

Wednesday fans followed, and started to throw rocks and bottles from the cover of the bushes, they hurled down on the fans and police like rain. The Wednesday fans continually threw bricks and bottles, one after another. The police took cover, Millwall fans were falling injured to the ground as they scattered.

The firm were walking at the back and could see what was happening in the distance, it was time to take advantage and work to the plan. They knew that the Shakespeare pub was about 500 yards away, but that meant they would have to run through the hail of bottles and stones. If they waited, the Wednesday fans would soon stop their attack and run, as the police would be giving chase. But, the police would also quickly regroup and gather the Millwall fans back together, there would not be another opportunity like this. Polly shouts. “Come on lads, let's make a run for it”.

The firm started to sprint along the road, as they got level with the Wednesday fans there was a wounded policeman and his injured dog laid in the road. Millwall Stbeing hit by bricks and bottles.
As they run past, the firm were looking up in the air and dodging the artillery, Jean saw the injured policeman, stopped, and walked over to him, he was laid flat out. Jean bent down and put his arms under his shoulders, and slowly dragged the policeman towards the safety and

cover of a terraced house, while bottles smashed at his side and bricks bounced along the road.

Polly looked around and saw Jean, he stopped, there was no time to think, Polly and his friends turned back and helped Jean pull the policeman to safety. They lent him against the wall were no bricks could hit him. Jean leant over and checked the policeman's face for injuries, he recognised the policeman. It was John, the same one that had teased him at the Wednesday ground. The policeman looked at Jean and they smiled at each other. The firm all stood around the policeman as he pointed to his dog, which was laid injured after being hit twice. Merit and Dean looked at each other and suddenly ran out to save the police dog Sully, they stood each side of him and gently picked him up. As they carried Sully over to the policeman, Dean was hit on the head with a bottle, smashing and causing a small but deep wound to the middle of his head, which bled heavily. Merit laughed. “Did that hurt Dean?”. Dean shook his head. “No, it's only a bit of a bottle”.
As they nearly reached the footpath and into safety, a brick came down hitting Merit on his left shoulder, he groaned and tried not to show the pain, it's Dean's turn now, Dean laughed. “I bet that hurt mate”. Merit tried not to show the pain with a smile. “No, it's only half a house brick”. Merit shrugs his shoulder, unable to rub it as he was carrying the police dog.

They quickly reach the safety of the terraced house and lay Sully next to the policeman, both are injured, but not critical, Polly becomes anxious. “Come on lads we have to go”. The policeman looks up at the firm, he's thankful for what they have done for him and his dog. “Thanks lads”. The policeman holds out his right hand, Jean takes it and holds it gently, leans over and kisses him on the side of his face, the policeman smiles and holds Jeans hand tight. Polly wants to go. “Can we go now Jean?”.

The throwing of bricks as stopped and there’s no more time for talking, the firm all start to sprint through the street, the Shakespeare pub is in sight and they are running like wild horses. As they get to the pub gates they quickly run into the entrance and hide behind the wall. The policeman watches, he knows they are going to set up an ambush, but as no sympathy for the Wednesday supporters. Dean grabs hold of the pub gate, “Let’s shut the gates”, Polly agrees. “Good idea”. Polly, Dean and Merit put their hands on one gate, Coop, Cracker and Jean on the other. The gates are heavy and hang crooked on the hole ridden tarmac ground, Jean counts. “One, two, three, push”. The firm give the gates a tremendous shove, they slowly start to move giving a screech as they close. Bang, the gates close, the firm now feel safe as they stand behind the wall. If the police pass they will not think that anyone could be hiding there. All the firm must do now is to wait for a gang of fans to pass. The Wednesday fans stopped their attack and ran, closely followed by the police, but as they dispersed they were not caught. The police had quickly started escorting the Millwall fans back to the train station, the firm watched through the bushes from behind the pub gates, as the fans passed by, many were bloody and injured.

The Wednesday fans were only ten minutes behind Millwall, as they had been held back to prevent any trouble. As the fans dispersed, or walked to the train station, the Worksop Skinheads where calmly walking back along the same route as the Millwall fans had took. They had no rush, it was only 5.30pm and they would only have to wait as shoppers, fans and people who had finished work would fill the train. They walked down towards the Shakespeare Pub, there were bricks and broken bottles everywhere, all the street had cleared of Wednesday and Millwall fans, it was quiet, and they decided to sit on a bench next to a small grass clearing. Duke knows they should be cautious. "Hey lads, it looks like there has been some trouble". Not knowing that it was the Wednesday fans that had started it. "We had better be careful as we walk to the train station, the Millwall firm are known as the bushwhackers". They were all on edge and started to look around, this was not a good place to be.

The Millwall firm had now recovered from their sprint and were waiting to ambush a Wednesday firm.

Jean put his hands-on top of the wall and slowly pulled himself up, and peered over the top. He could see the Wednesday fans in the distance, all wearing their blue and white shirts. One, two, three, Jean counted and dropped back down to the ground, the firm were looking at Jean. "What have you seen?", Cracker asks. Jean stands there, takes out his eyeshadow and lipstick from his ladies, small shoulder bag and slowly puts it on. The firm wait, Jean puts away his makeup, stands up straight and puts his right hand on his right hip. "Right, there are six or seven Wednesday fans sat on a bench just up the road. Their all dressed the same and must be a local firm. I can't see any police, so everyone must be in town". The Millwall firm stand in a circle, Polly as a plan. "Right, we will wait until they pass and then we will charge out at them".

The Worksop skinheads were sat talking about the match, Duke looked at his watch, it was 6 pm,
"Ok lads, we had better go, we can catch the 6.40 pm train and can be in the Vine for 7.40 pm".
Brady's cautious. "Keep your eye out lads, we don't know if there are any Millwall fans around, we don't want to be caught out by surprise".
They all quickly stand up and walk like they're on a mission. Merit hears the skinheads talking as they are walking down towards them, he wants to start the ambush.

“Let’s pull one of the gates open ready to ambush them as they pass”. Cracker, Jean and Merit pull the left-hand side gate back which is next to a large bush, which also provides cover for the firm as they stand tightly against the wall. Polly walks around the bush and peers from behind the gate, he can see the Worksop Skinheads quickly walking towards them.

The Worksop Skinheads draw level with the Shakespeare pub, Lez looks at the open gate. “Hang on a minute lad’s, I'm dying for a piss, I'm just nipping into this pub yard”. Rest of the skinheads join him. “Yes, we're coming to”. They all run through the pub gate in single file and stand in a straight line pissing up against the pub wall, Lez is relieved, “Are that’s better”. The Millwall firm were very surprised, this was not part of the plan, they can see clearly, Worksop Skinheads written on the back of their shirts. The pub landlord Frank, hears the lads outside, he open’s the bedroom window which looks directly down onto Lez. “Hey, what do you lot think you are doing?”. Lez looks up and seems to recognise the landlord, a woman wearing a dressing gown pops her head out of the window to see what is going on. Lez recognises her straight away. “Mom, what are you doing here? you’re supposed to be at work”. Lez is shocked. Frank and Val look at each other, the skinheads all look up smiling while having a piss, they know what Lez’s mom, is up to. The Millwall firm try to hold back their laughter, it’s a good start to a fight. Val tries to make up an excuse. “Lez, your

Uncle Franks not been too well, I've have come over to look after him, don't tell your dad, we don't want him to worry". Kenny doesn't believe that for a minute.
"That's the best story I've heard in a while". Frank puts his arm around Val. "I'll see you later Lez", they go back into the bedroom and close the window behind them, they've more interesting things to do than argue with the skinheads. Lez looks up, he can't believe what he as seen, his mom with his Uncle Frank. His friends have seen what has happened, he is so embarrassed and upset.

Polly makes a decision, he points towards the Worksop Skinheads, the firm charge silently taking them by surprise. Polly runs up to Kenny and punches him in the back of his head, knocking him straight down to the ground. The Worksop Skinheads hear the thud and quickly turn around, they stand in an orthodox boxing stance (leading with left arm and leg), with their zips down on their trousers and penis hanging out.
Brady is perfectly calm and comes out with a comment. "Do you know, I can't even have a piss in peace now". They all smile, the Worksop Skinheads have never fought with their zips down before, this will be one for the books. The Millwall firm manage to get in the first blows, they have the advantage of a surprise attack . Wolf gives the first war cry. "Millwall bastards". They all mingle as they rain blows and kicks down on each other and spill onto

the street, both gangs stand out clearly and know who is friend or foe.

<u>Wolf vs Dean</u>

Dean jumps forward and up into the air with a superman punch aiming for Wolf's head, Wolf side steps to his left, leaving Deans punch to miss. As Dean lands on the ground, he sends a left roundhouse kick to Wolfs right shoulder, pushing him back. Wolf steps forward, throws a left and right to Dean's head, Dean ducks and dives and takes a step back, Wolf resumes his orthodox stance. Dean jumps forward with a flying front kick, hitting Wolf in the chest which knocks him flat onto the ground, Dean stands upright and laughs at Wolf, "Come on you wanker".
Dean is exceptionally fast with his kicks, Wolf knows that somehow, he must hit Dean clean on the jaw to slow him down. Wolf slowly stands up and looks Dean dead in the eyes, and resumes his stance.

Duke and Polly are fighting, Polly hits Duke with a left jab to his nose sending him backwards, where he bumps into Dean. Dean is knocked off balance, this is Wolf's opportunity. He immediately steps forward hitting Dean with a left jab over his right eye and a right to the jaw, knocking Dean's head back. Wolf drops into a lower stance, throwing a left and right punch deep into Dean's ribs, Dean bends forward winded. Wolf follows up with a right uppercut, hitting Dean cleanly on the nose, breaking it immediately, Dean goes flying backwards onto the ground, dazed and breathless.

Duke vs Polly

Duke is stood in the orthodox stance, Polly can see Duke's name on the front of his t-shirt, he presumes he is the leader with a name like that. Polly throws a left jab which hits Duke on the nose. Polly steps forward and throws a right hook, hitting Duke in the left ear, making Duke's head turn to one side with the force of the blow. Polly throws a straight left but Duke ducks and spins around with a back fist hitting Polly on the left jaw. Polly responds with a left and right hook hitting Duke in the left jaw and above his right eye, causing a deep gash.

Brady sees what is happening and pushes Cracker in the chest with the palm of his hands, shoving Cracker three yards backwards. Brady then runs towards Polly and as he reaches him, brings up his right knee, hitting Polly in his right thigh. Polly feels a sickening pain, his leg goes limp and his arms drop, for that brief second his guard is down. Duke steps forward and kicks Polly in the bollocks. Polly's legs go together, he feels sick with the pain and drops down on his knees. Duke grabs hold of Polly's head and brings up his left knee, hitting Polly clean in the nose and mouth, breaking one of his teeth. Duke stands back, Polly falls forward, holding himself up off the ground with his arms.

Ian vs Merit

Merit runs forward and hits Ian in the throat with a forearm smash leaving Ian stunned. Merit then weaves behind Ian, puts him in a strangle hold and pulls Ian backwards onto the ground. Merit then wraps his legs around Ian's body and the strangle hold is secure. As Merit tightens his grip, the hold restricts Ian's ability to breath and he knows he has only seconds before he passes out. Ian puts his right hand on top of Merit's left thumb, he then grabs and twists it and gives it a hard pull. Merits thumb breaks and the joint dislocated, causing Merit to release his hold. Ian rolls over onto the top of Merit and pins his arms to the ground with his knees. Merit brings up his right knee and hits Ian in the back, knocking him to one side and they begin to wrestle.

B O vs Coop

Coop runs forward and kicks out with his right leg, aiming for B O, s bollocks. B O blocks the kick by bringing his right arm down in a striking motion. As Coop puts his right foot to the ground, he brings both arms around in a clapping motion, hands cupped, hitting B O on both ears at the same time. B O becomes dazed and stumbles, the blow to the ears as knocked him off balance. Coop spins around with a right roundhouse kick, hitting B O in the left ribs, breaking two immediately. He turns to one side, guarding them with his left arm from another blow. He stands in the southpaw position (leading with the right hand and right foot). Coop throws a left roundhouse kick, which hits B O on the left knee, B O falls to the ground on both knees. He looks up towards Coop, B O is dazed, and in pain, he has trouble breathing due to his cracked ribs, adrenaline kicks in, he must survive. Coop steps forward with the right knee towards B O' s head, B O moves his head to the right and Coops knee glides past. B O, dives forward and grabs hold of the back of Coops left ankle with both hands, puts his right shoulder above the knee, and pulls the bottom of Coops foot forward. As his shoulder pivots forward into his leg, Coop falls back onto the hard-tarmac drive, banging his head as he lands. B O still as hold of Coops ankle and wraps his left arm around it, holding the leg straight. He draws back the palm of his right hand and with a swift blow, hits Coops knee joint, Coop cries out in pain, his leg now goes limp.

Brady vs Cracker

Cracker steps forward with a right-side kick to Brady's chest. Brady is forced back and hits the pub wall. He looks around to see if anyone else is going to attack him and sees his friend Duke in trouble.
Cracker and Brady step towards each other at the same time. Cracker hits Brady with a left hook, grazing his left eye. Brady responds by hitting Cracker in the chest with the palm of his hands. Cracker stumbles back and Brady runs over to help Duke. Cracker starts to run after Brady, Brady's back is towards him, Cracker quickly catches up

to him and throws a right punch towards the back of Brady's head. As it lands Brady stumbles, as he bends over, he pulls back his fist and spins around, hitting Cracker above his left temple knocking him unconscious, and he falls to the ground.

Within thirty seconds the fighting is over, the Millwall firm on sat on the ground injured, they look over at Jean, they can see the Worksop Skinheads looking at him, probably thinking that they can easily finish the last member of the firm.

Lez vs Jean

Lez is upset, and as looked on as his friends have fought, but is now staring down at the ground, he can't believe he's just seen his mom hanging out of the pub window with his uncle Frank. Jeans been enjoying the fight between the gangs, he's also been watching Lez as he stands against the wall. Jean walks over to Lez and calmly stands in the front of him, then taps him on the right shoulder with his index finger. Lez looks up and sees a slim man wearing lipstick and eyeshadow.
Lez is surprised, especially as all his mates have been fighting with rough looking Millwall fans.
Jean makes his move. "Hello sailor." Jean leans over and gently kisses Lez on the lips.

Lez is shocked by being kissed on the lips by a man and turns away quickly, wiping his lips with his hands, he's forgot about his mom for now. "You dirty bastard".
Jean as taken two steps back, he stands upright, feet slightly apart, his shoulders straight and in line, hands on hips and smiling seductively. He looks at Lez with his piercing blue eyes. "Would you like to have a fight gay boy", he then blows Lez a kiss.
Lez is furious, he doesn't like being called a gay boy, or being kissed by a man in the front of his friends.
"You gay bastard". Jean decides to upset Lez even further. "Oh, and by the way, how long has your mom and Uncle Frank been close friends", he winks at Lez.
Lez is furious and runs forward towards Jean, his head down, he's upset about his mom and doesn't want to be kissed again. As he runs towards Jean he tries to hit him with a rugby tackle, but Jean just gently steps to one side, and as Lez passes Jean gently slaps him on the backside. He as seen the name Lez, on his t-shirt. "My what a lovely bum you have Lez". As Lez trips over onto the ground the rest of the skinheads start to form a circle around Jean, he's the last one they must defeat, before they can say they have beaten the Millwall Firm. They all look on battered and bruised and are quite surprised in the way Jean is fighting.

The Millwall firm stand up, they are all injured but not defeated, they have been here before. They look on, any other firm would jump up and fight with their friend, but

this is Jean, and he doesn't like anyone to get involved, or they receive the same punishment as his attackers. In Jean's words, "You have to be good little boys and do as you are told".
The firm looked on, thinking the skinheads do not know what they have let themselves in for. Jean is a sadist and masochistic, where he loves to receive and inflict pain, this is, *his exotic fantasy world*.

Jean stands in the middle of the circle and he is surrounded by the Worksop Skinheads. He calmly looks around. "My, what gorgeous, handsome, fit men you are". He opens his small black shoulder length handbag, and takes out a packet of long filtered Park Drive cigarettes. As he opens them, he smiles, pulls one out and then puts it into his mouth, it's all quiet, he closes the packet and puts it back, before pulling out a pink zippo lighter. He gives it a flick, it open's and it lights, he slowly puts the flame to the end of the cigarette and inhales very slow and deep, looking at Lez as he does so, he puts back his lighter and zips up the bag. Jean takes another puff of his cigarette, holding it between his index and third finger. Brady's getting fed up. "He's taking the fucking piss". Jean looks at Brady, takes another puff of the cigarette, has he exhales he smiles directly at him.

"My what pretty t-shirts you are all wearing, you all look so masculine and sexy, your every man's dream".

Jean walks over to Brady, his hips swinging from side to side and stands directly in front of him. Brady's eyes are glaring with anger. Jean takes a deep puff of his cigarette, this time he holds it with his index finger and thumb. It glows red, and he calmly sticks it into Brady's left eye. Brady screams and turns away, covering his face with both hands, before falling to the ground. Duke is stood next to Brady, he steps forward and throws a left jab towards Jeans nose, Jean quickly bends backwards, and Dukes fist just falls short of hitting him. Jean then crouches down, and in a circular movement, with his left hand and long nails grabs hold of Dukes bollocks, squeezing and pulling sharply at the same time. Duke gives out a large groan and falls back, wondering where that had come from.

Lez wants revenge. “You queer bastard”. Lez and B O both run towards Jean, from the front and back. Jeans stands and waits, B O puts his forearm around Jeans throat from behind, as Lez is about to punch him in the face, Jean suddenly grabs hold of B O’s forearm, drops down on one knee and sends him flying, he lands on Lez leaving them both laid on the ground. Wolf walks forward and hits Jean in the mouth with a tremendous right hand, bursting his top and bottom lips. Jean stands still, tastes the blood coming from his wound, before it runs down his chin. He takes the middle finger of his right hand and puts it into his mouth, as he pulls it out, it’s covered in blood. Wolf looks in amazement, no one has ever been able to take the force of his right hand, but Jean didn't even stagger. Jean stares into Wolf's eyes, he's memorised, his stare is like a snake when they hypnotize their prey, just before killing and eating it, Wolf has never seen a fighting style like this before. With his right finger, Jean wipes his blood along the nose of Wolf which quickly distracts him, and with the side of his left hand, hits Wolf in the throat. Wolf drops straight to the ground, he can't breathe, Jean steps back and smiles.

He looks around and sees Ian in a boxing stance, his left knee slightly bent to one side, has he walks with a limp from an old football injury. Jean walks slowly towards him, licking the blood from his fingers, eyes gazing excitedly, swinging his hips as he goes. Ian stands rigid, Jean jumps up and pounces forward onto him, knocking Ian down. As he sits on the top of him, Jean pins Ian's arms down by his side with his knees, he cannot move. Ian shakes his head as Jean puts his left thumb under Ian's nose and his fingers in his right eye. He slowly bends over Ian, their faces only an inch apart, Ian can smell the pleasure Jean gets from inflicting pain.
"I have saved you for the very last handsome". Jean pulls Ian's head to his right side, and starts to kiss the left-hand side of his neck. Ian struggles, but cannot move, he feels an excruciating pain as Jean bites deeply into him. Ian screams out in agony, Brady hears Ian scream and staggers up from the ground and runs towards Jean, kicking him in the head, sending Jean rolling along the ground, Brady holds out his hand and helps Ian up.

They hear the whale of the police sirens, Duke's worried about being caught. “Come on lads we'll just walk steady along the footpath as though nothing has happened”. The Millwall firm run into the pub yard and climb over the back wall leaving Jean. He stands up, his eye makeup is running from the tears in his eyes, and there's lipstick smudged on his face, but Jeans enjoying himself. “Hey boys, don't go, were having so much fun”.

The Worksop Skinheads hear Jean and start to sprint, Ian, who has a limp and is usually very slow, races past them all. He feels like his manhood has been taken away from him, and doesn't want any more of that. Both the Millwall firm and Worksop Skinheads concentrate on travelling to the train station, and catching the train home, there was not going to be any more fighting that day.

As the Millwall firm travel home, they hatch a plan to get their revenge, Coop wanted to take the battle to the skinhead’s home town of Worksop. “Let's go to Worksop next Saturday, we'll soon find out where the skinheads drink”. Cracker’s not too sure, “Look lads, Worksop is a long way off and is a small town, we need places to hide if we are chased by the police, we don’t want to do time”. Polly sits listening and comes up with a plan. “Right lads, this is what we will do. We’ll wait a few weeks until we are fit and then we’ll go down one Saturday, we’ll do what Coop said, but we’ll just go for Duke their leader, we need to look around Worksop town centre and find the nightclub the skinheads drink in, we’ll follow Duke home and jump him. If we dress in casual clothes while drinking around Worksop, no one will be able to tell who we are. If anyone asks, because of our cockney accent we'll tell them we're working on the roads. We'll take knuckle dusters and knives, who agrees". The firm nod, but it's time to think about going out with their friends tonight and having a drink, there's a lot to talk about, Duke is weeks away.

The Firm go to Worksop

It's early Saturday morning, it's five weeks since the Millwall Firm and the Worksop Skinheads fought. Polly makes his way through the old brick archway into the Queens Road Peckham train station. Its 5.45 a m, as he sits on the long old green wooden bench, waiting for the rest of his friends to arrive. Cracker, Merit and Dean come slowly walking along the platform, it's a bit early for them when they've been out the night before. As they meet they slump down on the bench, Merit looks at Polly.

"Where's Coop Polly?". Polly looks down the platform. "He won't be long, he's got another 20 minutes". They hear the sound of heavy steps, as they all look to their right, they see Jean walking towards them, holding hands with a tall slim man. Jean stops, looks at the firm. "Hullo boys, John's come down from Sheffield to take me on holiday for a few weeks, while he's on sick leave, that's sweet of him, isn't it"? The firm sit quietly looking from John to Jean, not knowing what to say. Jean looks at John, "John you've got something to say to my friends ". John's still feeling groggy after being hit on the head with a brick a few weeks before. "Yea of course, thank you lads for saving me and my dog, we will always appreciate it". The firm sit quietly looking at Jean and John, as they walk off together, Jean carrying his bunch of flowers and waggling his bum happily, as they leave to go on holiday.

The firm lay back on the bench, Cracker has a smile on his face. “Jean always liked men in uniforms, looks like he’s fell in love with one”.

People start to come into the train station, either going to work or shopping. They hear someone shout and they look round. “Come here, you dirty little bastard”. They see Coop running along the platform towards them, he's sweating and breathing heavy, followed a few yards behind by a middle aged, rough, mean looking man called Gunner, who’s covered in tattoos. Coop runs straight past the firm and into a small brick archway where the ticket office is. He quickly hides behind one of the large half-moon shaped old oak doors, that secures the office when it is closed. Gunner runs up to the ticket office, looks around, he then walks through the other side of the archway and looks up and down the road, he can't see Coop anywhere, he's very angry, “Bastard, I'll see him another day”. Gunner walks out of the train station and onto the main street and makes his way home, he's going to have a few words with his wife Jane when he gets back. But he knows deep down that she plays around when he is at sea, when in foreign ports he also goes astray, so it's not all one sided, she becomes lonely and he enjoys the fun, they'll soon make up.

Coop slowly pushes open the large heavy door, he peeps around, sneaks up through the archway and peers down the platform, he doubles back and looks down the road and sees Gunner marching away. Coop gives a big smile and wipes away the sweat from his forehead, and makes his way back to his friends. As he walks up to them, their bench is full, and he sits on the ground with his back against the old Victorian stone wall. Cracker, Polly, Dean and Merit stare down at Coop, wondering what was going off. Merits intrigued, “What’s all that about Coop?”. Coop looks up as he catches his breath. “That’s the fucking navy for you, I've been seeing a seaman's wife while he's been at sea, he wasn't due back for another week. Me and Jane were kissing and playing around on the sofa this morning, when I was due to go and meet you all. We heard the back-door open and quickly shut, we heard someone say, “Jane I'm home love, I've missed you, Jane was shocked to hear his voice and said, it’s Gunner my husband.

He must have quickly stripped off, and walked into the lounge, just as I was standing up pulling up my trousers. He was stood in his underpants with a bunch of flowers in one hand, and a box of chocolates in the other. He stopped, went bright red and looked very angry, he threw the chocolates at me and the flowers at Jane. I took the opportunity to run past him, and he chased me all the way down to the train station”.

Polly wondered why Coop didn't hide somewhere else. “Coop why did you run here?”. Coop put his hands over his face realising it was a stupid thing to do. “I don’t know, just that we arranged to meet here, and it was getting late, I didn't want to let you down”. The firm sat quietly shaking their heads.

The train pulls up, and the firm climb onto the train, they slowly walk to the back of the fourth carriage and sit down. A middle aged stocky man came slowly walking down the aisle. Polly recognised him from being a child, it was his dads old friend Rick. “Hey Rick”, Rick looked to see where the voice had come from, and sadly looked at Polly. “Come and sit with me “. Rick sits the opposite side of the carriage table. Polly wants to know where Rick has been. “What have you been doing with yourself, we've not seen you in ages”. Rick looks sadly at Polly, he remembers him as a small happy child and starts to tell his story, the firm gather round and listen with interest.

“The Millwall firm had gone to Manchester, I was the man at that time, your father was one of the main players. We stormed the pitch when united scored the first goal, and we started to the fight with the Manchester fans, usual fists and feet, nothing special, but I punched one young bloke in the head, he fell back and immediately collapsed, the police dived on me straight away. Well, this guy died on the way to hospital, and I was charged with manslaughter and given ten years. My wife left me for another man, the kids have grown up and live up north, and I'll probably never see them again, I can't get a job because of my record. I'm going up to Scotland to start a new life, and see what happens up there. I regret what I have done, and I feel guilty about taking a man's life, and sadly I have also destroyed my family”. It goes very quiet, the firm think about what they are getting into once again, but youth and adventure takes over from the sad

story they have just heard. Cracker lifts everyone's spirit by starting to sing one of their Millwall songs.
"Hello, Hello, we are the Millwall boys. Hello, hello, we are the Millwall boys, and if you are a West Ham fan, surrender or you will die, we all follow the Millwall boys".

The firm sit quietly on their journey and eventually arrive at Sheffield train station. They leave the train and find the Sheffield to Worksop platform, that the Worksop skinheads had used a few weeks before. The train is waiting in the station and they climb straight onto the double carriage train, and unusually, decide to sit in the middle of the first carriage, they usually like to sit at the back to see what is going on. It's 10.45a m. The train leaves the station and will arrive in Worksop at 11.30a m. It's time for the firm to check their weapons, there's no one else on the train, it only gets busy when shoppers are travelling back to Worksop. Polly takes the lead. "Ok lads, let's check our weapons". They take them out one by one, Polly, a short six-inch bar (cosh), Dean a short flick knife, Coop, a world war two pattern knife, Merit, Stanley knife and Cracker, a world war two, New Zealand knuckle knife, each weapon fitted neatly into the back of their jean pockets, hidden by their casual jackets. Polly has a plan. "Right lads, when we get off the train in Worksop, we'll suss out the town centre and local pubs", the firm agree and sit back in their seats waiting for the train to arrive at their destination.

The train pulls up at Worksop train station, they step through the door and onto the platform in line, feeling a little nervous as they don't know the town, or what really to expect. As they walk off the station platform and onto the main road, they see an old man Tom, carrying a shopping bag. Cracker asks him directions into town. “Excuse me sir, could you tell me the way to the town centre.” Old Toms impressed with the young man's manners. “Of course,”, and points down the road. “Just walk straight down past the Regal cinema and it takes you straight through town, all the way up to the old market, there's only one main street you can't go wrong”. Cracker smiles at old Tom, he reminds him of his old grandfather. “Thank you, sir”, the rest of the firm put up their hands and smile.

As they walk past the cinema, they see in the distance a few skinheads walking into a pub, wearing Wednesday colours. When they get close they see the pub sign for the Vine. They must explore the pub, Cracker volunteers. “I’ll have a slow look round, if you all wait across the road and look in Ken Ward’s sport shop windows we won’t look suspicious “. As Cracker walked into the Vine, it is full of Wednesday fans going to the match, he recognises Wolf who’s stood with his friends in their usual corner, but they don't recognise him as he’s dressed in a casual jacket, shirt and jeans. As he walks back out, he sees his friends across the road and walks over to them. They stand together looking in the sports shop window. “It looks like the skinhead's local, we've been lucky, if they meet there before the match they probably drink there after".

The Millwall firm slowly set off walking and follow the road down, becoming aware of the area as they go. As they walk through the town centre they bump into Jake, who apologises. "Sorry mate", Dean smiles." That's ok". This is an opportunity to ask about the nightclubs. "Excuse me mate, we're working away on the roads and we are staying in Worksop for a few nights, can you tell us about the night clubs". Jakes pleased to help. "Of course I can mate, on the corner there you can see the Carousel, it's more for the rough and ready's, but if you keep walking along the street you come to Barclays bank, next to it you will see two blue double doors, under a sign saying Dandy's night club, it's where all the skinheads go". Dean puts his hand on Jake's shoulder, "Thanks mate ". Jakes pleased to help. "That's ok", and Jake walks off.

The firm walk past the Carrousel and come to some crossroads. Polly looks to the right, "Come on lads, let's see if there's a side street that leads us back to the main road. Fifty yards down, there's a public toilet next to a small side street that leads behind the shops, they walk along and come to a crossroad across from the Queens pub. They walk across the main road and up the main street where they come up to Barclays bank, just as Jake said, they see the double doors with the sign saying

Dandy's. They now know where to go, all they must do is follow Duke through the streets, if their lucky, he won't have his friends with him, as they may be walking their girlfriends home like they do back home, if not, it will have to be a different plan.

They come to the market and see an old cafe, the firms hungry, they walk in through the shabby single door, the doorbell rings letting the staff know there's a customer. They sit at the end of the cafe next to the window looking out on the shoppers passing by. The tables are old, wooden and scarred with years of wear, and are lacking a table cloth, the seats are wooden benches more appropriate to old school days. An old, little lady called Hilda comes over to take their order, they ask for a bacon butty and a cup of tea. A young grey looking gentleman sits near them, he's strangely darkly dressed and does not have a drink. Hilda brings them their butties and teas on a large tray and puts it on the table. "Here you are lads, you'll enjoy these". She hands them around and walks away with a smile on her face, the cafe might be old and worn, but you can't get a better bacon butty anywhere. The take a bite of their bacon butty and can't believe how nice it tastes. Polly wipes his lips, "That is the best bacon butty I have ever tasted", the others mumble in agreement as their mouths are full.

The firm have their meal and chat, people come and go, but nobody seems to notice the tall dark man, the firm

keep glancing at him as he's making them feel uncomfortable. Merit has a cold shiver, he turns towards the stranger. “Excuse me mate, who are you, are you ok?”. The man slowly turns around and stares at the firm, they all stare back, wondering who this strange man is, he looks away, he has something special to say to them. “I am the Shadow Man, this is your last fight, and again, you will show your courage in a special way. In a short time, you will all be called upon to take on a special adventure with many battles”. The firm all suddenly feel dazed and find themselves opening their eyes. The stranger as gone, Dean can't believe what's happened, “Is that real or what?”, they all start to laugh.
Coop looks at the time on the old wined up clock on the wall, it’s 2.30 pm, the pubs shut at 3 pm and don't open until 6.30 pm. “Well lads, we've got four hours to kill, let's see if we can find a snooker hall “. Polly went up to the counter to pay for their meal, a young slim lady with blonde hair is drying a plate. “How much is that love? “. She looks at the tab next to the old metal till, “Five bacon butties and five teas, £1.25 please.” Polly looks though his change and gives her the correct money. “Excuse me love, do you know where the snooker hall is”. She looks and smiles. “Course I do duck, it's just down the main street, turn left at the Queens and it's a hundred yards on the right”. Polly nods, “Thanks love what’s your name”. She smiles at the stranger, she likes his cockney accent. “Dawn, why? “I would like to take you out one day, but today is not the day. Dawn looks deep into Polly’s eyes, she gives him a warm smile. “We’ll meet one day, but not

the way you think, you're very brave, please be careful", she then turns away, Polly nods, he feels that there is something special about Dawn.

.

The firm walk single file out of the cafe and shout together. "Thanks love", and make their way down the busy high street. As they come to the Queens pub at the crossroads, they turn left and soon see the snooker hall across the road on the right. They walk across the road and stand next to the brick archway entrance with a stone slab along the top saying, snooker hall 1911. The firm walk through the old brown wooden doors, as they look around it as twenty-one snooker tables, with old wooden benches spaced out evenly around the hall, where retired men sit and talk. At the far end is a kiosk where you pay for a table and collect your snooker balls. They walk down the middle row of tables and come to the kiosk, there is a middle aged, well-built lady, with short black hair and a fag in her mouth called Daffodil, who's in charge of the hall. She peers over her glasses as she looks through the glass window. "Yes lads, what do you want?". Merit stands at the opening in the window with a smile on his face, he likes to play snooker. "Could we have four hours on a table please". The lady looks across the snooker hall at the empty tables. "Of course, table seventeen, here's some chalk, the queues are hung on the wall, that's £2 please". Merit gives the lady the money, picks up the chalk and they make their way to their table. The numbers of the tables are on the top on the snooker table lights, table seventeen is in the far corner next to a bench, where some old gentleman are chatting. The firm take off their jackets, put them on the coat hooks on the wall and discretely hide their weapons in the inside of their jacket pockets, and slowly, but quietly, play snooker for the rest of the afternoon, lightly joking and laughing as they play.

Polly looks up at the clock, it's 6.40 pm, time as flown, it always does when you're having fun. “Come on lads it's time to go, we'll start off at the Vine.” They pick up their jackets, put their weapons in their back pockets and slowly make their way to the pub, they are going to keep a low profile tonight, so they don't attract attention. They walk into the pub and up to the bar, Dean buys the first round, “Five pints of lager please mate”. They pick up their drinks and stand next to the jukebox, they can see all around the pub from there.

It's 7 pm as the pub doors burst open, Duke and his gang barge in singing their Wednesday songs, they stand in a circle talking and laughing about their day. Duke wants to move on. “Come on lads let's go and meet the girls, they will be waiting for us at the Marquis”. The firm hear what Duke as said, they've seen the pub as they have walked through town, they drink up and follow on. The skinheads walk into the Marquis, it's a small pub with one long narrow lounge and a bar at the far end, their girlfriends are stood waiting for them in the far corner. They pair up, and for the rest of the evening slowly walk around the pubs together. They finish off at Dandy's nightclub, dancing to *Red Red Wine* and *Moonstomp*. The firm have followed Duke around town and casually stand next to the dance floor, watching everyone dance. People start to leave and there are just a few couples left, Duke will be walking home alone as his girlfriend as left early, because she is at work early that morning. Duke drinks his pint of cider and walks out of the night club, followed distantly by the firm, they smell the scent of revenge.

It's cool, raining but calm as Duke walks home from Dandy's nightclub, after a good day out with his friends. As he walked through the town centre which leads close to where he lives, it was quiet, five men suddenly passed him walking in the same direction, one was polite, "Good night mate", Duke was too drunk to reply straight away. "Ok lads". As he walked towards the canal bridge, the firm were stood in a shop doorway waiting, they decided it was time to take their revenge, Polly would start the attack. Duke noticed a youth nearby of medium build, walking slowly towards him, but being drunk he didn't sense the danger, the rest of the firm followed. As they reached each other, Polly spoke. "Ae up mate". Duke managed to reply. "Ae up". Duke suddenly felt a sharp pain at the back of his head, causing him to slump down on one knee, he heard someone swear. "Clever Bastard".

He felt another heavy blow to his right shoulder, causing extreme pain, which made him slump down on both knees, he knew from his violent past that he must not go down onto the ground, as they would stamp on his head.

He looked around, feeling dazed, he could see around five guys, either with skinhead or short straight hair, covered in scars and carrying knives and wearing knuckle dusters. A youth holding a 6-inch, short iron bar looked down at Duke. “Remember us from the other week?”. Duke looked up, he looked tall, broad and very mean, part of his left ear was missing and there were scars down the right-hand side of his face from previous battles, he remembered them from the Wednesday match, it was Polly, leader of the Millwall firm.
“Yes, we fought, and you caught me with a lucky punch, now I am here to return the compliment”, Dean, Coop, Cracker, and Merit looked on. Polly stepped back with his right leg and brought his knee forward, striking Duke clean in the face. Duke briefly blacked out and fell straight to the ground, his left forearm was under his head, his right arm was totally disabled which laid down by his side.

The Millwall firm circled around Duke, who was now dazed and unable to move, they had plenty of time and they were going to slowly punish him. Duke was laid on the ground looking up, Polly put his foot of Dukes right arm, making him groan with pain. “Were going to make an example of you Duke, no one fucks with the Millwall Firm”.

Polly nodded to Dean, who walked around Duke until he was level with the right-hand side of Duke's body. He took three steps back and then quickly ran forward, kicking Duke in the ribs, making him cry out. He was now totally vulnerable and at the mercy of the Millwall Firm. Dean laughed and mocked Duke. “Come on Duke, who's the tough guy now?”, as he knelt by the side of Duke’s head.

Steff was walking along the street with his girlfriend, they had been at a friend’s house for a late-night drink. He saw the Millwall Firm attacking a man on the ground, unknowing to him it was his arch enemy Duke. “Bastard’s, leave him alone”. Steff was only about 50 yards away and started to run towards the gang. Dean drew his knife level with Duke’s face, Duke was so badly injured, he was unable to know what was happening. The firm looked round and saw Steff, a 6ft 8’ tall rocker with long black hair, coming running towards them like an apache warrior. They quickly lined up and formed a spear head, first one with the iron bar and the others with their knifes. As Steff ran forward he began to scream, Polly stepped forward and drew back his cosh, Steff, as he ran jumped up into the air and as he flew forward, hit Polly in the face with his knee, breaking one of Polly’s bottom teeth and knocked him back onto his gang. The Millwall Firm stepped aside, knives are drawn, Steff had dropped to the ground on his feet, ready for the fight. This was Steff's world, being a Hells Angel, he loved the excitement, challenging lads who were tooled up and ready to go to war, this was another medal of honour for him, and hopefully another scar to tell later tales.

The Millwall firm were well rehearsed as they surrounded Steff, Dean had quickly joined them, Duke was laid a few yards away, but Ruby had attended him to see if he was alright, and administered first aid, but she was still aware of the dangers Steff faced. She could see that this gang was exceptional in the way they fight. Dean stepped forward lashing out with his knife towards Steff's chest, while Cracker at the same time attacked from behind. Steff took one step forward, hitting Dean with a right jab to the nose breaking it immediately, which sent his head back before he collapsed onto the ground. This gave Steff the small space and time to quickly make his manoeuvre. It was obvious that he was going to be attacked from behind. From the right jab position Steff span round spinning his right arm out as he went.

Cracker walked straight into a backfist, which hit him in his right ear. He was in agony and stepped back as the blow had knocked him off balance.
Merit stepped in, as Steff struck Cracker, he bent down lashing out with the knife, deeply gashing Steff's right thigh. Steff felt a burning pain down the side of his leg and went limp.
He turned to his left side, took two quick steps back, his wound was pouring with blood, he knew it was serious and at to end the fight quickly. Coop jumped onto Steff's back from behind and tried to put him in a strangle hold

with one arm, but Steff was too strong, and he just dangled from Steff's neck, but was determined not to let go. Merit stepped in and this time lashed out towards Steff's chest, he lent back, as the knife whizzed past he quickly stepped forward throwing a left jab, hitting Merit clean on the temple, and he was knocked clean out.

Coop had held on to Steff with his right arm, as he dangled he held his world war two pattern knife in his left hand. The knife was easily held, but Coop found it difficult to hold on while he brought it round towards Steff's throat, Ruby was watching closely. "You Bastards".
Ruby had seen what Coop was about to do, she quickly circled around the back of him, took off her black high heeled shoe, held it in her right hand, and in sheer desperation, launched herself into the air, striking Coop at the back of the head on her way down. Coop felt a sickening blow, making him release his hold on Steff, which caused him to drop his knife. Coop stood back as Steff's leg gave way, he felt dizzy from the loss of blood, Coop saw this, he looked at Ruby who was stood right in front of him, he grabbed Ruby with both hands by the throat squeezing as hard as he could. Ruby gently put her arm in between Coops, put her right hand over the top of his right fingers, with a neat quick flick twisted Coops wrist. As he released his hold she twisted his right arm, stepped in, turned and put his arm straight over her right shoulder, as she bent down threw Coop flying,

where he landed, back first on the side of the kerb of the foot path.

The Millwall Firm knew they were beat but had got their revenge, they helped each other up and walked off singing. “Fight, fight. Wherever you may be. We are the boys from Bermondsey. And we hate you all. Whoever you may be. We are the boys from Bermondsey”.
Ruby was concerned about her boyfriend. “Are you ok Steff?”. Steff nodded, and she ran to the phone box to phone for the ambulance and police. When Ruby ran back, Steff was kneeling at the side of Duke. “Do you know who it is Ruby?”. “Yes Steff. Its Duke, you have just saved his life”. Steff smiled, he was pleased that Duke was ok.

The ambulance and police arrive, there were two ambulance men, called Harry and Daniel, they went over to Duke, Harry recognised Ruby straight away. “What are you doing here Ruby?, while you're here, can you give us a hand”.
Ruby gave them a rundown of what had happened and Dukes possible injuries which she had earlier assessed. Ruby then went to help with Steff. “Pass me some bandages for Steff’s wound”. “Here you are Ruby”, Harry threw her one of the first aid kits. When Harry and Daniel had tended to Duke, they put him on the stretcher and carried him into the ambulance. As Duke laid there, he began to regain consciousness, but was a little dazed.

Ruby had bandaged Steff's leg, Daniel came over to help Steff into the ambulance and Steff sat opposite to Duke. Peter the policeman, was stood there just waiting for the ambulance crew to finish their work. He walked over to Ruby who was stood next to the ambulance door.
"Excuse me lady, do you know what as happened ?".
"Yes, I do officer, but can I call in at the police station to give a statement, my boyfriends injured and must go to hospital". The policeman was happy with the reply. "I can always check up with the hospital for the address of the injured".
Ruby jumped into the back of the ambulance and Daniel closed the door behind them, he drove while Harry monitored Duke's condition.

Duke was now wondering where he was. "Where am I?". Daniel explained what had happened.
"You have been attacked by a gang of lads, they must have been looking for you. If it had not been for these two-young people, they would have killed you".
Duke blinked his eyes and gained his vision. He looked, looked again and realised it was Steff, is enemy, his anger had suddenly turned into respect. He remembered what had happened and could see that Steff had been injured while saving him. He looked and smiled at Steff.
"Steff come here". In a quiet tone
Steff went and sat next to Duke, this big tall rocker with long hair, was smiling down at him in a reassuring way, blood still dripping down his Jeans from his bandaged

wound. “Thanks Mate”. Steff smiled. “Ok mate, I hope you get better soon”. Steff rested his hand on Duke’s shoulder all the way two the hospital.
Skinheads and rockers were always arch enemies, but both have learned how strange destiny can be, when it wants to turn foes, into friends.

As the firm walked away, the road forked to the right past the Vine, but Polly has a strange feeling. “We’ll keep to the left lads, they'll be a side road up to the train station. The rest of the firm look at Polly, Cracker can't understand why they are taking a different route. “Why don't we go the way we came Polly?”. Polly looks at Cracker with determination in his eyes “. I don't know mate, I feel we just have to go this way”. Polly starts to walk off and the firm follow, they’re not really bothered which way they go, as long as they get to the train station, Polly as a good sense of direction, which has never let them down.

They walk up past Woodlands motorbike shop, on the right they see a large church. As they walk on, they come to some flats, they can hear a lady screaming, they look up and see a young woman and two children on an upstairs balcony, there’s smoke coming out of the open upstairs windows. Polly takes charge. “Coop you go to the phone box we have just passed, phone 999”. Coop looks across the road for a road sign, and sees the sign for Saint John's Church and runs to the phone box, Polly deploys his men. "Cracker, you stand under the balcony, Merit, Dean come with me. "The flat is on the second story and they will have to work out how to get the family to the ground. The firm are used to making their way through different flats, in towns and cities, where they've been chased after matches and are aware of how the flats are laid out. They run around the side of the flats, through the double doors, up the concrete stairs and onto the walkway. A neighbour is stood outside the door, there is smoke coming out through the kitchen windows, and she is calling out their names in panic, not knowing what to do. The firm start to quickly walk along the balcony pulling down the washing lines as they go, they've used them before to escape.

They walk past a flat with Sheffield Wednesday curtains in the window, they all glance at the colours, which catches their attention. They come to the back door of the burning flat, it's time to act. Polly steps back, they all take a deep breath, he runs forward, and kicks open the door, smoke and flames burst out. They run into the flames and smoke, holding their breath, the lounge door is still open, and they run through. Merit closes the door behind them and they make their way to the balcony door. Polly pulls down the handle, and the door opens, they fall through, and Dean closes the door behind them. They gasp for breath, the lady is holding her two children, she screams in terror for the safety of her two kids. "How are we going to get out?". Polly Is used to having to think fast, a wrong

decision in the past would have got the firm into trouble. He looks over the balcony, Crackers stood waiting and waves to him. "Come on Polly, what are you fucking about at, let's get them down". Polly ties the washing line under the young girl's arms and lowers her slowly down, Cracker catches her and releases the knot, he puts up his arm and waves and Polly pulls up the rope. Flames are now coming out of the lounge window, Polly quickly ties the rope around the young boy, the lady puts her hand on Polly's shoulder, she's relieved her children are now safe, and calms down, has Polly lowered him slowly down. Cracker takes the child, he's fine and unties the rope and they both sit on the grass looking up for their mom. Merits getting worried. "Come on Polly, the flats going to blow". Polly looks at the lady. "Come on young lady it's your turn", giving a reassuring smile. He doubles up the washing line and ties it around her, they all slowly lower her down. She's about ten feet from the ground, Crackers watching, the heat from the fire makes the balcony windows suddenly explode behind the lads.
They let go of the rope, Cracker catches her as she falls.

The fire brigade arrives and see what is happening, Polly Merit and Dean quickly stand behind the short wall on the balcony, which is briefly protecting them from the heat. Polly shout's. "Right lads". He runs forward, puts his hand on the top of the balcony and leaps over, Dean and Merit follow without thought. They all fall through the air screaming with excitement. They hit the ground, roll and quickly stand up grinning. Polly looks up at the fire. "The flats aren't as high has the ones we jumped from in Manchester". A fireman walks over. "Well done lads, you should be proud of yourselves, where are you from?". Dean doesn't want the fireman to know. 'Were just working on the roads, were from down south". The lady and the children run up to the firm. 'Thanks lads you saved our lives", the little girl puts her arms around Polly while the little boy gives Merit and Dean a cuddle in turn.

It's time to go, the ambulance arrives, the fire engine is putting out the fire, and people gather round to watch, the firm slowly but quietly walk away. Polly leads them across the road and they come out just below the train station. Merit is relieved, "You were right Polly, it's a good job you took us that way". They walk onto the station platform covered in smoke and blood, they make their way to the toilets and have a wash and rinse out their shirts and jackets. They sit quietly on the platform bench, it's been an eventful day. Merit looks at the station clock". I can't believe it's 6 a m", the train arrives, times travelled fast.

They take the train to Sheffield, then back to Queens Road Peckham train station. The excitement as turned into tiredness, has they reflected back Polly decides to change the course of his life. "I'm tired of this fighting lads, it's time to call it a day while we are still in front, I want to do something useful ". The rest of the firm are relieved, they've thought the same since the fight at Sheffield after the Wednesday match. Merit shows his support for Polly. "Your right Polly, we need to do somethings different, let's sing our final song together".

Cracker starts to sing and all the passengers on the train join in.

“I'm Millwall until I die. I'm Millwall until I die. I know I am.

I’m sure I am. I'm Millwall until I die”.

They all stand up, cheer and shake hands.

The train arrives at Queens Road Peckham train station, as they stand on the platform they put their arms around each other, these fans are no longer known as the Millwall firm, but others will take their place. They walk off in different directions, not glancing back as they go. Gunner is walking past the station with Jane, and see’s Coop walking off the end of the platform. “Coop you bastard “. He takes his arm from around Jane's shoulder and start to run towards him. Coop starts to run down the road pursued by an angry Gunner, leaving his friends with a happy farewell smile.

Duke came out of the hospital the next day, and Wolf took him back to his flat on crutches. As they drove past St. John's church, Duke looks up at his home, and he is shocked to see the smoke damage to his neighbour's flat. “Fucking hell Wolf, what’s happened here?”. Wolf looks over, “I don't know Paul, we’ll soon find out”. Wolf drives around the flats and parks in the carpark, next to the concrete stairs that lead up to Duke’s flat. He helps Duke out of the car and gives him his crutches, Duke’s keen to find out if his friends are ok. Wolf helps Duke up the stairs and when they get onto the landing they see a neighbour.

June stood looking over the balcony, having a cup of tea with a fag in her mouth. Duke limps up to her. "June what's happened? ". June turns around, takes a drag of her fag and blows the smoke into Duke's face, he coughs. "Val did some baking and forgot to take some buns out of the oven, she had left the tea towel on top of the cooker. Next thing they knew, the kitchen was on fire, they had to be rescued from the balcony". Dukes worried. "Are they ok June? where are they now?". June takes another drag of her fag. "There at their Aunt Elsie's, flat 22, just up from yours ".
Duke knows Elsey and limps to the door and knocks. Elsey opens the door and is glad to see Paul (Duke), "Come in Paul". There's a shout from the lounge. "Who is it Aunty Elsy?". Elsey smiles. "It's Paul love". There's a cheer, Val, Ross and Kirsty go running into the kitchen, the kids grab hold of Paul's legs, while Val throws her arms around his shoulders and hugs him tight, they all start to cry with relief that their ok. Paul cannot feel the pain from his injuries, he's more concerned about Val and the kids, Elsey puts on the kettle. "Go and sit in the lounge Val before Paul falls down, looks like he's had a rough night". Val and the kids help Paul into the lounge and he sits down on the sofa, Kirsty and Ross sit on one side of him and Val on the other. "What's happened Val?". "All I know Paul, is that the flat had caught fire, we made our way onto the balcony and I was screaming for help. Suddenly four men came to the rescue, one stood on the ground and the others burst in and lowered us down with a washing line, before jumping to safety

themselves. Their hero's, they ran through the burning kitchen to save us, without them we may have died". Duke wondered who it could be, he knows a lot of people from Worksop. "Do you know them Val?". She starts to cry. "NO, but it looks as if they had been in a fight, they were covered in grazes and had blood on their shirts, one had half his ear missing and they had a cockney accent, they wandered off when the fire brigade came, one of their friends must have called them". "Duke looks up at the ceiling, and gives a big sigh, his enemies who had inured him the previous night, had now become his heroes, his hatred had become gratitude, these unknown lads are true soldiers, and have earned his respect. "Come on everyone you're going to live at mine". Another cheer goes up, the kids are happy as they help Paul back to his flat. Wolfs been listening as he follows. "I'm going now Paul". Paul puts his arm in the air. "Thanks mate ". As Wolf walks along the balcony and out of the flats, he agrees with Paul, the Millwall firm are true warriors.

Duke eventually finishes with his girlfriend and later develops a relationship with Val and the children, they move into a Coal Board house, get married and after a few year's have a child together. Duke as found what he has always been looking for, someone to love.
Polly went on to join the fire brigade, Cracker joined the police force, Merit became a paramedic, Dean trained as a social worker helping violent kids, Coop became a male

escort and Jean went to live with John in Sheffield, where he became a lady's fashion designer.

Souls Final Destiny

It's been a few weeks since the trouble at the youth club, and Jan is worried about the threat Soul as made against her. It's Thursday night, 7. pm, and Jan has difficulty in concentrating on her homework. Mary, Jan's mom is ironing and her dad, Patrick, is watching TV. Jan walks down stairs and sits on the sofa. "Mom, dad I need to talk to you". Mary stops ironing and her dad looks over at her, wondering what it could be, maybe she was pregnant. "Ok love, you know we love you and you can tell us anything".

Patrick walks over to Jan, sits on the sofa and holds her hand, Jan has a tremble in her voice.
"Mom, can you remember when Sam and his friends got attacked at the youth club". Mary has a worried look on her face. "Yes". "Well, I walked into the youth club that night because I was looking for my friend, Sue, there was a young lad there who grabbed hold of me. The hall doors were open, and I saw Sam and his friends, they had been beat up. He then pushed me into the caretaker's cloakroom and locked the door. He said I would be safer in there and he was right. I then heard someone shout, Who's there? The young man replied. It's a young girl Soul, looking for her friend, she's not seen anything. But he knew I had. Soul must have walked over and stood close to the door, he gave me a warning and said. If you say anything about tonight girl, I will find you. I have kept quiet until now, but I have been worried, what happens if he comes back?".

Mary and Patrick look at each other, they know something will have to be done. Mary reassures Jan. "It's ok Jan, he won't come after you, you're not worth the trouble". Jan smiled and felt reassured, she gave her mom and dad a big hug, and looked at the time. "It's 8.30 pm, I have some more homework to do for tomorrow, I'll go and do it now. Goodnight mom, good night dad ".

Mary and Patrick smile, but Mary's concerned. "We will have to find out who Soul is, and what he looks like". Patrick has an idea. "Sam will know". Mary decides to find him.
"I will take the dog for a walk, and see if I can find Sam, I can ask him about Soul". Patrick knows, that Mary always gets to the bottom of things. "Ok love". Mary shouts Max her pet Labrador and he runs into the room. "Want to go for a walk Max", Max looks up and wags his tail. Mary picks up the lead and her coat from the coat hooks on the back of the kitchen door, puts the lead on the dog and puts on her coat. As they walk out of the house, it is dark and raining, but feels warm.

As she walks along the street, Sam's friend comes walking past. "Hey Dan, have you seen Sam?". "Yes Mary, he's stood outside the off licence, having a drink with Pete and Russ". Sam had only been home briefly that evening to make a fire for some hot water, he fancied having a bath later that night, as the pit showers always left him feeling dirty. Mary walks down the road and comes to a row of small shops, Sam, Pete and Russ are stood outside of the beer off. As Mary grows closer, Sam sees her and shouts. "Mary are you alright?". Mary waves and Sam runs over to her. "Is everything ok Mary, is Jan ok?". "She's fine, but I need to talk to you, but first here's £3, fetch me four bottles of Guinness and a drink for yourself".

Sam takes the money and walks into the old off licence, it is small and narrow, all the doors and shelves are varnished brown, with one pump for draught bitter. There are bottles of different beer stacked on the shelves and at the top of the wall behind the counter, is a 30lb pike in a glass case, which was caught in the Sheffield canal basin by the present off licence holder, Albert, a small slim man in his late sixties, who liked to chat. Old Ed was sat at the end of the counter on a bar stool, drinking a pint of bitter and smoking his pipe. "Are you ok Sam?". "Yes, thanks Ed". Albert stands in front of Sam to serve him. "What do you want Sam?". "Half a bottle of Bells whiskey and four bottles of Guinness please Albert". Albert takes the drinks from the shelves. "£2.95, please Sam". "Thanks Albert, keep the change".

Sam gives Albert the money, picks up the bottles and walks out of the off licence, pleased with his free bottle of whiskey.

Albert presses the black key for £3 and it registers on the top of the till as £3 cash, he presses the red key and a bell rings, the cash compartment shoots open, hitting Albert hard in the stomach. “Fucking thing, it's never been right since the engineer put a new spring on the till draw”. Old Ed laughs, “You get caught out with that every time Albert”.

Mary is stood waiting in the rain and Max is sat down waiting to go for a walk. “Sam, we need to find somewhere quiet to talk, there's a bench on the street corner just down the road”. Sam's worried, he hopes that Jan is ok. They walk up to an old green wooden narrow bench, well used by old miners during the day, which is positioned on a small grass verge next to the path. Sam doesn't want to sit in the rain. “But Mary, it's raining, let's sit in the bus shelter”. “No Sam, no one will hear us talking on the bench”.

Sam shrugs his shoulders and they walk over to the bench and sit down, Max lays under the seat where it is dry. Sam lays the drinks safely on the ground and passes Mary a bottle of Guinness, then picks up his bottle of whiskey.

Sam wonders how Mary is going to open her drink. He sees her looking round at the bench and finds a small nail stuck out. She gently puts the lid on the nail and gives it a slight tap, the tops come off without disturbing the Guinness, she picks up the bottle, holds it to her mouth and pours the Guinness in, without it touching her lips, within a split-second half the bottle had gone, Sam’s well

impressed. “That’s some trick Mary”. Mary puts her drink on the bench next to her.
“Ah, that’s good, you can't beat a Guinness. Right Sam, there's something I need to know, can you remember when you had the trouble at the youth club?”. Sam looks forward. “I remember well Mary, look at the scar on my face”. Mary looks straight at Sam; his scar means nothing to her. “Well, tell me about the man that did it, his name, what he looked like”. Sam pauses, takes a deep breath, the incident still angers him.

“His name is Soul, he works as a debt collector and hit man for Johnny the gangster who beat me up, he is evil, we fight, but he enjoys torturing people, if he says he is going to do something, he does it”.

Mary starts to think that this man may come back for Jan to intimidate her, so she may not be a witness to any of his wrong doings. “What's Soul look like Sam, where does he drink?”. Sam looks down. “Mary, all that I really know is that he drinks in the Peacock near Sheffield city centre. Soul is a very dangerous man, why do you need to know?”. Mary looks seriously at Sam.
“Sam, promise me you will never talk about our discussion”. Sam stares at Mary and wonders why she doesn't want anyone to know. “I won’t Mary”. Mary’s relieved, this must be a secret. “Cheers Sam”. Mary and Sam have a drink, for the following five minutes sit quietly, thinking in the pouring rain. Mary, how she could

protect her daughter, and Sam, reflecting on what happened in the youth club that night.

It was time for Mary to go, she had the information she needed. “I'm going home now Sam, I will see you around, here, you can have these three bottles of Guinness”.
Mary stood up, she was drenched with the rain, her long ginger hair hung down, but she did not appear to feel the cold, she had more important things to be concerned about. “Come on Max let's go home”.
Sam watched Mary, as she slowly walked away, he's puzzled about what she may do.

He quickly drank his half bottle of whiskey, and was looking forward to the next three bottles of Guinness. He picked one up and put the tin lid on the nail that Mary had used earlier. Sam hit the top of the bottle and the lid stopped on. He tried again, hit the lid harder with the palm of his hand, the lid came flying off, making the Guinness bubble out of the bottle.
Ten minutes later, Sam had managed to open all three bottles and lined them neatly up on the bench, just to see how quickly he could drink them. The footpath was only three feet wide, and there was a deep pool of rainwater in the front of the bench, were the grate was blocked on the road.

An old blue transit van came speeding up the road, Sam looked as he heard the van's engine being thrashed. It

was his friend Pete, and he recognised Sam as he drove towards him. Pete beeped his horn, then slammed on his brakes, there was a loud screech and the sound of skidding. Pete stopped and quickly reversed, as he got level with Sam, he drove through the large pool of water which had gathered, sending a large wave into the air, hitting Sam and the bench, in a torrent of muddy water. Pete jumps out of the van, fag at the side of his mouth, he looks at Sam in a concerned way. "Are you alright Sam, you look wet through?". He then laughed, "What did Mary want?".
Sam looks up at Pete, there's muddy water running down his face, he's wet from head to foot, he has that lost puppy look. "I'm fine Pete, Mary just wanted to make sure me and Jan was ok, just a worried mother discussion, and now I'm just having a drink in the rain". Pete slowly shakes his head. "Why don't you do, what most people do and go and have a drink in the pub where it's warm. See you later Sam". Pete jumps back into his van and speeds off with sparks and smoke coming from his exhaust.

Sam watches him drive away, as he throws his fag end out of the window, he can't tell Pete what he has been talking to Mary about, and that's the real reason he has been sat in the rain. Sam sighs, but now he can enjoy a drink. He puts his left hand down to pick up a bottle of Guinness, but it wasn't there. He looked down and all three bottles had gone, he despaired, and looked at the back of the bench, there was three broken Guinness

bottles on the ground, the wave of water had knocked them off the bench.
Sam took a deep breath, he was pissed off, he stood up from the bench, the rain was pouring down, he was wet and covered in mud, he looked up in the air and shouted out, "BOLLOCKS".

Sam made his way home, he had a day's holiday the following day and once he'd had a warm bath, everything would be ok.
Sam walked into the house, he was glad to be home, his mom was sat reading a magazine on the lounge settee. "Is that you love? ". Sam's pleased to hear his mom's voice, "Yes mom". "Are you wet son?, it's raining heavy outside, I thought you might be cold, so I left you the water in the bath". At last something was going right for Sam, he could relax in a nice warm bath. He runs up the stairs into the bathroom, quickly takes off his clothes and jumps straight in. His dog Rover is laid on the towel on the floor, looking up at Sam with his tail wagging.

He suddenly feels the shock of cold water, more shocking when you think it's going to be warm. Sam jumps straight back out of the bath, shivering.
"Mom, the baths freezing", Linda is watching TV. "Is it love". Sam's stood naked and shaking from the cold. "What time did you have a bath mom?". "6-30 pm love, when I came in from work love". Sam looks into his bedroom at the old wind up double bell clock. "It's ten thirty now mom". "That's why its cold love, you should

have come in earlier". Sam grumbles to himself. "How should I know, when my mom his having a bath". Sam pulls the plug out of the bath and drains three quarters of the water out. He looks for the bubble bath and soap, but there's none there. He turns on the hot water tap, puts his hand under it and waits for the hot water to come through. The baths now half full and still there's no hot water, the bath water is now colder than before. Sam shouts to his mom. "Mom, there's no hot water ". Linda is looking down at her ladies' magazine. "I know love, thanks for making me a small fire when you came in from work, it heated the water up nicely. There was just enough hot water in the tank to have a nice warm bath, so I let the fire go out ". (In those days, hot water was stored in a copper cylinder and water was heated by a coal fire, it only stored enough hot water for one bath). Sam decides to have a wash in the cold water. "Mom, where's the bubble bath and soap?". "There isn't any love, I forgot to buy some from the shop".

The bath water is now discoloured, from the mud and dirty water from Sam's hair, he now decides to have a quick rinse. There is only one towel and Rover is still laid on it. He goes to the small airing cupboard at the top of the stairs, opens the door, it's just a bare cupboard and there are no clean towels ". Mom, there's no clean towels". "I know love, I had the last clean one". He goes back to the bathroom and looks down at Rover, there's only one towel left and his dog his laid on it. Sam bends down and picks up a corner of the towel, he tries to pull it

from under Rover, but his dog refuses to move and slides along the floor on the towel.
Sam, stands with his hands on his hips and looks at his dog, going comfortably to sleep. He is stood there, wet, cold and tired, he puts on his underpants and goes to bed. As he lays there, he hears people laughing as they walk past from the pub, he wonders why Mary as asked him so many questions, and then his thoughts go to Jan. He feels Rover jump up onto his bed and he laid his head on Sam's feet, he sits up and pats his dog, who then wags his tail, Sam then lays back down and smiles has he goes to sleep.

Mary as made her way home in the rain, not feeling angry, but determined, determined to make Soul pay for threatening her daughter Jan. She walks down the path, past her neat front garden and into the house. Patrick is sat in the small kitchen on a chair between the kitchen sink and the twin tub washing machine. He looks at Mary and sees that she is worried. “How did it go Mary”. Mary takes off her coat and hangs it on a coat hook on the back of the kitchen door, Max shakes himself down and lays under the table. “Sam’s told me as much as we need to know, let's go into the lounge and talk”.

Mary walks into the small lounge, Patrick follows, there's a new grey settee against the right-hand side wall, in the far corner is a black and white TV. On the left-hand side of the room, there's an open coal fire and an alcove in either side, one where there is a fold up table with two chairs and the other, an old brown varnished cabinet full of books.

Mary sits on the settee as Patrick closes the door behind him, before sitting next to her. They both sit and stare at the coal fire, before the conversation starts. “Well Mary, what as Sam said?”.

Mary looks deep into the fire as she speaks. “The man's name is Soul, he is a debt collector and hit man, he does some work for Johnny a bare-knuckle fighter from Sheffield, he's vile and he always keeps his word. If he has threatened Jan, he will be back”. Patrick’s concerned. “Ok, I will get in touch with the lads tomorrow, we need to act quickly”.

Patrick and Mary are members of the Sheffield folk music group and have many close friends in the area. Mary needs to be organised. “Patrick, we need a plan”. They sit and have a discussion for about an hour and then decide what they will have to do.

The next day Patrick picks up the phone and phones one of his friends. “Is that Collin, it's Patrick”. “Yes mate” in a slurred voice, “What do you want, are you ok?”. Patrick doesn't answer Collins question. “Collin, this Saturday at 8 pm, we have a gig at the Peacock near Sheffield train station, it's Irish songs”. This is Morse saying we have trouble with the English, and we need to act fast. “Ok

Patrick ". Patrick puts the phone down and leaves Collin to phone the rest of the band.
He goes and sits down next to Mary and puts his arm around her, Mary looks deep into the fire, turns to Patrick and they hold each other tight, Mary remembers why they came to England to live. "I hope the trouble doesn't start again", Patrick talks quietly and is confident. "We've been here before, the same plan, you know it". Jan had heard the lounge door close and she wondered what her parents were talking about. She had crept downstairs and had put her ear to the door. She has heard her mom say, Soul, and her dad, I'll phone the lads. Jan heard the phone being put back down, and she had run back upstairs and got into bed, and is now worrying about what could happen, and what her parents plan to do, but there's a lot Jan doesn't know.
The next day (Friday) Mary phones one of her friends, "Hullo is that Shannon? ". "Yes, is that Mary",

"Be at mine for 6 pm tomorrow night, (Saturday) please phone Vicki", Mary puts the phone down.

It's 5 pm Saturday and Mary is in her bedroom, preparing to go out that evening with her friends. She spends time putting on her makeup, tight skirt and high heeled shoes. She puts on a very special Paris perfume, Empreinte Rose by Robert Gonnon from Paris (1970), which she was given from one of her late friends. As she looked into the mirror she looks quite stunning, with her white blouse and short black skirt, she gives an appearance of being vulnerable, an attraction to the men she will meet later that evening.

Patrick walks into the bedroom, “How’s things Mary?”. Mary turns around, stands up and looks at Patrick. “How do I look Patrick?”. Patrick smiles as he looks her up and down, he knows what she is capable of, and kisses her on the cheek.
Mary as two wardrobes, one white and new, the second for her special clothes. She walks over to the second, set in the far corner of the bedroom, an old, light wood varnished wardrobe, with a plain door on the right and the left door holds a full-length mirror. She puts her arm around the back and picks up a small brass key hanging from a hook, puts it into the well-worn brass lock and opens it. She first takes out a green blazer from a wooden coat hanger, and slowly puts it on with pride, before pulling it tight from the bottom. Then, she slides her hand under her shirts on the left hand top shelf, and pulls out a small slim black wooden box. She walks over to her oak stained dressing table, places it respectfully down and sits in the front of it. Mary, lovingly strokes the top, lifts the two silver clips on the side, then gently opens the lid. Inside, there are three, old, small items which all have an history. She lifts them out one at a time, admiring them as she does so, laying them out side by side before slowly putting them on.

First, a silver ring, grazed and scratched with wear, this is from the Pirate Queen (1530 – 1603) Grace O’Malley of the famed O’Malley clan of Mayo. Her father was a chieftain and sea trader and she learned how to handle herself on his ships. Striking out on her own she became known as the Pirate Queen, capturing English ships and taking their cargo, she slides this onto the third finger of her right hand.

Second, an old Irish brooch badge, sea gems, Celtic green with aqua gold around the side owned by Betsy Gray (died 1798), who was an Ulster-Scots Presbyterian peasant girl, from outside Lisburn in Co. Antrim, in what is today Northern Ireland, who was killed as part of the 1798 Rebellion of the United Irishmen. She is the subject of many folk ballads and poems, written since her time down to the present day.
She fought in the Battle of Ballynahinch, against the Yeomanry and was killed in retreat along with her brother and lover. She had her right hand cut off before she was decapitated.
Mary places this brooch on the right-hand side, of her green jacket lapel.

Third, a green Celtic knot hair pin, used by, Constance Gore Booth who was an unlikely 1916 revolutionary. She was from wealthy Anglo-Irish stock and grew up on a rich estate in Sligo. She married a Polish count.
However, she soon identified with Irish nationalism and became a major player in the Irish Citizen Army, founded by James Connolly, and dedicated her life to the poor.

She fought at St Stephen's Green in 1916 and was sentenced to death, which was later commuted. She was the Minister for Labour in the first Irish government, only the second woman in Europe to get a government ministerial role. She fought on the Republican side in the Irish Civil War. She died in 1927 at 59 from complications from appendicitis. Mary, slowly slides the hairpin into the right-hand side, of her long, ginger wavy hair, just above her ear.

She gets a cold shiver, maybe her ancestors are with her. Mary walks back over to her wardrobe, on a small hook in the middle, is an orange berry, which is only worn on special occasions. Mary slowly picks it up, stands in front of the mirror and puts it on, she tilts it to the left-hand side of her head.

She stands up straight and proud as she looks at herself, Patrick's been stood watching, he's proud of his wife Mary.

There's a peep of a car horn, Mary looks through the bedroom window and can see Shannon and Vicki sat in a small, yellow mini cooper, waving through the open windows and smiling, they appear to be looking forward to the night out.

She closes the net curtains, picks up Patrick's hand and reassures him. "Patrick, everything will be ok, I'll see you when I get home". Patrick gives her a kiss." Here you are Mary, half a bottle of John Locke whiskey to share with your friends later in the evening ". Patrick is to stay at home, if there's any trouble, he can say Mary has been with him all evening. Mary picks up her bottle of whiskey, walks proudly down the stairs and out of the house to her waiting friends.

Shannon and Vicki are now stood next to the car, both dressed the same as Mary, as she reaches them they all put their arms around each other, and give each other a kiss on the cheek, before getting back into the car. Sam's stood further up the road with his friends, they are just on their way to the welfare, he sees Mary going out and becomes suspicious. "Sam what are you looking at". "Nothing Pete, let's go to the welfare".

Shannan pulls back her seat, Mary climbs into the back and puts her drink in the side pocket of the car., Shannan sits down and closes the car door, Vicky starts to drive off. "Well Mary, where are we going?".
Mary looks out of the side window as they drive through the Manor Estate. "To the Peacock, close to Sheffield train station". Shannan looks round at Mary. "All you need to know, is that we are with you". Mary knew this, but was pleased to hear it from her friends once again. "Thanks girls, would you put some music on please".
Shannan takes a cassette tape out of the glove compartment, puts it into the stereo and presses a button, *Rocky Road to Dublin* starts to play and the girls begin to sing all the way to Sheffield.

They pull into the Peacock car park, their spirits are high, as they look around they see transit vans and pickups. There is a dark blue, open top, 1972 Mercedes Benz 450 SL, parked near the front of the pub, Vicky decides to park next to it. Shannan turns off the music, they listen and wait, but do not look round, they don't want to give people the feeling they are being watched, but one of waiting for someone.
A couple of young men walk past, bang on the car roof and shout. “Are you ok girls?” and carry on walking towards the pub.

A large black transit van pulls up at the side of their mini, the passenger side doors open. A medium build, young Irish man, knocks on Shannon's window, she winds it down, the girls recognise them and are happy to see them.
Its Charlie and the Bhoys, a well-respected Irish band, four other band members gather round, Jimmy, Rob, Tam and Wardie. They open the mini doors and the girls all get out, they all look at each other, laugh, and have a big hug. Charlie has a surprise for them. “Wait girls, I've got someone you might like to see”.
Charlie walks round the back of the van, the girls wait to see who they have brought along. Out steps, two very large, broad shouldered Irish men. Mary recognises them straight away, it's two of Patrick’s old friends, Kevin Barry and James Connolly. They tower above all their friends,

one thing they have today, stronger than anything else, is tried and tested companionship and trust.

They can hear a band playing in the pub, it's time to make a start, Mary looks round at her friends, she's feeling good. "Ok lads, and of course girls, just wait here while I check out the pub".
Mary walks in through a new blue double door, to the right is the men's and lady's toilets, and a passageway that leads to a fire exit, on the left is a small bench, often used when people are waiting for a taxi, which looks over towards a juke box. This leads to another set of wedged open double doors and down to a long, oblong concert hall. There's a small stage on the right, and a bar on the left, the tables are set in four rows. At the bottom of the hall there are two tables placed together with three chairs, two at the back and one at the front.

The pub is busy with people of all ages, laughing and drinking, the odd person sees Mary and whistles and laughs with their mates. Mary smiles at them, then they carry on talking, she scans the room as she slowly walks out. When she gets to the toilets she walks down the passage and is met with a double fire door, she pushes the handle and the doors open. As she walks through it leads onto the bottom of a dark alley, lit up with a small orange blinking street light. There's broken bottles and blood on the floor, nettles and weeds are growing round the edges of the wall.

Mary walks back through the fire exit doors and closes them behind her, she makes her way out of the pub and is passed by regulars on their night out. Some stare, as though to wonder who Mary is, but the way she is dressed, makes her look far more attractive than threatening.

Mary walks over to her friends. “Ok Charlie, time for you to set up”. “Ok Mary, right lads, let's go on play some good music”. As Charlie walks off to the pub, the girls put on their makeup and have a fag, they laugh about what they used to do together when they were young. Jimmy, Rob, Tam, and Wardie pick up their instruments from the van and follow Charlie, Kevin and Barry slowly walk behind, they've no rush.
As the Bhoys band walk through the entrance and into the main hall, everyone looks, the Savoy’s, who are on the stage stop playing. The Bhoys band stand in front of the Savoy’s, Charlie walks up onto the stage and speaks to the lead singer Collin. The audience all stand up, they're expecting trouble. Kevin and James sit at a table next to the wedged open double doors, which is the entrance to the hall.

“Look mate, it's time for you to go, we will be playing for the rest of the evening”. Collins frightened, he only wants to sing. Charlie, takes out a large roll of five-pound notes and puts them in Collins top shirt pocket. “Go and buy yourselves a meal and come back in a couple of hours, just leave the drums".

The band have seen and heard what Charlie as said, they pick up their guitars and walk off the stage and out of the pub. The Bhoys walk up onto the stage, Charlie picks up the microphone. "Ok everyone, it's just a mix up, we were due to play tonight, the Savoy's will be back later.

The audience sits back down, their suspicious as their not sure what is happening. The Bhoys set up their instruments and they're ready to play, Charlie picks up the microphone. "Ok everyone, I'm sorry again for the mix up, please sit back and enjoy the next few songs, the Bhoys start to play an *Irish Pub Song* by the Rum jacks. There's a man stood looking into the jukebox, he has a double brandy on the top, with both his arms stretched out leaning, as he reads the songs that he could play. The Bhoys begin to sing, there's a fantastic rhythm to the music, the audience begin to clap and feel at ease. People start to comment, how the Bhoys are a better group than the Savoy's and they start to join in with the songs.

The girls are stood next to their mini having a laugh, and they hear the band beginning to play, that's the sign for them to begin their scene, Mary throws her fag to the ground. "Vicky, Shannon, it's time for us to dance".

Mary leads the way, Vicki and Shannon follow, the band plays, *I'm Shipping up to Boston* by Dropkick Murphy. As

they walk across the car park, men whistle and stare as they pass, they all look stunning as they are dressed the same, in their green, white and orange colours.
They slowly walk up the steps and in through the double doors, looking straight in front of them as they go. They turn to the left and just before they walk into the main hall, there's a very tall, elderly man, known as Captain, wearing a blue jacket with a navy emblem who is selling entry tickets to the pub.
"Hey girls you need to buy a ticket before you can go in".
Mary looks straight forward, she only has two words for him. "FUCK OFF". Captain can't believe what Mary as said. "Hey, you can't talk to me like that".
As Vicky walks by, she looks at Captain's emblem and recognises that he must have been in the navy, she smiles. "Hey sailor, how many free blow jobs have you done?".

A young couple who are waiting for their friends start to laugh, Captain's face goes red, he becomes angry and shouts. "I was young and vulnerable, we were at sea for months".
Some of captain's friends are stood nearby and hear what he has said, they give him an undesirable look. When he has told them of his heroic stories, he's not included that.
Cookie, a very small, middle aged fat man is stood next to Captain and asks him a question. "Are they still free Captain?", with a smile on his face. Captain, throws the tickets and money into the air, turns around and slaps

Cookie on the head before walking down to the bar to get a drink. Cookie puts his hands on his head frowning. "Oooh, what's happened to the drunken sailor?".

The girls walk past Kevin and Barry and stop. The band plays *Star of the County Down* by the Orthodox Celts. Vicky looks to her left, Shannon to the right, Mary is walking in front. There's a middle aisle that leads up to two men, who are now sat at the bottom of the hall behind a table. Mary presumes they may be the leaders of the gang. She started to walk forward, followed closely by her friends, the band plays, people look and become suspicious, these three women are now standing out from the crowd.

Mary comes level with the end of the row of tables at the bottom of the hall, she stops and now stands in the front of the two gangsters.

Trigger Mike is sat on Mary's left and Digger sat on the right, they have been watching her walk towards them, the crowd start to take an interest, they look and nudge their friends. Johnny is away on business and as left Digger and Trigger Mike in charge. Digger always does the talking and Trigger Mike listens and weighs them up. He shouts out loud, so everyone can hear.

"Look lads, I wonder what these girls want?". Digger laughs out loud, he's trying to intimidate Mary and her friends. "They've come looking for a man". Trigger Mike smiles at Digger. "It's no good looking at you then

Digger". People around smile, Digger and Trigger Mike giggle, they are having fun. Mary's relaxed, she first looks slowly at Digger, then Trigger Mike, their arrogance is showing their weakness.

They stop giggling, it's time to find out what Mary wants, Digger points to the seat in the middle of their table directly in the front of them. Mary pulls the chair back and sits down, Shannan and Vicky step forward and stand like two disciplined soldiers a yard behind Mary, their eyes slowly looking around without moving their heads, they can hear and see everything that is going on. Digger looks into Mary's eyes, she looks so innocent, more becoming of a saint which makes Digger feel comfortable. "What's your name girl?". Mary's not going to give anything away, she's straight to the point. "I can't tell you, where's Johnny?". Digger's not impressed, she carries a hardness about her, Trigger Mike puts one hand on the table, he's doesn't like what he's heard, everyone always answers their questions, but, it doesn't seem it's going to be that way tonight, Diggers losing his patience. "He's away on business, what do you fucking want?". Mary is polite, "I'm looking for someone ".
Trigger Mike suddenly asks a question, he supposed to keep quiet, but can't help it today, Mary worries him. "Are you the police?". Mary looks at Trigger Mike, she slowly shakes her head with a grin on her face. It's time for a reality check. "Yes, I'm Sergeant Dixon of Dock Green, do we look like the fucking police you dim fuck?". Trigger

has half a smile, he's a bit embarrassed. “Well, you do in a way”.

Digger looks at Mary and they start to laugh, her straight talking and confidence are attractive to him, it's something he’s never come across before. Mary leans over and picks up the newly poured double whisky in the front of Digger, she puts the glass to her mouth and slowly drinks it all in one, she takes the glass away, licks her lips and puts the glass down in the front of him. Diggers impressed, drinking whiskey that slow without coughing is some feat. Trigger laughs out loud, no one's ever dared to do that to Digger before, some of the gangsters start to gather round Mary and her friends. Vicki and Shannon are not worried and calmly carry on looking forward.

It's time for Mary to find the man she has come for. “I’m looking for a man called Soul, I have a business proposition for him, I've heard he is professional and reliable “. Digger looks at Trigger Mike and wonders whether he should give Mary the information she has asked for. He looks into Mary's eyes, she looks at him, she looks so beautiful, his heart rules his judgement. “Ok, I'll tell you”. Digger points to a man at the far end of the pub stood next to a jukebox, Mary looks, she can just see him through the crowd. “What, him with the scar and black polo necked jumper?”. Trigger Mike doesn't trust

Mary and puts his hand on Diggers shoulder. “Don't tell her anything Digger”.
Digger, puts both of his hands flat on the top of the table, Mary puts her hands on the top of his, he can't resist her charm. “Yes, that's him, with the scar”. Mary leans over the table and gives Digger a kiss on the cheek, she smells gorgeous, he will never forget that perfume, he's never known any woman smell that nice. She finishes the discussion, it's time for business. “Thankyou”.

Mary stands up and walks away, followed by her friends, they walk along the hall and back through the wedged open doors, she walks over and stands next to Soul who is looking at the songs on the juke box. He is aware that Mary is stood there. *(The band plays the Irish Rebel Song- Come out and Fight).* Mary speaks in a quiet, soft spoken voice. “Excuse me”. Soul turns around and looks Mary up and down, he then looks back at the list of songs on the jukebox, it’s a long time since a woman spoke politely to him, but he’s been aware of Mary and her friends since they first walked in. Soul starts to scowl. “I’ve been watching you, I don’t trust you. Ok, what do you want?”.
Mary looks straight at Soul, “I'm looking for a man called Soul, he’s been recommended, the gentleman at the bottom of the hall said you’re the man”. Soul looks at Mary, he would usually ask who had recommended him, but she flutters her eyes and stands sexually flirting her body. “It’s important that no one hears “. Soul is attracted

to Mary, he thinks she as something special to offer in return for his business, he doesn't usually mix business with pleasure, but it's not going to be that way tonight. “So where would you like to talk?”. “Outside the back of the pub please Soul”. Soul stares at Mary with his angry eyes, “Ok, I'll lead the way”.

Soul drinks his brandy and puts his empty glass back on the top of the juke box. “Come on then”. Mary follows, and her friends are walking closely by, Soul sees them and stops.
“Wait! no friends, they can stand outside of the pub”. He doesn't want anyone to watch if Mary returns a special favour. Three of Souls friends are stood close by, they have been watching what was going on. Soul shouts them over. “Billy, you and the lads stand outside with these two girls, make sure they don't cause any trouble”. Souls taking control and being cautious, Billy is looking forward to the company.
“Ok, we will look after them”, he as an evil eye on the girls. Mary looks at Shannon and Vicki, she nods, they stand expressionless, prepared for anything that could happen next. They walk out of the pub with Billy, and stand next to the steps to the right of the pub entrance doors.

The band as seen Mary and her friends walk out and they start to play, the audience start to feel nervous, there could be trouble. Soul walks out of the entrance, down the steps and turns left behind the back of the pub, he looks behind and sees Mary two steps back, she is now smiling, they walk to the bottom of the dead-end alley. Mary, walks straight past Soul and stands with her back against the high, old, red brick wall, her back is now covered, and she can see anything that happens.

The orange street light flickers, as she stands on the nettles and broken bottles, her ginger hair and orange berry stand out in the light. Some would say, this is dangerous, there's nowhere to run, but Mary would say, she never runs anywhere. Soul towers over Mary, he looks far meaner and bigger than he did in the pub, he looks down at her with his mean face. “Well, what do you want? weather we do, or don't do business, you're going to look after me tonight”.

Mary looks up at Soul, she’s now expressionless.

Pleasantries are now over, it's just Soul and Mary, she puts on her true Irish voice. “Can you remember, when you came over to the Manor Estate a few months ago?”. Soul looked and wondered, what this skinny, weak looking woman really wanted, he started to laugh. “What, those tosses’ from the Manor, I had a good time taking care of business with them, how's Silver by the way?”. Mary is now serious. “I’ve not come to talk about Silver “. (*Rocky Road to Dublin)* echo’s down the alley. Mary lifts up her orange berry, brushes her long ginger hair back with her right hand, secretly pulls out her hairpin, and replaces her berry neatly to the left-hand side of her head, she’s now ready for battle.

“Can you remember the young girl in the caretaker’s closet?”. Soul starts to get angry, he thinks Mary is taking the piss, he points at her. “Ya, that young bitch, if ide the time, I would have fucked her and then slashed her face. I told her, that if she said anything to anyone, I would come back for her “.

Soul starts to look nasty, he feels like he has been set up and he will punish Mary for this. Mary takes a small step forward with her left leg, her arms slightly bent by her waist. “THAT WAS MY DAUGHTER”. Soul shouts out loud, “Bastard”, his gang members hear him, they start to walk towards the alley. Shannon and Vicki run around them and stand side by side in front of the entrance, the gang stop and look, they can see Soul and Mary talking, for now they will observe, Billy warns the girls.
“I’ll tell you now, you fuckers are going to get leathered and fucked before the night is out “.
It's not the first time the girls have been threatened, besides there are only three men.

Soul suddenly steps forward and grabs Mary around the throat with both hands, squeezing tightly, he then brings his right knee upwards towards Mary’s stomach. Mary throws a block with her left elbow, hitting Soul just above his right knee, his leg goes limp, his knee joint is knocked out of place. From this position, she drives up both arms in the shape of a triangle, which forces Souls

hands from her throat. Soul steps back in pain, he can hardly put any weight on his right leg.
Mary puts her hands back down, stands feet apart, waiting, her breathing is calm, she's relaxed.
Billy sees what his happening, he fears, that this is no ordinary girl, she could be another gangster, he gives an order to his friends. "Come on lads, let's help Soul", as they start to walk forward, Vicki and Shannon are stood directly in the front of them, they stare at each other with determination, the girls have a cause and no one that night, will beat them.
Soul throws a left jab, hitting Mary on the nose, her head goes back, and it starts to bleed, he throws a right hook hitting her on the left-hand side of her head, knocking her head round, she quickly recovers. Soul has an evil smile. Overcoming the pain, he kicks out with his injured right leg. Mary strikes down with the outside of her left arm, pushing Souls leg away. He is off balance, is guard is weak, until his foot touches the ground. Mary steps forward and hits Soul under his jaw with the palm of her right hand. Soul stumbles back, a shooting pain goes straight through his head.

He stops, his vision his blurred, Mary steps forward with a left side kick to just above Souls right knee, it breaks, he screams in pain and falls to the ground, Billy shouts, "Quick let's help Soul".

Shannan steps straight forward, puts her hands-on Billy's shoulders and headbutts him on the nose, breaking it immediately, he falls to the ground in a crumpled heap, she stands still looking at Vicky out of the corner of her eye, ready to give assistance if needed. Crazy Joe throws a right jab at Vicky, hitting her above the left eye, leaving a small gash. She twists to her left side, drops to the ground on her left hand, and spins backwards along the floor, kicking Crazy Joe's legs from underneath him. He falls heavily, Vicky rolls straight over and as the back of her heels come down, she hits Joe in the solar plex, leaving him struggling to breathe. Baron steps forward and with his left leg, he throws a roundhouse kick, slightly catching Vicky on the left-hand side of her face causing a long graze. As she sits on the ground, Baron puts his left foot down, she twists to her right puts her right hand out, grabs hold of Baron's right foot and pulls, he drops into the splits tearing the muscles in his groin. He's now sat up next to Vicky. She rolls round the back of Baron, kneels up, and strikes with the side of her right hand, hitting him at the back of his head, he slides to one side motionless. From a kneeling position, she jumps up onto her feet, and stands in a fighting stance.

Crazy Joe stands up taking deep breaths, he looks at Shannan, he starts to throw a left and right hook and then a roundhouse kick at Shanan's head, she ducks and blocks with the outside of her arms. He hits her with a straight kick to the chest, sending her flying to the ground. Shannon is temporarily stunned, Crazy Joe quickly steps in, brings up his right foot, and brings it down hard towards Shannan's face. Shannan instinctively throws both arms up, and as her wrists cross she deflects Joe's blow. As he put his right foot down next to her head, she half rolls over and jumps up and quickly steps back. She steps forward, throws a double left jab to Crazy Joes nose, followed by a right, left, right to his ribs, he bends over, and she throws a right uppercut, knocking Crazy Joe backwards onto the ground leaving him semi-conscious

Mary is stood looking down at Soul, who is now on his knees, he knows it's his time and it's all over. He looks deep into Mary's eyes. “Who are you?”. “Look at my colours Soul, you know”. He remembers the orange white and green, he should have known. Mary puts her left thumb under Souls nose, tilts back his head, it's her turn to do the staring, she looks into his eyes, he is at peace and there is no anger, he doesn't struggle. She pulls back her right fist with the old hairpin protruding, she strikes Soul in his Adam’s apple, the old hairpin is driven deep into his throat, killing him immediately, and he dies knelt up.

Mary straightens her clothes and walks towards her friends who are waiting for her, she stops at the end of the alley, looks back, there's two grey silhouettes of a man and woman, Soul is now laid on the floor behind them. The gangsters watch as the girls walk past them, they can't believe what's happened.

The fight is over very quickly, but captain has heard a noise outside and goes to see what his happening, he sees the fights, he rushes back into the pub and runs straight up to Mike and Digger. "Hey Mike, some of our lads are fighting outside, there's something going off". Digger stands up and shouts, he knew something was wrong with the girls. "Everybody outside we've got trouble".

Kevin and James are ready, they go and stand either side of the entrance doors, James opens his jacket, he pulls out two Smith and Wesson 44 magnum handguns and holds them up in the air. At the same time, Kevin has six M26 fragmentation grenades strapped onto a belt on his chest, he takes one out and pulls out the pin.

The gangsters stop where they are, Trigger and Digger sit back down, one grenade would injure everyone in the pub. The band plays, there enjoying the action, it's time for Kevin to take charge. "Right you fucking English wankers, one move out of you lot and you're all going to fucking die".

Everyone sits down and stays quiet, they wonder who these men could possibly be, no one has ever fucked about on Johnny's turf before, he will go mad when he finds out.

Mary walks back into the pub, followed by Shannan and Vicky, they walk straight to the end of the hall, up to Digger and Trigger Mike, who are now sat down waiting for something to happen. Mary kicks over the table onto

the two brothers, leaving them covered in whiskey, she has a word of wisdom for them. "When you see Johnny, tell him the girls from the IRA have been".
Mary turns around and walks out, followed by her friends, the band pack up their instruments and walk off the stage, still covered by Kevin and James. Kevin gives out a final warning before leaving. "The next time we call, won't be as much fun". They put away their weapons and make their way to the car park. As James passes the dark blue open top 1972 Mercedes Benz 450 SL, he stops and smiles, he goes over to the petrol cap, twists it off, takes off his blue waxed tie for special occasions and puts one end in the top of the petrol tank, and the other end hangs down, he shouts his friend Kevin.
"Hey Kevin, have you got a light, I don't smoke", Kevin's stood looking at the front of the car and walks over.
"Here, it's about time you did ", he passes James a box of matches. James takes out a match, strikes it on the side of the box and lights the end of the tie. It burns very slowly as they go and join their friends back at their van.

The girls make their way back to their mini, a small black van pulls into the car park. Charlie puts up his hand and points to the alley way, the van goes over and reverse's back, the injured gangsters are now sat at the bottom of the pub steps watching what is happening, but wise enough not to get involved.
Mary and her friends climb into the mini, as they sit there Shannan picks up half a bottle of whiskey, she had left in

the side pocket of the car door, she hands it round, they sit quietly before Vicky breaks the silence.
“What do you think to the new Boots range in lipsticks”, they all start to compare notes as they drive off. The band, Kevin and James get into their van and go quietly on their way, briefly followed by the black van, before it turns off in a different direction. They hear a loud explosion, as they look back they see a large flash coming from the direction of the Peacock car park. Nobody asks any questions, what they don't know they can’t lie about.

Digger and Trigger run outside of the pub, they find three of their friends injured and Johnny's car in flames, Digger walks up to Crazy Joe who is still sat on the steps. “What’s happened to you lot?”. “Digger, you don't want to know, what's happened to Soul, he’s down the alley”. Digger runs to the bottom of the alley, he can't see Soul anywhere, he sees a glitter on the ground and he walks over and finds a gold ring, he picks it up, he can't see it clearly with the street light, he takes out his petrol lighter, gives it a flick and it ignites. He puts the flame near the ring and he can see some writing. He looks closely, scribed on, it says: *With love to Soul*. It must have been from Souls old girlfriend he killed for cheating on him, his one and only love. Digger knows Soul as gone, he's no loss, they will find another hit man, and wonders how much he can get for the gold ring.

Digger walks back into the pub, some of the gang have took the injured to hospital, captains phoned for the fire engine as Johnny's prize car in now a mass of flames, he sees Trigger Mike stood at the bar. “Hey Mike, we’ve fucked up this time, Johnny’s left us in charge and we’ve let another gang destroy his patch, he’s going to go mad when he gets back”. They both take a deep breath and decide to get pissed, it's seems it’s the only thing they can get right tonight.

As the girls drive home they discuss what dress they would like to buy, shoes they like to wear and what's happening at work, the night is behind them, just as though it has never happened.
They arrive at Mary's house, Vicky gets out and lets Mary out of the back seat, it's dark and starts to rain, she waves goodbye to her friends as they drive off, she walks down the garden path and into the house.
Patrick is waiting for her, he walks straight over to greet her, he gives her a kiss on her lips and holds her tight, she's safe.
“Ok Mary, this is what we will have to do, now we need to go back to Ireland and keep low for a few months, we'll get a phone call when we can come back, we will tell Jan her gran is ill, and we have to care for her. When we get there, we will tell her the truth., It’s time for her to know our history”, Mary agrees, they can both relax now Jan is safe.

Jan's Farewell

It's 7am, Patricks not going to work today, they have more important issues to resolve. Soul is no longer a threat to Jan, but Mary must keep a low profile for a short while, just in case Soul is reported missing, and the police start to ask questions. Mary and Patrick have a discussion of what their next move is to be.

"Right Mary, as we agreed, we need to move to Northern Ireland for a while, until we are sure everything is quiet here". Mary gives a big sigh and nods in agreement. "We'll go and live with my gran in the countryside. I'll tell Jan she is ill, and we are going to look after her for a short while, just to give the rest of the family a break. I'll have a word with my gran and sister Kate, they know the score, we'll have to tell Jan right away. I'll pack some clothes and we'll leave this afternoon". Patrick agrees, but knows Jan is going to be devastated.

Mary shouts upstairs. "Jan!", Jan has a feeling something is wrong, as she hears her mom call, she gets up out of bed, picks up her pink dressing gown and slowly walks down stairs, she feels nervous. Jan walks into the lounge, her mom and dad are sat on the settee, both look sad, Mary breaks the news. "Jan, please sit down, I've something important to tell you". Jan knows this is bad news, but what could it be, she looks seriously at her mom.

"Jan your gran is ill, your aunty Kate as asked us if we can help out for a while, until her daughter has had her baby, I have said we would, it's only for about three months". Jan panicked. "What about Sam, mom my friends, what will they all do?". Jan started to cry, her mom and dad sat on the arm of her chair next to her, Mary felt sorry for Jan, she knows how much she loves Sam. "Jan, go and have a word with Sam now, he loves you, he will wait". Little does she know that temptation will test their love. "When are we going to Ireland mom?". "As soon as we have packed some clothes, we are catching a train from Sheffield train station to Manchester, and then a plane to Northern Ireland'.

Jan rushes out of the house in her slippers and dressing gown, and runs up the street to Sam's. She runs down the garden path, dodges the dog shit and jumps over a mop and an old silver bucket, she doesn't stop, and bursts through the back door. Sam's making a cup of tea on top of the twin tub washing machine, he's wearing a tea stained white t- shirt, and black shorts, he's surprised to see her.
"Ae up Jan, I didn't know you were this keen to see me". He smiles at Jan, is happiness is to be short lived, Jan starts to shout hysterically. "My mom says we are going to live in Ireland ". Sam couldn't believe what he had just heard, he's shocked. "What do you mean? ". Jan's crying. "I've told you, we are going to live in Ireland, my grans ill, it's for about three months, then were coming back to the Manor". Sam puts his arms around Jan, she holds his waist, and they both cry. Jan pushes Sam away, she

doesn't understand her emotions, she's both angry and sad. "I've got to go now Sam". He grabs hold of Jan's hand, "Then I'll see you off."

He walked her home, Jan dressed in her dressing gown and slippers, Sam in his stained t- shirt, shorts and bare feet. As they arrived at Jan's house, the taxi was waiting outside. Mary and Patrick were just putting their cases in the boot, Mary had arranged for Jill her Irish neighbour to look after the house, and their dog. Mary wanted to quickly leave. "Come on Jan, get straight into the taxi, you can get changed on the way". Caitlin, an Irish friend was driving the taxi, no one will know where they have been dropped off. Jan needs to say goodbye to Sam. "Mom, please get into the taxi, I need to have one more minute with Sam". They will wait, this goodbye is important for both Sam and Jan. They both put their arms around each other for the last time.

"I'll be back in three months, please wait for me Sam"'. He holds her tight, "I will always wait for you Jan".
Patrick feels that they should leave, he shouts to Jan out of the front passenger window.
"Jan, we will have to go". They let go of each other, Jan kisses Sam on the cheek and quickly walks to the taxi, she stops, looks back and waves, she knows they will meet again, but for good next time. As she gets into the car Jan turns around and blows Sam a kiss, she closes the door and the taxi speeds off.

Sam feels empty, he doesn't know when they will next meet, but makes a vow to himself. "I will always love you Jan and will be faithful until your return".
Sam slowly walks home in his shorts, stained t- shirt and bare feet, not knowing of what to make of his young emotions, but he feels that things will quickly change as he waits for Jan's return. A thought, that turns out to be true, but not the way he imagined.

Sam arrives back at his home, he is just about to open his gate as he feels something sticky, warm and muddy ease between the toes on his right foot. He stops, looks down, picks up his foot. "Fucking hell it's dog shit". He looks behind him and sees Roy walking his dog, laughing as he goes, he knows it's his dog that has shit on the footpath, he looks at Sam and smiles. "Hey Sam, it's supposed to be lucky to stand in dog shit, but you usually have your shoes on, you want to bottle that fucker Sam, IT'S PURE PEDIGREE ". Roy walks off laughing as his dog wags his tail.
Sam stands with one hand on the gate, as he holds his right foot in the air shaking his head, there was only one thing to do, and that was to wipe his foot on the long grass in the front garden. He starts to rub his foot until it is clean.

Linda, Sam's mom has been watching him and opens the front downstairs window. She's wearing her hair curlers and has a fag in the left-hand side of her mouth. "Sam do you want a cup of tea love, it's already made". It's just what Sam needed, Linda passes him the white stained mug without a handle and a slice of toast, he takes the mug in his right hand and holds the toast in the left. He stands in the garden and takes a sip of his beautiful sweet tea, and a bite of his burnt toast, it tastes gorgeous. He starts to think of Jan and decides to pace himself, until she returns. He's halfway through his tea and toast and life is feeling a little rosier. Sam watches two young kids playing football in the street, with a big old brown leather case ball, that's wet with the rain from the night before. Linda knocks on the window, Sam looks around. She points to the road, Sam feels a heavy wet thud on the back of his head, his nice sweet tea and burnt toast fly through the air, as he is knocked face down to the ground. He pushes himself up and hears someone shout.

"Can I have my ball back please mate?". Sam looks to his right and next to him is a brown leather case ball, he smiles, stands up, picks up the ball and kicks it back to the kids in the street.

Dan and Russ come walking past, "Hey Sam, what are you doing this weekend?". Sam stands holding the back of his head. "I'm going over to Jake's". Russ and Dan are a bit disappointed. "Why don't you come out with us, we'll have a laugh".

Sam would love to, "Sorry lads, I found out this morning, that Jan is going to live in Ireland for a few months, I'll

really miss her. I'm going over to Jakes for the night, it'll take my mind off her".
Dan shrugs his shoulders. "Never mind Sam, I'm sure she will find a slick, good looking Irish guy to keep her company". Sam looks angrily at Dan, Russ agrees as they slowly start to walk off. "Yes, one with a great big Irish knob, you'll be no good to her when she comes back Sam".

Sam goes mad. "You bastards ", Dan and Russ laugh and start to run, they have wound Sam up nicely. Sam jumps over the privet hedge, Dan and Russ have now run well down the street, Pauls bike is laid on the footpath as he is delivering the papers. Sam grabs the handlebars, picks it up and jumps on the bike, he started to peddle as fast as he could. As he chased Dan and Russ down the street, he hears a shout, and glances round, he sees Paul waving but can't hear what he says. Sam starts to pedal even faster, he gets funny looks from the neighbours as he rides in his shorts, tea stained white t-shirt and bare feet.

He comes up to a parked car, there's another coming up the road, he pulls on the brakes, but they don't work. He turns into the footpath to swerve away from a car, but the curb is too high, and the bike somersaults, throwing Sam high into the air, he then falls hard onto the ground. Sam lay's winded, Dan and Russ have seen what had happened and walk back, they are laughing as they pick

Sam up. He shakes himself down and starts to laugh with them, he should have known they were winding him up, and he fell for it, hook, line and sinker.
“Ok lads you win “, Dan pats Sam on the shoulder, “It’s like this Sam, Jan will be back, we've got the concert coming up and that will keep us busy”. Sam had forgot, “Yah right, I'll see you next week lads”. Dan and Russ start to walk off, “Ok Sam have a good time “. Sam knows Russ and Dan are good friends and he likes to go out with them, but Jake is different, his cheeky personality attracts excitement, and you don't know what's coming next. A night out with Jake is going to be exciting.

A Night Out with Temptation

Its Saturday, Sam had daydreamed his way through the day, he’s had chance to wash and iron his clothes and had made a fire to heat the water, it's suddenly afternoon and it's time for him to get ready. He has a nice warm bath, pulls out the plug and slowly gets dried, the new grey towel is very small, as he dries his body the towel quickly becomes wet leaving him damp. He walks into the bedroom and looks at his half-ironed clothes on the chair, he's quite impressed with the old iron Bill had repaired, usually Sam doesn't iron them at all. He slowly puts on his tight black jeans, black socks and then sits on the bed, and slides on his black winkle picker boots. He stands up, stamps his feet, they feel comfortable and he feels so smart. Next, his black shirt, as he pulls it tight from the bottom it fits snugly around his slim body. Sam looks in the mirror and feels good about himself, but there was only one thing missing, his girlfriend Jan.

He picks up a twenty-pound note from his old scratched brown dressing table, and puts it into his pocket. It's time for his Brut deodorant, which his mom bought from Marie's across the road. He pours it into his hand and rubs it under his arms and all over his body. It feels refreshing, but as he smells the fragrance, it seems to smell like a woman's perfume, more elegant than manly. Sam shrugs his shoulders, he doesn't mind, at least he smells nice for a change. He picks up his slim black button up leather coat and puts it on, it's time to leave for the train station. As he opens the back door his mom shouts. "Have a good time Sam". Sam looks towards the voice coming from the room, he's forgot to say goodbye, his mind is on other things. "Goodbye mom", he walks out of the house and closes the door gently behind him.

Sam makes his way through the estate, kids are playing football, buses are busy with shoppers, and dogs are walking around in packs. As he walks along he continually thinks about how the day as gone. He walks past the local shops, kids and women stare as three large blue, 1971 convertibles are slowly driving along the street.

Johnny is a front passenger in the lead car and is looking around. Sam gets a cold shiver down his back, Johnny sees Sam and points for his driver to pull over. Sam carries on walking as Johnny takes off his black sunglasses and stares at Sam. "Hey Sam I want a word with you, come here". Sam stops, he then looks cautiously as he starts to walk across the road to Johnny, and stands next to his car. Sam's a little frightened, he doesn't know what to expect. He looks down at Johnny, who's looks as though he wants to uncover a mystery. "What do you want Johnny?", Johnny looks straight in front.

"You lads from the Manor, think you're a set of clever fuckers, coming onto my turf with them Irish bastards. When I find them, I'm going to kill them, I don't know why,

but I feel kind today Sam, so I'm going to give you two choices.
One, I find everyone who was at the youth club that night, the young girl who was locked in the closet, the old man, your young friends, Silver, what's left of him and yourself. We'll torture all of them, until we find out who blew up my fucking car and thumped my lads. Two, you and your cocky mate, fight eight of my best bare-knuckle fighters, no rules, two on two, four back to back matches, no rounds only knockouts. If you win, we'll call it straight, you lose, you tell me what I need to know, and I'll officially be cock of the Manor". Johnny smiles', he knows that either way he will get the information he requires. Sam makes an immediate decision, Sam looks at Johnny, his eyes glare, as Johnny is threatening Jan. "I'll tell you what Johnny, me and Jake will go back to back with your fighters, but when we win, I'll be coming for you". Johnny laughs, he's got what he wants, "I'll choose the time and place, maybe the fight will just happen, be prepared Sam".

Johnny slowly drives off as Sam looks into the open top convertibles, as they pass he doesn't recognise any of the men in there, but there's one man missing that always goes with Johnny on these jobs, which is Soul. Sam wonders where he could be, Johnny's talked about the Irish and is prepared to go any distance to find out who they are. Sam saw Mary going out with her friends on Friday evening, all dressed up, and suddenly they have had to leave, he wonders, could Mary be behind the trouble on Johnny's turf.

The gangsters have driven away, and people start to talk, two women, Shirley and Elaine have been stood near to Sam, listening to what was happening and have heard everything that has been said. People gather round, as Shirley and Elaine pass on the gossip.
Old Ted and Bill the local policeman has been watching and shout Sam over. “Hey Sam, I want you”. Sam slowly walks over the road, “What do you want?”. They've got an idea of what Johnny is up to.

Old Ted wants to help. “Sam I'll train you every Saturday morning, I’ll show you a few techniques I learnt off an Indian Gentleman when we were prisoners of war in Burma”. Sam needs all the training he can get. “That’s great Ted, can I Bring Jake?”, Ted as a half-smile on his face, he likes Jake. “Of course, you can Sam, that’s even better, you two can train together”. Bill the policeman runs the local boxing club. “Sam come down and get some extra training with us, I'll get you into shape”. Sam’s pleased with the support he has got and carries on with his journey to the train station. As his day goes on, it becomes more intriguing, from his girlfriend recently leaving for Ireland, to being set up for a bare-knuckle fight, with eight of the best bareknuckle fighters in Yorkshire.

Sam's stood at Darnall train station waiting for the Worksop train to arrive, he's looking forward to a night out with Jake, he knows they going to have a laugh and for a few hours, put all the problems the Manor brings behind him. The train arrives, the conductor is an old Indian gentleman wearing a turban called Rashid Anwar, of medium build and height, he stands on the platform as Sam slowly climbs aboard. When everyone is on the train, Rashid checks his watch, the trains keeping good time, he waves his flag and blows his whistle. A Pakistani train driver, Jamal, pops his head out of his train drivers window, smiles and shouts. "Come on bandage head, let's go". Rashid puts his two fingers up to his friend, "Fuck off you Paki bastard", and climbs onto the train laughing.

Sam sits half way down the first carriage and is surrounded by Wednesday fans. As they sing their football songs, he looks out of the window and wonders what Jake will say about the fight he has got him into, or even worse, he may not want to fight at all, then what will Sam do. As Sam listens to the Wednesday fans singing, he remembers the incident at the youth club, and how Dan, Russ and himself stood and sang their favourite united song, which lifted them all and prepared them for the battle. He forgets where he is, he suddenly stands up and starts to sing. Kenny and B O, two Worksop skinheads are sat behind him.

"Oh, when the Blades. Oh when the Blades.

B O nudges Kenny. "Have you heard that fucker, he's a united fan, they start to listen, the fans in the carriage go quiet. Sam finds himself stood up with his right arm in the air singing loudly.
Oh, when the Blades. Oh, when the Blades. Go marching in, go marching in. Oh, when the Blades go marching in. We want to be in that number. When the Blades go marching in.

Kenny's not too chuffed. "Bastard you're taking the piss", Kenny grabs Sam from behind, as he puts both hands on Sam's shoulders, grips his leather coat and pulls him backwards over the seat.

Sam his laid helpless on the floor as he put his hands up to protect his face. B O and Kenny start to stamp on all parts of his body. Rashid, the ticket inspector sees what is happening and walks down towards them. "Hey lads, stop now". B O's not bothered about an old train conductor.
"Fuck off old man". Rashid suddenly steps forward and hits B O with a right forearm smash under his chin, B O is immediately knocked unconscious and slumps slowly to the ground. Kenny carries on kicking Sam. Rashid steps onto the seat with his right foot, puts his left for arm around Kenny's throat, the back of his right-hand rests securely at the back of his head. Snatch, and with a quick flick, Kenny's head shoots to one side, he feels an excruciating pain at the back of his neck and down his back, he screams out as he falls helplessly onto his seat.

Rashid is very angry, “Any more trouble from you two and I'll fuck both your arms up as well, now both of you, fuck off”. B O slowly stands up dazed and helps his mate Kenny from his seat, they stand and look at Rashid, he suddenly claps his hands, Kenny and B O jump back, Rashid laughs as they walk off to find their friends. Sam slowly stands up, his forehead and cheeks are grazed. Rashid's is concerned for his passenger. “Are you ok young man?”, Sam’s brushes himself down. “Thanks mate, you sure sorted them out, where did you train?”. “In India, many years ago”. Sam is grateful to Rashid, he shakes his hand and puts his arms around him. “Thanks mate I really appreciate what you have done”. Rashid has a strange feeling and whispers a message into Sam’s ear. “You have a new friend, trust him, he will never let you down, he will lead us in a spiritual war”. Sam sits quietly down as Rashid carries on checking and selling tickets to his passengers. The Wednesday fans have been stood quite as they looked on, usually they would have got involved and helped Kenny and B O, but most of them have met Rashid before, and no one fucks about on his train. Sam is now sat in Kenny and B O’s seat, this has been his second experience of meeting an Asian guy from a different culture, which he now as a great deal of respect for.

The train carries on its journey, Rashid goes and as a word with Jamal, the train driver to let him know what has happened. The train pulls up at Worksop train station,

Jake's chatting to a young girl on the platform as Sam climbs off the train. "Hey Jake", Jake looks around and waves, "Ae up Sam", Jake gives the young girl a kiss and walks off towards his mate. "Who's that Jake?".
"You'll find out in a minute Sam". The train driver Jamal climbs out of his cab, Rashid is stood looking out of the back-carriage door, he points to Kenny and B O, who are holding their head and arm. As they walk along the platform Jamal puts up his hand, he as seen who they are, one thing he hates is skinheads. As Kenny and B O reach Jamal, he steps in front of them blocking their path. "Hey, you, Paki bashing bastards." Kenny looks down at this 4ft 8in tall Pakistani man dressed as a train driver. They both burst out laughing. BANG, Jamal headbutts Kenny on the bridge of his nose breaking it immediately, Kenny bends over and holds his nose, and is in pain as the blood drips to the floor. With a quick shuffle, Jamal throws a left and right hook to B O's ribs, as B O drops his head down, Jamal follows up with a right uppercut to B O 's chin. Crack, B O falls to the ground. Jamal calmly climbs back into his train cab; the passengers are now on the train for the next stage of the journey. Rashid waves his flag, blows his whistle, the doors close and the train leaves the station. It's just another day for Rashid and Jamal, while Kenny and B O have had a train journey they will never forget.

Wolf has seen Jane kissing Jake as they had queued to climb off the train. "Look Duke, Jakes been kissing your

girlfriend". Duke shouts, "You bastard Jake", Jake looks around, gives a cheeky smile. "Right Sam, this is where the evening begins". As Sam and Jake stand at the bottom of the old wooden footbridge the Wednesday fans walk past. The Worksop skinheads walk along the platform, Brady sees Kenny and B O, they are just standing up from the ground.
"What's up with you two lads?", Kenny doesn't want his friends to know what's happened. "We've just bumped heads when we were messing around". Brady looks at their faces, "It looks a bit more than that to me, your faces are covered in bruises and blood". Wolf spots Jake standing with Sam in between the fans. "Duke, Jake's there, he's stood at the bottom of the bridge". Duke spots them and starts to run towards them, his face is red with anger, thinking the lesson Jake was given hasn't taught him anything. "Jake, you little bastard, you're going to die". Kenny and B O have other ideas. "Duke, you get Jake we'll get his mate", the rest of the gang don't know what had happened on the train.

Jake and Sam are getting ready to run, but Sam wants to ask Jake about the forthcoming fight, he needs to know. "Jake will you join me in a?". The skinheads are close, Jake decides it's time to go. "Sam run, the Worksop skinheads are after me", they run up the wooden steps and onto the footbridge. As they run along the top, Sam wonders why the skinheads are chasing Jake. "Why are we running Jake?", Jake as a cheeky grin. "Because Duke had seen me kissing his girlfriend ". Sam's confused, “Why have you done that Jake?”. Jake looks at Sam and grins. “Because I like to wind them up”. Sam’s made the right choice, he knows Jake will fight with him.

They carry on running down the wooden steps, onto the opposite platform for the Lincoln train, through a white wooden spiked gate that leads them onto a gravel car park. The skinheads are in close pursuit, as Sam and Jake run along the footpath next to the main road, they hear the skinheads shout.” BASTARDS”. Jake and Sam laugh as they run past the old Regal cinema. The footpath is closed, there's a seven-foot trench surrounded by three-foot-high barriers. They jump over the barrier and land on the mound of earth which had been dug out. They then jump with both feet together, as they land on the other side of the trench they vault immediately over the fence.

They stop and look back, the skinheads fail to make the first hurdle, as Brady stops his friends crash into him and they fall into the fence knocking it over. Kenny tries the long jump and lands on the far side edge of the trench. The side crumbles and he fall’s backwards into the hole. He looks up, the sides are too steep to climb out. Brady sees Jake laughing at him. “Come on lads, we'll cross the road we can still catch them”. Jake and Sam carry on running, past the Old Vine pub, down the underground steps to the public toilets and along the old beige tiled floor. They see a man and what looked like a small collie dog talking to him. They stop, Sam's amazed. "How does your dog talk mate?". The man laughs, "He doesn't, I'm just throwing my voice, I'm a comedian and come here to practice my show". They hear the skinheads running down the steps." See you later mate, hey what's your name? "The man pats his dog, "Neil Down and my dogs called Gimme". Sam starts to walk off, "See you later mate", They run up another set of steps and stand at the top waiting for the skinheads.

As the skinheads run down the steps, they see Neil listening to his dog, Gimme talk. They all suddenly stop and watch in amazement, Wolf loves what he sees." Wow mate, that's a talented dog ". His friends nod in agreement. An old, Scottish man called, Suk Ma' Cock, (unknown to everyone is Neil's friend,) with a walking stick walks by, with his dog called Some.
Suk throws his voice to Some; the small grey mongrel stops and appears to talk to Gimme. '"Are you ok Gimme?". His friend answers, Neil throws his voice", "Yeah I'm getting bored though, I'm ready for a run, what are you doing". Suk throws his voice, "Just studying tonight mate, nothing special, who's these guys?". Neil throws his voice, "I don't know, can you read their names on their shirts". Somme looks at the skinheads and Suk looks their way. All the skinheads are watching and listening, they've forgotten about Sam and Jake. "Well, we have, Duke, Wolf, Brady, Lez, B O ", each skinhead nods their head in turn, Dukes amazed, "I can't believe it,

your dog is more intelligent than the other one over there, (Gimme) he can read the names on our t- shirts as well has speak". Neil and Suk try not to laugh, they can see their Wednesday colours, and the dogs start to sing a united song together.
"You fill up my senses. Like a gallon off Magnet. Like a packet of Woodbine. Like a good pinch of snuff. Like a night out in Sheffield, like a greasy chip butty. My Sheffield United, come thrill me again".

The Worksop skinheads aren't impressed any more, time to give chase, Kenny comes running up to them, covered in soil, a passer-by as helped him out of the trench. Duke leads, "Come on lads let's go, where have you been Kenny? ", Kenny just shrugs his shoulders. As they run up the steps, Sam and Jake are waiting at the top for them. They run across the road onto the canal bridge, over the metal fence, across the locks and under the road bridge. They are met with a six-foot-high blue water board fence. They jump up, grab hold of the top and quickly pull themselves over, and fall into the waterboard yard. There's an old hand winched crane on a swivel, which was used for loading barges. Jake explains to Sam what he must do. "When I push the crane arm it will slowly turn around, when you're over the wall drop onto the road", Jakes thinking of his friend first. Sam climbs quickly onto the crane arm and stands ready. Jake gives it a gentle push, Sam waits, it slowly moves round, as soon as it is level with the wall he jumps, there's no cars coming, it's a quite road as he rolls and then stands up onto his feet. He walks over the road to the footpath and waits for his friend. As the crane arm comes slowly back round, Jake jumps on and quickly climbs along the crane arm, a loose rope is now twisting around the swivel. It's Jake's turn to jump, and as it goes around he drops to the other side of the wall.

The crane slowly comes to a stop, Duke as seen them as they have dropped over the wall. “Come on lad’s “, Brady Duke and Wolf stand on the crane as B O gives it a big push, it quickly moves around, B O as pushed it hard. As it grows level with the wall, the rope suddenly pulls tight and the crane stops dead, throwing the skinheads off the crane arm. As they fall, they hit the top of the stone wall, before falling heavily onto the road. The crane is now stood. B O walks along the crane arm and lowers himself down onto the road. Sam and Jake have been stood laughing, while watching the skinheads pick themselves up from the road. Jake thinks it’s time to freshen the scent for the chase. “Hey Duke, your girlfriend smells nice”. Duke is stood up against the old stone wall on the other side of the road, brushing himself down as cars are passing by, he looks over red faced. '' Jake, your cards marked”.

Jake and Sam start to run, the skinheads stagger as they give chase. Jake and Sam run into Woolworths, passed the broken biscuit counter, along the side of the clothes department, and back past the stationary items. The skinheads jump over small bikes, manoeuvre prams and seem to get stuck in ques. Sam and Jake run out of the shop and have been purposely slow to allow the skinheads to gain ground, Jake knows a place to hide. "Come on Sam, we've got to try this". They run past Freestone's bakers and are tempted to call in for a cream bun, but there's no time today, they carry on around the corner from Jays toyshop, past Novak's cafe and into the old bus station, the skinheads are now close behind. As they run back out of the far side of the bus station, they come out onto a main road in between the billiard hall on one side of the road, and the Salvation Army Hall on the other. They stop as they hear the salvation army singing, they must make a decision. "Well Sam, what is it? snooker or hymn time ". That's an easy decision, Sam loves music. "Hymn time Jake, let's go".

They see the open doors and they can hear the band playing, they look behind, there's no sign of the skinheads. Sam and Jake casually walk into the hall, there is a band of young musicians sat in three half circle rows, with a young conductor at the front. The band stops playing, the young conductor looks around and smiles, Jake introduces them. "Ok friends, I'm Jake and this is my friend Sam, do you mind if we join in". Tom's pleased, he likes new talent. "Ok lads, there's guitars against the wall, and a cap and Jacket on the coat hangar at the far side of the room". They run over, put on their uniform, pick up their guitars and sit at the back, Jake hears a familiar voice shout. “How is it going Jake”. Jake looks to the right and sees Johnny, the local hand job champion. “Ae up Johnny “. Johnny smiles, his secret is out, but he doesn't care.

Tom decides to have a change of music, “Right everyone, let's play our favourite song”. A young lady stands up, she appears to be shy as she looks down. The orchestra starts to play, *‘My Sweet Lord’*, Jake and Sam start to strum their guitars, the young lady starts to sing, a few friends join in the chorus, she makes Sam and Jake tremble as she sings so well. Sam becomes so emotional he could cry, “Jake, this girl is fantastic”, Jake is lost for words, “You’re right Sam, she sings like an angel”.

Meanwhile, the skinheads are stood on the street corner wondering which way Sam and Jake could have gone, Brady and Duke look at each other. “Brady, I wonder if they could have gone into the Salvation Army Hall, come on let's have a look”.

The skinheads walk into the hall and stand in a line behind Tom, he puts his conductor's baton down and the orchestra stop playing, Tom looks at them. “Hullo lads, have you come to join us?”. Jake and Sam pull their Sally army caps over their noses, and slide down in their chairs so not to be seen.

The skinheads look through the musicians, but they don't recognise Sam and Jake sat at the back.

The skinheads have had enough, it's time for a drink, Duke needs to have a serious chat with his girlfriend. “Ok lads, let's go to the Vine”.

As the skinheads leave, Jake puts up his hand to gain Tom's attention. “Yes, young man, what do you want?”. “Can you play *Shout by the Shangri-Las?”*, cheers went up from the young musicians, Tom throws off his jacket. Jake stands up and walks over to the young girl who sang the last song, he holds out his hand, she looks, “What's your name? “. She looks at Jake with her beautiful blue eyes “. Angella”, Jake gives her his cheeky smile, she feels attractive as she returns the smile. “Angella, can you sing Shout*?”.* She nods, takes Jake's hand and they walk over to Tom.
Sam can't believe how confident Jake is and walks up to join them. Jake reassures Angella, but little does he know, that under that shy character, there's a talented singer waiting to climb out. “You'll be fine, let's sing the place down”, Angella smiles shyly.

Tom starts to conduct the band, the music plays and Angella starts to sing, Sam and Jake join in the chorus. Everyone stands up to dance while playing their instruments. The air is full of musical rhythm, people from off the street come walking in to see who is playing and join in the dancing. The song finishes, everyone cheers, Jake gives Angella a big hug, it's time for them to leave, and Jake gives a fair well. “I like to thank everyone, it's

been great", Sam gives them an invitation. "I would like to let you all know there's is an amateur band competition at the Sheffield Lane working men's club, it would be nice if you entered". Angella stands quietly, Tom fancies the idea. "We'll do that, thanks lads ".
Three girls come up to Angella and congratulate her, as they stand together Tom fancies some more fun. "Ok girls, could you sing for us, *Under the Moon of Love".* As the orchestra plays, Angella and her friends sing, Sam and Jake slowly make their way out. They look round the entrance to the hall and look down the road to see if it's all clear. "Come on Sam, let's go to the Swan on Lead Hill". As they make their way they can hear the Salvation Army singing and playing, they look forward to meeting their new friends again.

It's a short walk up to the Swan on Lead Hill, an old pub known for its rougher characters and planning of criminal jobs over the years. Sam and Jake walk up the narrow, small stone cobbled side street. On the right is the Swan, it has four large stone steps that lead up to a large brown single door, half wood, half glass. As they walk through the door the floor is made of thick, old oak wooden planks, like the ones used on old sailing ships. Half way up the wall, is a small shelf used for placing drinks on, and runs all the way round the pub. Bar stools are left where people have sat and talked. The bar is rectangle, made from old timber and as hand pulled pumps for serving beer, the far side of the bar looks out onto the tap room where people played darts, dominoes and cards. The front of the bar looked towards the lounge and music room, which was painted in a strange pink, with an old battered jukebox, that has been pushed over in many fights, and is now sat in the middle of the far wall. There were two lights set on the ceiling that should have changed colour, but were stuck on blue and red.

Jake walked up to the bar, he is surrounded by middle aged, tough looking men and women, who were stood drinking in their work clothes. Some worked in the woodyard and were covered in creosote, others were builders covered in plaster and cement, which gave a strange body odour and smell to the place. The women were of a mature age and wore short cut dresses and were covered in tattoos, and swore as they spoke.
The landlord was known as Keith, a tall slim middle-aged man, who was very polite in his manor, but known for being a very good boxer in his day. "What would you like lads? ". Jake buys the beer. "Two pints of bitter please mate". Keith slowly hand pulls the beer, two young girls walk up and stand behind Jake and Sam, Sam looks around, he smiles, they smile back. Keith puts the drinks on the bar. "20p please young man". Jake gives Keith the money and picks up the drinks. "Here you are Sam", Jake passes Sam his pint of bitter, with the froth flowing over the top and dripping onto the floor. "Come on Sam, let's go into the music room". Jake smiles at the two girls as he walks past. They walk over to the juke box, Sam puts

10p in the slot and selects the song, *Wonderer.* "'This is for you Jake", they start to mess about dancing to the music.

The two young girls, dressed in blue miniskirts and yellow t-shirts come over and stand near them, Jake likes them, "Are you ok girls?". One looks, "Fine thanks". Jake walks over to them, "What's your names? ". "I'm Kate, my friends called Nicky, who's your friend, he seems quite ". Sam looks at Kate, she looks so much like Jan. "I'm Sam from the Manor near Sheffield", Kate's attracted to Sam and stands next to him as Nicky talks to Jake. "It's nice to meet someone from out of town, I hope you don't mind me saying, but you have a cheeky smile on one side of your face, I love that".
Sam laughs, "I know, it comes with a story ". As they chat, Sam finds comfort in talking to Kate.

They've finished their drinks, "Come on Sam let's go", and Jake suddenly starts to walk off. Sam looks at Kate, "I'll see you Kate, I've got to go". He feels like kissing Kate, and she feels the same. "Where are we going Jake?".
"To the Legion, there'll be loads of Grebos in there".
They walk up the hill and across the car park, where they come to a pub, it looks very like the welfare at the Manor. As they walk through the double door and down the corridor, they can hear *Brown Sugar* being played. They walk through the double glassed doors into the concert room, it is packed with young people, mostly wearing

leather jackets. As they walk up to the bar, they must squeeze in between everyone. Jake sees Buttony getting served. "Buttony, here's 20p, get us two pints of bitter please mate". Buttony laughs, "Fuck off Jake, get it yah sen ", and then holds out his hand for the money. Buttony passes Jake and Sam their drinks, they walk over to Jake's friends sat in the far corner near the stage. People are dancing to the Stones music, others are laughing, couples are kissing and having a good time.
Foxy, Jimmy, Hoggy, Steff and Ralph are sat around a table, Jakes pleased to see them. "Are's it going lad's?". They all look up and laugh, Steff shouts over, "Ae up Jake, who's your mate?".
"It's Sam from Sheffield, he's a warm lad", Steff laughs. "Come on, sit down next to me Sam". Sam sits down next to Steff, and Steff puts his arm on Sam's shoulder, his hands are as big as a dinner plate and Steff looks like a giant. The lads have a laugh as they drink and dance, and the night flies by. It's 11 pm and time for Sam and Jake to move on. "Come on Sam, it's time to go to Dandy's". Steff looks concerned, his mates laugh. "You're not taking Sam to Dandy's are you Jake, it's full of skinheads, you know you'll have trouble in there ". Jake can't help himself, "I know Steff, come on Sam".

They walk back across the road and down the cobbled side street towards the Swan on Lead Hill. Billy is walking up with a few of his friends. "Hey Jake, you little bastard, I want a word with you". He steps towards Jake. Sam, automatically steps forward with a superman punch, hitting Billy on the nose, sending him staggering back. Jake's quite impressed. "Nice one Sam, but he will come again". Billy shakes his head as he walks forward, he's more cautious this time. Sam stands with his left leg leading, Billy throws a left and right punch to Sam's head, Sam ducks and weaves, he steps in with a roundhouse kick, his right leg hits Billy on his left knee. Billy lifts up his leg in pain, Sam brings up a left hook, hitting Billy on the chin, his head goes back, Sam then throws a right hook hitting Billy on the left jaw. Billy falls back unconscious as he hits the ground, Billy's mates stand back, Jake's enjoyed the show ". Nice one Sam ", Billy quickly comes around, but to dizzy to get up from the ground. Jake looks at him, "Hey Billy, have you got a chip?". Jake and Sam laugh, Billy's caught Sam on a bad day.

As they walk to Dandy's night club, Sam takes the opportunity to ask Jake that burning question. "Jake, there's a special favour I have to ask you, and it's very dangerous ". Jake looks and wonders what it could be. "Sounds good to me mate, what is it?". They stop and look at each other. "Johnny's told me I've got to fight eight of his best bare-knuckle fighters, in a back to back two-man tag team. If I win, he promises to leave the Manor alone, if I lose, I will have to tell him who may have beaten up his lads on his turf. I think Jan's mom Mary, may have had something to do with it. I'm frightened for Jan's safety, would you fight with me Jake?". Jake tapped his lips with his fingers, Sam waits anxiously for a reply. “Do you know Sam, I can't think of a better way to pass on a night, when do we fight?”. Sam’s pleased and hugs his friend. “I don't know when we will fight Jake, Johnny will suddenly call the fight at a day's notice. When I find out, I will get my mate Pete to come over and pick you up. Old Ted says he will train us every Saturday”. Jake ponders, it’s an opportunity. “Great Sam, meanwhile I'll train at the Manton Inn boxing club with Terry Moor, we'll show um what us Yorkshire miners are made of”.

Sam and Jake reach the entrance to Dandy’s, stood at the door are two large bouncers, dressed in black suits, white shirts and dicky bows. Kenny has long ginger hair, and Brian with short black hair, he’s the one who always does the talking.
“Are you ok lads?”. Sam and Jake look up at the bouncers, Jake knows them, they are two woodyard men who live up Manton, just up the road from him. Their friends of Keith from the Swan and they used to train together. “We’re ok thanks mate”. Brian gives them a warning. “You know we don't have any trouble in here lads”, Sam doesn't want any. “There won't be mate”.

Sam and Jake walk past Kenny and Brian and make their way up the long narrow stairs, until they reach a young lady sat behind a glass hatch selling entry tickets to the club. She opens the window, “25p each please lads”. Sam gives the lady 50p and she hands him two blue raffle tickets. “Have a good night lads”, and she closes the hatch window. The top of the stairs leads straight into the night club, there's flashing lights hung from the ceiling and it's dark. There's a typical oblong bar, with seating on two sides and the front looks onto the dance floor. As they walk up to the bar the club is full of skinheads. Jake sees Duke at the far end of the bar. “Sam, you get the drinks, Duke is over there, I'm going to make peace with him for tonight”.

Duke stands up straight, fists clenched as Jake walks over, the rest of the skinheads stand and watch. Jake stands in the front of Duke, calm and relaxed. Duke thinks Jake is taking the piss, coming into his club. “Duke, I know it looks like I’m taking the piss, and I haven't learnt my lesson, but enough is enough. I've given up, you've won, can I buy you a drink?”. Jake holds out his hand, Duke’s surprised that Jake as finally given up, but could still be taking the piss, for a pint, it doesn't matter anyway. If Jake has given up, they will have to find some else to chase. Duke shakes Jake’s hand, has they grip, Duke nods, the chase is over. “Ok Jake, I'll miss our chase but one final competition, we’ll take you and your friend on at dancing”. Jake’s smiling, as Sam walks over with the drinks.

“Ay Sam, where in a dancing competition”. Sam shakes his head, it's a fun filled day. Dukes gang have heard the discussion, they're going to have some fun. Duke walks over to Don Man the DJ, a small middle-aged man with long curly black hair and explains what is happening. Don Man looks over at the bar, he sees Jake and Sam stood near two young girls they have been talking to earlier in the Swan." Yes Duke", Duke shouts into Don Man's ear. "Don Man, we're going to have a dancing competition between Jake, Sam and the skinheads, will you be the judge?". "Sure Duke, what songs shall I play? ".

"Play these in the following order ". *Red, Red, Wine, Moonstomp, Skinhead Girl, Try Me Best, One Love.* Play each song twice, first the skinheads will dance, then Jake and his friend". "Ok Duke". Don Man looks through his records to find the songs.

The DJ looks straight onto the dancefloor and will have a clear view of the contest. Don Man picks up the microphone." Ok everyone, we've got a dancing competition, the Worksop Skinheads vs Jake and Sam ". Sam looks at Jake, "What's that all about, I thought you was joking?". Jake puts his hand on his friend's shoulder. "You've got me into a fighting competition, I've got you into a dancing competition. I hope you can dance as well as you can fight". Kate and Nicky have heard what is happening, Nicky loves to dance, and they walk over to Sam and Jake, "Can we join in? we can dance ". Sam and Jake look at each other, Sam winks at Jake," Ok girls you can join in".

The first song starts to play, *Red, Red, Wine,* the skinheads dance in a line holding their braces and are impressive. It's Jake, Sam, and the girls turn, they step backwards and forwards to the rhythm of the music, there on par with the skinheads. Next, *Moon Stomp.*
They jump up and down and dance to the song, Sam dances with Kate as Jake danced with Nicky. The DJ plays *Skinhead Girl.* The skinhead girls dance backward and forwards to the rhythm of the music. Its Nicky and Kate's turn, the music begins, and they twist and move their shoulders from side to side, Jake and Sam join in their having fun. Next, *Try Me Best*. All the skinheads stand up and dance, Jake, Sam and the girls are lost in the crowd and join in the dancing. Finally, *One Love,* Kate dances in the front of Sam as she looks into his eyes, he looks at her and it seems that all his troubles no longer exist for that brief song.

The competition ends, the crowd cheers, both for Duke and Jake. Don Man announces the winner. Well after a very close dancing competition, the Worksop Skinheads win by a whisker. The crowd applaud, Jake walks over to Don Man and picks up the microphone. "I would like to congratulate the Worksop Skinheads on winning, but I would like them to know about an upcoming event. In a few months' time, there is a singing competition coming up at the Sheffield Lane working men's club in Sheffield, I would like to see the Worksop Skinheads there".
The skinheads shout, "Nice one Jake, we'll be there", the skinheads and Jake are now at peace.

It's 2 pm and the club is due to close, Jake walks over to Duke. “Look mate, I meant what I said, I've stopped taking the piss”. Duke laughs, his mates join in. “I've heard that before Jake, but it's been fun”.

Jake, Sam and the girls walk out of the club together, Sam and Kate stand on the footpath looking at each other, Kate really likes Sam, the night as been so much fun, Sam holds Kate's hands. “Kate, I must tell you, I've had a fantastic time and you're a lovely person, but I love a young Irish girl called Jan, who's had to go and live in Ireland for three months. I have promised to be faithful to her and wait for her return”. Kate like's Sam's honesty, squeezes his hand and kisses him on the cheek. She turns and walks away with a tear in her eye, she had fell in love with him.
Sam watches as she walks away, “Hey Kate”. She stops, looks around, Sam runs up and throws his arms around her. “Kate, thanks for tonight, this is something special I will always remember “. Kate looks at Sam and gives him a sad smile. Sam lets her go and she slowly walks away. Nicky and Jake have been kissing and Nicky sees her friend walking away. “Hey Kate, wait for me, see you Jake”, she runs off to catch up with her friend.

Jake sighs, “Well Sam, we've had a laugh, lets walk back to my place”. They both quietly walk through the street, both full of beer and pleasure from the evening. They reach the old Priory Gatehouse, inside, there are old stone seats were nuns used to sit. "Hey Sam, lets kip here for the night, it's more interesting". They lay down on the old stone seats, Jake is snoring straight away, but Sam slowly looks around the old gate house, with the orange street light shining through the arch, he thinks about his first love Jan.

Jake and Sam wake up to the sound of church bells, it's 8am and sunny, they sit up, yawn and stretch out their arms. "What time is your train Sam?". Sam rubs his eyes. "Every hour after 10am Sunday Jake. I'm hungry". Jake smiles and rubs his eyes, "I know a cafe back in town near the bus station, we'll go there". As they make their way, they talk about the night before, throw stones into the river and throw a punctured case ball they have found to each other, catching it in the air. As they approach Novak's cafe, they see a young man dressed in old Victorian working-class clothes, sat on a garden wall playing an acoustic guitar. He begins to sing, *Imagine.* As they walk by, Sam and Jake stop, Sam likes his music. "What's your name mate?" He looks innocently at Sam and Jake ". I'm Józef, the Shadow Man, I've been watching you both for a long time". He looks courageously at Jake with honour." My friend, you are going on a long, dangerous journey, you will take with you, both knights, female warriors, wise men and a lady with two young children ". Jake and Sam feel a cold breeze and shiver. Sam's interested in the young man's singing. "Ok mate, there's an amateur singing competition at Sheffield Lane working men's club, you need to join us, phone up and book a place ". Shadow Man goes pale, "I'll be there ". Sam's pleased, it's going to be packed with young competition, "See you Shadow man". A few yards further and they arrive at Novak's cafe, they look round and Shadow man as disappeared, Sam and Jake glance at each other, but they are hungry and quickly walk into the cafe.

The cafe is small, with only four small oblong tables with benches on either side, a juke box is half way down the cafe, and the pinball machine is next to the window where you walk in. Sam and Jake sit down at the first table, a young girl walks up and takes their order.
"What would you like gentlemen?", Sam orders for them both. "We'll have a full breakfast please, by the way, what is your name?". The young girl shakes her head and smiles, "Elleska, why?". Sam wonders if she knows who Shadow man is. "Do you know who the young man is, who's playing the guitar in the street, just next to your cafe?". Elleska looks at Sam. "No one's been playing the guitar this morning, look, you can see down both sides of the street from the window". Elleska walks away. An old polish man Klimiuk, brings their breakfast through, Sam's been waiting to talk to Elleska. "Where's the young lady, Elleska my friend". The polish cafe owner looks at Sam puzzled. "We have no female waitresses working here today". Sam's confused, "Who took my order then". Klimiuk doesn't understand what Sam means. "You came

up to the counter and ordered your breakfast before sitting down". Sam apologises, "Sorry mate, I must have had too much to drink last night". Sam and Jake scratch their heads. "Oh well Sam, next time we won't have so much to drink ". As they eat their breakfast, it tastes good, especially after a night in the open air. Sam looks at the clock on the wall, it's 9.40 a m. It's time for Sam to go, "Come on Jake it's time for my train".

Sam arrives at the train station, the train arrives, he looks at his mate Jake and shakes his hand. "Thanks Jake, I'll see you again". Sam boards the train, there's plenty of spare seats, as Sam sits at the back of the first carriage he looks through the window, wondering what further challenges life is going to bring him. Jake watches the train pull away, as he slowly walks home he thinks about his friend Sam, and how they have developed a bond. He's brought a new excitement to Jake's life and looks forward to fighting for his friend.

Jake goes on to train with Terry Moore at the Manton Inn boxing club, it's in an old barn next to the pub. Terry teaches him the street fighting style of punching and kicking, he has developed over the years as a bare-knuckle fighter. Meanwhile, Sam trains with Ted, learning martial arts and boxes with Bill the policeman, both preparing for the day they fight for the pride of the Manor.

The Concert

Sheffield Lane Working Men's Club

Its Saturday morning, a few months later, Jan has returned to the Manor, and Sam and Jan are now happy together, the birds are singing, and sunlight is coming through Sam's window. Ring, ring, ring, Sam rolls over and turns off the alarm, on the old double bell wind up clock, he tries to move his feet, but his dog Rover is laid on them, "Move Rover". Rover moves his head as Sam pulls back the blankets, he sits on the side of his bed and wipes his eyes. There's a ruffle on the bed behind him, it's Rover, he's moved to the top of the bed and is laid flat, out with his head on the pillow. Sam smiles as he pat's his dog, he wags his tail and goes back to sleep. As Sam stands at the top of the stairs, he feels excited, Jan as returned home, and today they are going to the amateur singing competition. It's not so much for who wins, but for the fun and experience of the live bands and dancing. He finds one of his shoes at the top off the stairs, he looks down and sees the other at the bottom. Sam walks into the bathroom and has a wash, he looks for a towel, but there isn't one. "Mom, where's the towel? Linda's sat reading her magazine at the kitchen table while smoking a fag. "In the wash basket love". The radios on in the background, there's a news flash presented by Wally Whyton. *"We have just heard from American scientists working for DARPA (Defence Advanced Research Project Agency), on Project Pegasus, at the Curtis Wright Aeronautical Company*

Facility in Wood Ridge, as just successfully teleported a chromonaut to Mars, we will keep you updated with the latest events".

Sam looks in the wash basket in the corner of the bathroom, it's full of dirty clothes. He finds a towel at the bottom, all dirty, smelly and stained. Sam holds it up, shakes his head and dries his face, a quick rub and he throws it back into the wash basket. He then walks down the stairs and into the small lounge where the coats and clothes are usually thrown. He walks over to the ironing pile, which is on the top of an old sofa and looks for his trousers and shirt. He finds his mom's blouse, pants, bra, and knickers, his dad's socks and vest, but none of his clothes.

"Mom". Linda's filing her nails. "What love?". Sam's stood looking at the wash pile. "Where's my shirt and trousers?". Linda blows the dust from her nails. "There in the spin dryer love". Sam walks into the kitchen and squeezes past his mom sat at the table. The washing machine is an old twin tub, Sam opens the lid and sees his trousers and shirt inside the spinner. He pulls out his red shirt, shakes it and holds it up, it's covered in creases, Sam lays the shirt flat over the top of the washer.
He looks into the spinner and sees his trousers at the bottom, he reaches in and pulls them out. Laid in-between his two hands is a small wet ball of his best blue jeans. Sam shakes them out and lays them next to his

wet shirt, he gives a big sigh, looks up at the clock and it's 7.30 a m, he as to get a move on. Sam wonders what he can do, he has good idea, if he irons his clothes they will dry out. He picks up his clothes and takes them over to the table in the lounge, which is covered in plates from the meal the night before. Sam puts his clothes on the back of a chair, picks up the pots and takes them into the kitchen and places them in the sink. He then walks back and picks up his shirt, walks over to the table and lays it between the gravy stains on the old ripped white table cloth, ready to be ironed. Sam's quite proud of this manoeuvre and starts to look for the iron. He looks in the cupboards, draws, behind the settee and under the table, but he can't find the iron anywhere.
"Mom". Linda's sat reading her magazine. "Yes dear ". "I can't find the iron mom". "It's on top of the potato bag dear". Sam walks back into the kitchen, squeezes past his mom and walks into the pantry, he sees the iron on top off the potato bag and smiles. "Ah, found the iron", he's really pleased with himself, all Sam must do now is iron his clothes to dry them out.

He walks into the lounge, finds a socket and plugs in the iron, he then picks it up and walks towards the table, but the cable is too short, and the iron doesn't reach, Sam gives another big sigh. He then decides to pull the table closer until the iron can sit comfortably, and then makes a cup of tea while the iron warms up. Sam goes to the pot cupboard, opens the door and there no clean cups.

“Mom”. Linda’s varnishing her nails. “Yes Dear”. “There's no clean cups”. “There in the sink dear”. Sam knows that, but he was hoping there was a clean one. He walks over to the sink and stares down, there are the plates he as just put in, a small frying pan, and peeping out, are two cups covered in grease. Sam pulls out a cup, he runs the hot water tap but there’s no hot water. Sam moans, but he washes the cup in cold clean water from the tap and dries it with a dirty tea towel.

The kettle boils on the cooker, Sam puts a spoonful of tea in the tea pot, and then pours in the hot water. While the tea is brewing, Sam goes over to see if the iron is getting hot, he picks up the iron, turns it bottom side up and spits on it, but it doesn't sizzle, he then gently touches it with his fingers. The iron is still cold, he checks the socket and it is switched on. Sam knows that the iron is very old, and it may take a long time to get warm. He goes back into the kitchen, picks up the teapot and pours the tea into the cup. As he looks into the cup, the hot water as released the fat inside, bringing it floating to the top. Sam gives another sigh, he thinks that today is not going well, but never mind.

Sam goes into the pantry and picks up a half bottle of opened milk from off the old stone slab, which was used for keeping food cool, he pours the milk into the cup and it immediately curls. He goes to the bottom of the stairs and shouts. Linda’s gone up to the bathroom. “Mom”.

Linda looks in the mirror wondering which lipstick to put on. "Yes dear". "Mom, the milk is sour". "I know dear, it's three days old, I've used the last of the fresh milk".
Sam shakes his head, walks over to the cold water tap in the kitchen, turns on the cold water and takes a drink straight out of it. "Oh well, it's time to iron my clothes".
Sam walks back into the room, walks over to the table, picks up the iron, turns it over and spits on the metal bottom plate. There's no sizzle, he gently touches it with his fingers, the iron is stone cold. He pulls the cord, checks the wire and switch but the iron still doesn't work.
Sam goes back to the bottom of the stairs. "Mom", "Yes dear",
"The iron doesn't work", "I know dear, that's why it is on top of the potato bag, with the rest of the rubbish ready to be thrown away, Sam gives another big sigh.

He thinks about what he could do now and as an idea. "I will ask Bill next door, he will know how to dry my clothes, I can ask him if he has an iron to lend me." Bill is known for being a practical joker, but Sam's back is against the wall and he needs to dry his shirt and trousers. He walks outside and climbs over Bill's fence in his underpants and knocks on his door.
Knock, knock, knock. Bill opens the door, he is short, fat, with a cap aged about 40. "Ok Sam, what are you after?". Bill smiles as he looks Sam up and down, standing there in his underpants, he senses that there may be an

opportunity brewing for a trick. “Bill, can I borrow your iron?”. Sam's first mistake is showing his vulnerability. “Sorry Sam, my mother- in -law as it”, Bill's wife Edna is looking over Bill's shoulder, listening to the conversation, she slaps him over the head.
Sam's desperate. “Bill, I've got to dry my shirt and trousers, I’m going to a concert today, what shall I do?”. Sam’s second mistake, asking for advice from Bill, Bill has a serious face. “Well, what I once did, was to put on my wet clothes and run up and down the street, Sam’s pleased. “That's a good idea Bill”. Third mistake is believing anything that Bill says.
Edna’s not too happy with Bill. “Excuse me Sam I need to have a word with Bill”. Edna points to the lounge, Bill puts his head down, and closes the door.
“What have you been saying to Sam about my mom having the iron, she's only been dead a week and the iron is in the cupboard”. Bill makes out he's sad. “Sorry Edna“, while trying to hold back a smile.

Sam runs into the house, puts on his wet shirt, trousers and shoes, as he walks out he can hear Edna shouting at Bill, but can't understand what she is saying. He walks up the garden path and into the street, and slowly starts to run up and down the road. The neighbours stand at their gates, wondering why Sam is running. Doreen, a middle-aged lady, with curlers in her hair and a fag in her mouth shouts. “What are you doing Sam?”. Sam stops. “I’m drying my clothes, what does it look like”. Doreen laughs,

“I put mine on the line love, or Ide never get through all the washing”. As Sam runs he says to himself “Ide put them on the line love”.

After running up and down the street for 30 minutes in front of a cheering crowd, Sam is out of breath, he stands bent over the wall outside Bill's house, he feels his trousers and shirt, they are still wet.

Bill's been looking through the bedroom window watching Sam run. He sees Sam stood outside leaning over the wall. He walks downstairs and out through the back door. As Bill walks up the path to the front gate, he smiles, Sam sees Bill walking up. “Bill, Bill, I thought you said my clothes would dry if I ran up and down the street”. Bill has a big smile on his face, another victim. “No’, all I said was, I have run up and down the street with wet clothes on to see if they would dry”. “And what happened Bill?” “They did not dry either”.

Sam stretches his arms in the air and gets his breath back, he sits on the wall thinking what he could do and as lost track of time. It's 9am and he hears a, peep, peep, peep. Sam looks down the street, Pete is just pulling up in his blue transit van.

Dan and Russ are sat in the front seat waving and smiling, Sam goes up to the van and opens the passenger door, they both look smart in their blue jeans, black boots and red shirts. They look Sam up and down with a grin, Sam knows how he looks. “What’s up with

you two?'. Dan's smiling. "Sam, your clothes are wet and creased". Russ shakes his head. "What have you been doing?". Pete leans over from the steering wheel, listening intently.
"My clothes were still in the washer when I got up, Billy told me that if I put them on and run up and down the street they would dry". Pete laughs, "Billy, your next-door neighbour, Billy talks bollocks". Sam looks at Pete, realising what Billy has done. "Yes, I know Pete". "They all start to laugh. Pete looks at Sam, with both hands on the steering wheel. "No one believes Billy, he's a right joker, hurry up Sam, we are going to be late".

Sam rushes into the house, picks up his guitar and rushes back out to the van, he makes his way to the passenger side and opens the van door, Russ and Dan are smiling, "Move over lads". Pete's got a special place for Sam to sit. "Sorry Sam, there's no room, you will have to get in the back".
Sam was looking forward to sitting in the front with his mates. "Ok Pete". Dan nudges Russ with his elbow. "I can't wait to see Sam's face", they nod to each other. Pete jumps out of the van and stands next to the back door with his hand on the door handle, Sam walks around the back. Dan and Russ jump out and follow Sam and stand closely by. Sam's stood with his guitar, excited and ready to go. Pete opens one of the double doors, a chicken suddenly flies out past Sam, he jumps back.

“What's that?”, Pete panics, “Quick catch it, it’s one of my chickens”, Russ and Dan chase the chicken as it runs down the road. Pete pulls back one of the double doors, Sam looks into the van, it's covered in straw and six chickens are wandering around.
“Pete, what are you doing with chickens in the van?”. The chickens are stood next to the open van door waiting to be fed. “That's a stupid question Sam, you know I live in a flat and I have nowhere to keep them”. Russ and Dan come back with the chicken and throw it into the van.

Pete decides it time for them to go. “Come on, we're going to be late”. Sam gives a big sigh and climbs into the van, he ties his guitar up next to the others as Pete closes the door. Sam shouts to Pete through the small window that looks into the cab, covered by chicken mesh. “Where's the seat?”.
“I took them out, so the chickens would have more space, you will have to make do with the straw”.
As Sam sits on a seat of straw, the chickens are sat in his lap, or keep jumping on his head, the van tilts from side to side as they turn the corners, rolling Sam out of his straw seat and across the back of the van. A mile down the road, fumes start to come into the van from the faulty exhaust, leaving the air with a blue smoke. Sam coughs and splutters, the chickens move closer to the van doors, which seems free of fumes.

The three-mile trip seemed to take forever, as they arrive at the Sheffield Lane working man's club and pull into the car park, Pete slams on the brakes. "Sorry lads, I can never be sure if they are going to work". Sam goes rolling forward to the front of the van as it skids to a stop. Pete, Dan and Russ jump out and walk to the back. Pete opens the doors, they all look in. Sam is laid on the floor with chickens jumping all around him. "Come on Sam, stop messing around". Sam climbs out of the van, as he does so, he stands upright, straw in his hair and on his clothes, Dan and Russ brush him down. Russ brushes the last pieces of straw from the back of Sam's shirt. "That's good Sam, your clothes are nearly dry". Sam smiles, brushes back his hair, Pete climbs into the back of the van and passes out the guitars. "Make your way lads and get us booked in, I'm going to feed and water the chickens". Dan looks at the chickens. "Pete, what you going to do with them?". "I'll leave the van doors open, they'll wander around the car park, they'll be fine".
Dan, Russ, and Sam walk off smiling shaking their heads, nothing surprises them about Pete. Sam looks back into the carpark he is looking forward to seeing his friend Jake.

Jake wakes up early, it's morning of the concert, Foxy rolls up with the guitars in the back of the van and pips his hooter. Jake walks out of his house and onto the footpath, hair ruffled and stood in bare feet. Foxy wines his window down. "Come on you lazy fucker, it's time to go, I've got some news for you. Buttony's selling his bike if you want it". Jakes pleased with the news, it's just right for him to knock about on. Foxy is about to wind up the window, but needs to do something first. "Here Jake, I want you". Jake walks up, puts his head through the half-opened window and looks into the van, his t-shirt neck is wide open, and the bottom is tucked into his trousers. Foxy takes a draw on his fag. As he holds it with his finger and thumb, he suddenly throws it down Jake's open top. Jake feels a burning pain and jumps back, hurriedly trying to find the fag, but it is trapped down his t-shirt. Foxy's sat laughing, he can't believe he's caught Jake out with that old trick. "Hey Jake, I didn't know you could dance that well, I'll see you at the concert, you're bound to win". As Foxy drives off, he turns on the radio, the music is interrupted with a news flash. "*The American government has announced that as the chromonaut returned to earth through the time portal, at the Curtis Wright Aeronautical Company Facility in Wood Ridge, powerful entities have followed him through. It appears that scientists have been unsuccessful in trying to close the portal and all contact has been lost with the facility. We will keep you updated with any further news".*

Buttony pulls up on his 1969 pink Honda 50, Jakes rolling about all over the footpath, he eventually pulls out the fag from his t-shirt, Buttony is sat on his bike wondering what Jake is doing.

“What are you fucking about at Jake, are you rehearsing for later? “. Jake stands up, covered in sweat, he’s ripped his t- shirt to retrieve the fag end and his covered in grazes from the rough surface of the footpath.
“You ok Buttony, I’ve a question for you?”, Buttony is sat on his bike smiling. “What’s that Jake? “Foxy says I can buy your bike off you”. Buttony thinks it's his lucky day, he's being trying to get rid of this pink Honda for ages. “Course you can Jake, I said you could buy it. I want £20, give me a pound a week and I'll be happy “. “Great Buttony, I'll have it”.

Texas pulls up on his BSA 500 Twin Cylinder A7 with Hoggy on the back. “Come on Jake, let's go”.
“One-minute Texas, I'll just get my leather jacket. He runs into his house, changes his t- shirt, puts on his jacket and runs back out. “Come on Buttony, I'll ride the bike, you get on the back. “Buttony smiles, he still can't believe he's sold Jake the bike. Texas looks on.” See you there lads “, Texas and Hoggy ride off. Jake kicks up the engine, pulls in the clutch, puts the bike in first gear. The bike shoots off with the front wheel in the air, throwing Buttony off the bike. As Jake rides down the street he looks around and notices that Buttony’s not sat on the back, and sees him sat up in the middle of the road. Jake turns around and rides back, he pulls up next to Buttony. “What’s up with you Buttony?”. Buttony looks at Jake, his back and legs are hurting him. “You daft fucker Jake, you threw me off “. Jake laughs. “Sorry Buttony, jump on”. Buttony slowly

stands up and climbs onto the back of the bike. People start to stand at their gates, wondering why two rockers are riding a pink 50cc motorbike.

As they ride the bike down the road, it jerks backwards and forwards as Jake gets used to the gears. When they arrive at the local petrol station, one eyed Brenda is serving the petrol.
"Ae up lads", she peeps at them through her good left eye. "Fill us up please Brenda". Jake watches as Brenda makes three attempts to find the petrol cap, before making another three attempts to get the nozzle into the petrol tank. "Ok Jake that's fifty pence". Jake gives Brenda the money and their ready to go. Jake kicks up the engine, again and again, it doesn't start. They both get off and push, the engine fires, Jake jumps on, Buttony misses the seat and runs behind the bike. "Jake, Jake' wait, ". Jake looks round and slows down, Button catches up and leapfrogs onto the back. As they ride down the road people stare, bikers smile as they pull up next to them, shaking their heads and give them the hand job sign.

It's a long ride to Sheffield, as they arrive at the working men's club they pull into the carpark, there's vans and cars with young people walking around, all with their different fashion and styles.
Jake and Buttony meet their friends and walk up the concrete steps and through the double doors, where they

are met by two mature men stood in a wooden kiosk, taking the bands names. Bernard asks the names, William writes them on a list, they all have a specific job, just like when they are working down the pit. Bernard looks at the band. “What’s your names lads? “. Foxy speaks up. “Where the Worksop Rockers mate”. Bernard as a bored look on his face, he must keep repeating the same question. “And your name's? “. Foxy smiles, “Texas, Foxy, Hogger, Jake and Buttony”. Will writes the names down. “Ok lads, the presenter will call you out when it's your turn to play, just make your way up to the stage, there's specific areas around the hall where you can stand your guitars, good luck”. Bernard picks up the phone and makes a call, William can’t hear who he is talking to.

The Worksop Rockers make their way through another set of double doors, as they walk into the hall, bands and their fans are bustling around and having a laugh together. A young girl casually dressed, is stood in the top far corner of the hall on her own. Jake sees her and walks over, she's dressed in jeans, blue shirt, and is wearing a Salvation Army hat. Another young man looking very quiet was stood near her, Jake was pleased to see her. “Angella you've made it, come and stand with us, “Angella is shy. “No thanks Jake, I'll be fine“, Jake takes the hint, “I’ll be here if you need me”. Jake walks back to stand with his friends, he sees Sam as he walks

into the hall, they've been playing darts in the tap room and had booked in earlier.
“Sam, over here “, he puts his arm in the air. Pete Sam, Dan and Russ walk over and start to chat with the rockers.

Time flies by and the presenter walks onto the stage, it's 12.05 pm, he picks up the microphone.
“Good afternoon ladies and gentlemen, my name is Chester, your presenter for the evening, I would like to welcome you all to the 1974 Sheffield Lane, Working Men’s Club, Amateur Concert. We have sixteen bands. There are three judges at the far end of the hall, Dee, Alice and Gillian. Most bands have brought with them a small group of fans. Anyone can join in the singing and dancing. Each of the sixteen bands will sing three songs. The qualification stages are, the final six, semi-final and final. As you all know, there are no prizes, this is a competition for singing, dancing and having fun. Has I announce each band, they will need to make their way up to the stage, and now it's time to start “. Chester looks at his sheet with the list of the bands. “First up, from the Manor Sheffield, The Pink Ladies”. They walk up onto the stage, Jan picks up the microphone. “Hullo everyone I'm Jan, to my right is Clare and my left Sue, we will sing for you, *Can the Can, Devil Gate Drive and Rock Hard”.*
Everyone gives a welcoming cheer, as the band begins to sing the audience start to dance and join in. The Pink Ladies finish their songs and the audience clap.

They leave the stage as Chester makes the next presentation. "Ok everyone next up, also from the Manor at Sheffield is the Manor Lads", Dan, Sam Russ and Pete. They walk onto the stage and Sam introduces the group, he has feathers in his hair and his clothes are badly creased. "Ok everyone, our songs are. *House of the Rising Sun, Run Through the Jungle and Born to be Wild".* The audience casually listen to the songs, some dance and enjoy the atmosphere, but the Manor Lads seem to be lacking a special buzz in the music. As the Manor Lads finish, they've enjoyed playing and that's what it is all about.

Chester walks up onto the stage, "Next up ladies and gentlemen, Duke and the Royals", Kenny, Brady Duke, Lez and B O. They plug in their guitars, skinheads line up on the dance floor, the audience look on, Chester walks off the stage. Duke picks up the Microphone." You'll know these famous songs, just have a good time and dance". The Royals start to play *Red, Red Wine,* their fans start to dance in line, holding their braces, some members of the audience join in, they like the rhythm. The group lead straight onto their next song, *Moonstomp.* As they play, people start to jump from side to side to the rhythm of the music, singing with the group, the dance floor is busy with youngsters, the song finishes, and people cheer. They start to play *Bad Boys,* the young dancers walk backwards and forwards in line to the beat of the music, rocking their shoulders as they go, their now lined up

across the hall. Worksop Rockers look on, they've got their work cut out to beat the skinheads. As the Royals finish the dance floor is full, a cheer goes up and the skinheads put their arms in the air as they walk off the stage.
It's the turn of the Worksop Rockers, Chester presents the group, "Jake, Foxy, Hogger, Buttony and Texas, "What an act to follow ". The Rockers look at the crowd, Texas gives his opinion as he takes the microphone from Chester and shouts. Bollocks". The group begins to play without announcing their songs, just the same as the skinheads, there's a competition on. The band begin to play *Brown Sugar,* the Manor Lads walk onto the dance floor and start to do the Grebo dance, bending backwards and forwards towards a partner in rhythm with the music, shaking their shoulders as they go. The audience rock to the music, which is followed by *Honky Tonk Women and Jumping Jack Flash.* The audience give a polite applause, as the Rockers walk off the stage feeling proud.

Chester introduces the next group, "Ladies and gentlemen we have the Four Jacks, Karly, (Asian), Poppy, (English) Daisy, (African), Molly, (Irish). Molly announces the group's songs. "Hullo ladies and gentlemen, we will sing for you tonight, *Mr Postman, Shout, and Downtown".* As the four girls begin to play, the girls in the audience immediately walk onto the dance floor and start to dance, it's the ladies' kind of music, the lads look on admiring the young girls and join in.

The group finish and the audience give their applause, Chester takes the stage. "Next up ladies and gentlemen are all Teddy Boys, the Three R, Ron Rick and Rupert". Ron takes the microphone from the stand. "Are we ready to rock", the audience cheer, the three R fans walk onto the dance floor dressed as teddy boys and girls, with long checked dresses. The band starts to sing, *At the Hop,* the audience start to click their fingers and thumbs, while the fans spin, clap, and dance. Next *Jailhouse Rock,* everyone loves Elvis. As the audience walks onto the dance floor, lads take hold of a girl's hand and they dance together, there's only the rockers and skinheads that will not join in. A young man called Steve looks over at Angella and they smile at each other, as people dance in their own different styles and have fun. Finally, the Three R sing *Keep on Dancing*, the audience cheer and applaud, as the songs end everyone is out of breath.

Next up the Silhouettes, Anna, Claire and Maria, an all-black group, sing *Baby Love*, everyone slowly smooches together, a loving atmosphere takes over, Steve musters up the courage to walk over to Angella and says hullo. They both stand silently listening to the music, each hoping that one will ask the other to dance. Maria starts to sing *Chain Reaction.* The girls in the audience start to swing their hips and sing with their arms in the air, the lads step from side to side, the air is electric. The final song, *Momma Said,* gives the audience chance to calm down and carry on dancing, some walk to the side of the dance floor and look on. As the song finished, the audience give a fantastic applause, some shout for more as the girls walk off the stage.

Chester announces the next group. "Here we have, the Bhutto's, Asseem (India), Sabeen (Pakistan) and Chang (Chinese) singing *Bully Bully. The Wanderer, and I'm Into Something Good.* As they start to sing Bully Bully, people in the audience line up and hold each other's arm, stepping from side to side, kicking their legs up as they go. They start to play the Wanderer, this time, it's the turn of the rockers and skinheads and they get up and dance, as the others on the dance floor sit down. They clap, dance around, mess about and are being stupid, all giggling as young people do. Finally, they sing, *I'm Into Something Good*. The skinheads, rockers, Manor Lads and the blue tops dance together, which makes the others who are stood watching, bend over with laughter, their having so much fun.

It's the turn of the Celtic Warriors, Connell, Drew, Rhona, and Charlotte, they play. *Five Hundred Miles, Sweet Dreams are Made of This, and Ob La Di,* the audience chat and gracefully listen to the songs.

It's the turn of the Blue Tops, they walk up onto the stage, Liam, Bubbles, Duddy, and Caspar. Liam takes the microphone, "Ladies and gentlemen, please take these songs as they come, sit back or dance. Their gay friends stand on the dance floor, dressed like the flying pickets, the band start to sing, *Only You,* the fans slowly dance in a circle, Liam's voice echoes out across the hall, the audience quietly listen and enjoy the song. Next *Chama Chameleon.* People sing and dance as they walk around the dance floor.
Liam smiles as he speaks into the microphone. "You'll all like our final song, *Another One Bites the Dust*", the audience sit down. The rockers and skinheads walk onto the dance floor and stand in opposite lines, pointing at each other as they dance, the atmosphere becomes a little tense. As the song ends, they stand glaring at each other.

Chester quickly brings on the Irish group, Irish Heather, Koran, Devlyn, Dorrell and Tam". Quick lads let calm everyone down", the band starts to play, they laugh as they look at the skinheads and rockers, they like trouble and they start to sing the, *Irish Pub Song,* their wearing caps and have their shirt sleeves rolled up, Dorrel is playing the flute. The rockers and skinheads jump up and down, doing an Irish jig, they wanted to fight, but now the rhythm of the Irish music makes them want to beat each other at dancing. Jakes bouncing up and down in the front of Duke, with a stupid cheeky grin. Duke head butts him and knocks him to the ground, everyone laughs as

Jake quickly gets up, slightly dizzy, he deserves it and it's all in good fun. They all start to mingle, the audience stands back as they wait to see what happens. Sam's watching his mate Jake, any trouble and he will be in there to help him. The band go on to play, *Green Ginger* Wine, and *I'm Shipping up to Boston,* there all determined and will not to give in. There out of breath and sweating as the music stops, fatigue takes over from anger, the skinheads and rockers look at each other, stand still, and have a serious face, the audience gasps, some get ready to run away. They hold off for a few seconds and suddenly, Duke bursts out laughing, they all follow, and they walk up to each other and shake hands. The audience are relieved as the rockers and skinheads walk off the dance floor together.

Next up, the Sugar Girls, Candy, Kate and Carmel, singing, *Gypsy Tramps and Thieves, Georgy Girl and Da Da, Doo Ron Ron.* Followed by the Mod Heads, Nathan, Ryan, Jacob and Grace singing, *Telegram Sam, Get it On, Hot Love.* The fans are dressed as mods and casually dance.

Chester likes this next group, their dressed like characters from the *Rocky Horror Picture Show.* "I'm pleased to announce, we now have performing for us today, The Trafalgar's, Chloe, Grayson,

Layla, and Isaac. "They sing *Time Warp, Hot Patootie, and Sweet Transvestite.* Their fans line up on the dance floor, dressed as rocky horror characters, as the Trafalgar's sing, the fans dance to the rhythm of the music, the audience look on swinging their hips, some join in and follow the style and technique.

Chester presents the next singer, "Next up is Steve". Chester looks on, no one walks up to the stage, "Steve please come up to the stage". There's a shout. "Here", the crowd look around, they see a medium built, tall young man with long black curly hair, slowly making his way up to the stage, he walks up the steps and stands quietly next to Chester. Chester looks at Steve", Steve where's your band?". Steve looks out into the audience, their waiting for an answer. "I've only ever sang on my own, except for once at the club on the Manor". There's a shout goes up, it's Liam from the Blue Tops, "We'll play for him." The band march onto the stage, the audience clap in remark of respect. Chester's happy now, he doesn't want any of the singers or groups fail to perform this day.

"Ok Steve, what are you going to sing?". Steve looks nervously at Chester, he takes the microphone. "Under *the Moon of Love, Come on Let's Go, and Dream Lover.* The band begins to play, Steve starts to sing, his voice throws out rhythm and style. Jake, Sam, skinheads and the rest of the audience walk onto the dance floor, clapping and singing. Everyone swings to the music, the judges stand up and start to dance. Chester's rocking at the back of the stage, singing into a broom handle, pretending it's a microphone.

As Steve sings, Come on Let's Go, the audience pair up with whoever is next to them and rock and roll on the dance floor, people dance in the corridors, car park and toilets. Finally, Steve sings, *Dream Lover*, the audience begin to smooch, others stand and listen, all the audience smile with the atmosphere, everyone's relaxed and enjoying themselves.

Chester walks onto the stage, "Our last competitor before the judges make their decision is Angella". Chester looks across the hall, Jake sees Angella stood quietly in the corner, he walks over and stands in the front of her, she's looking down at the floor and appears frightened. "Angella, this is your time", she looks sadly at Jake, he holds out his hand, she takes it, he smiles, and she smiles back." Remember how you sang when I first met you, trust me, I'll be with you". Jake slowly leads Angella through the crowd and up onto the stage. Jake takes the microphone from Chester". Sam, Duke, Foxy will you play for Angella?". "Yea they shout", and all walk up. Sam and Duke are playing the guitar, Foxy's on the drums. "Angella's going to sing for us this evening, *I Know a Place, it's a Heartache and I Will Follow Him* ".
The band begin to play the intro, Angella remains quiet, looking at the floor of the stage, she's stood in her casual clothes and salvation army hat. Steve shouts out, "Come

on Angella you can do it". The audience is silent, the bands stops playing, Angella looks around at Jake. "Come on Angella you can do it, think we are back in the salvation army hall, look out into the audience and be proud, you look beautiful". Angella looks out, there all stood quietly waiting, she takes the microphone from Jake and the band begin to play. She starts to sing, *I Know a Place*. She sings with rhythm and heart, her voice echo's through the hall, which momentarily turns into a cathedral, girls and boys can't help but dance to the music. Next, it's *a Heartache,* Angella is starting to enjoy herself as the audience enjoy the splendour of her voice. As she finishes her song, Jake takes the microphone, "Could we have some male and female singers to support Angella with her last song". She stands still, as the Royals and Silhouettes walk onto the stage, and they stand behind Angella. Steve is now stood in front of the stage, looking up at her, she looks down at him and smiles. Jake and Sam laugh, she's getting confident. Angella announces her last song. "My final song is, *I Will Follow Him*".

Angella starts to sing as she looks down at Steve, he looks up at her from the dance floor, the backing group sing the chorus as they dance. As the song finishes, people cheer, the judges look at each other in agreement, they walk off the stage and Chester walks back on. "Ok everyone, we're having a fifteen-minute break, while the judges make their decision".

People go out into the car park, others stand and chat or have a drink, It's easy for the judges. As Chester stands next to them waiting for the results, they double check their decision, Chester walks back onto the stage, with his list of groups who qualify for the final six. The audience and competitors all walk back into the hall, waiting for the decision, Steve and Angella stand next to each other. A young blonde-haired lady walks in and catches Jake's eye, she smiles as she stands next to the fire exit door on her own.

Chester picks up the microphone, "Ok everyone, we've had some fantastic singers, and now we have the names of the final six". He looks at his list. "Ok, the final six are: The Blue Tops, Bhutto's, Irish Heather, Silhouettes, Steve, and finally", the audience go quiet. Angella holds Steve's hand, he squeezes hers, there's a long pause, Chester shouts! "Angella". Steve jumps up in the air, Jake does a chicken dance around the hall, but Angella calmly smiles as everyone claps.

Chester announces the next contestants. "The first contestant from the final six is, the Bhutto's". They walk onto the stage, Asseem takes the microphone. "Our two songs are, *Hound Dog and All Shook Up",* there's plenty of Elvis fans in the audience. As they walk onto the dance floor, Asseem starts to sing, and the audience rock to the songs. The band finish and the audience wait for the next band to play. Chester makes his announcement. "It's the Irish Heather, singing *Seven Deadly Sins, and Rose*

Tattoo". The Irish songs make everyone jig on the dance floor. Steve's next, singing, *Take it Easy and Runaway.* Silhouette's follow singing, *Then He Kissed Me and Be My Baby, Blue* Tops then play *Walk tall and YMCA.*

The bands finish playing their songs, the audience are enjoying their evening. Chester makes his last announcement. "And, finally, it's Angella". Angella walks up onto the stage, her Salvation Army hat half cocked, the Royals follow her up to play for her, the audience gather on the dance floor, Angella takes the microphone." My two songs are, *I Couldn't Live Without Your Love and I'll Never Find Another You".* She starts to dance as she sings, the Royals dance from side to side as they play, the dance floors packed with people dancing to the music. Chester walks back onto the stage. "Ok ladies and gentlemen the judges are making the decision on the final four". Gillian brings the list up onto the stage, Chester takes the microphone. "Ok ladies and gentlemen the final four are. Steve, Angella, Bhutto's and Irish Heather". Each group will play one song. First up is Steve who will sing, *Pinball* Wizard". The Bhutto's follow playing, *On the Eve of Destruction,* people dance but are becoming a little tired. As Irish Heather play Star *of the County Down*, some of the audience dance, others stand and chat. Angella starts to sing *Locomotion* backed by the Silhouettes and played by the Blue Tops. The audience walk back onto the dance floor, everyone always dances to this song, but the concert seems to be losing its excitement after a long day, the judges make their decision.

Chester walks up onto the stage with an excited grin, holding his list of finalists, he picks up the microphone. “Ok, it’s getting interesting ladies and gentlemen”, the hall goes quite.” Steve is through to the final but Angella and the Bhutto’s have drawn on points and will have to sing again”. The crowds nervous for Angella but the Bhutto’s are also a great group.
“Ok first up is the Bhutto’s”, as they walk onto the stage, they're all smiling and having fun. Asseem picks up the microphone. “Ok ladies and gentlemen we're going to sing *Mony Mony “.* This song suits them, the young people dance and sing, as the band finish, they are given a great applause.
Angella’s up next, she’s no need to be announced, the Worksop Rockers follow to play for her, and the Royals are to back her up with the singing. Duke makes the introduction, “Angella’s song for this evening is *Unchained Melody”.* She stares across the hall and feels calm, she wants this song to be special for her friends, both back at Worksop and at the competition this evening. As she starts to sing, people are frozen and feel a cold shiver, her voice seems to penetrate their souls, bringing a special glow. They all take hold of the girl or boy next to them and hold them tight, some girls and boys start to cry. As the song ends there's a fantastic cheer, that goes on, and on, and on. Duke takes the

microphone from Angella. "Ok ladies and gentlemen, let's find out who's won".

The judges make their decision and after ten minutes give Chester the list, he walks up onto the stage and slowly picks up the microphone, he knows the audience are anxious to find out who's won. He waits as he looks up, people shout from the audience, "Come on Chester who's won? It's time to let the audience know".
"Ok everyone, from that playoff, the winner is Angella", the crowd and the Bhutto's cheer. "Steve and Angella, please come up onto the stage". They walk up together, Angella stands to the right of Chester and Steve to the left, their smiling, they can't believe they've got this far. Chester takes both their hands. "Ok Steve and Angella, your both in the final, what are you going to sing?".
Steve looks at Angella, he holds out his hand in the front of Chester, she takes it and Chester stands back has they hold hands together. They walk off the stage, down the steps and walk into the middle of the dance floor, the audience look on in anticipation. Jake runs over to Chester, takes his microphone and takes it to Steve. "Ok ladies and gentlemen, we don't want to compete with each other, so we are going to sing together, Angella will choose the first song". She takes the microphone, "Our first song will be *Dead Ringer for Love,* I'll need all the ladies on one side of the dance floor behind me, and the men behind Steve ". Angella then passes Steve the microphone." That sounds interesting, is there anyone

who could play our first song? ". The Bhutto's shout out, "We'll play", they make their way up onto the stage. Angella and Steve start to sing their first song as they stand in the middle of the dance floor.

Everyone is dancing, the lads dance behind Steve and the girls behind Angella, their all having a great time. The young blonde-haired lady and Jake look over at each other. As Angella and Steve finish singing their first song, Jake walks over to her, he takes her hand and leads her outside. Angella sees them walking away together, she has a bad feeling and Steve starts to sing their final song, *Bad Moon Rising*. Jake and the young lady walk across the car park and stand at the side of Pete's van, which is next to Jake's pink Honda 50, their surrounded by other vans, and chickens are stood around their feet, waiting to be fed. Pete's left the radio on, there's an urgent newsflash, the news reader sounds very worried. "*The moon appears to be changing and earthquakes are now breaking out all over America. Scientists fear it may be the result of portals being opened or powerful entities that may have come through, which was reported earlier, contact has been lost with Washington and New York. The president Richard Nixon is now on-air force one and American citizens are being told to gather supplies and seek shelter.*

The pope and other religious leaders around the world say these events may signal the return of the antichrist.

Islam leaders say this is the sign for Armageddon. We will keep you updated on any further news "

Jake and the young lady don't take any notice of the news and begin to talk, she leans against the side of the van, Jake looks into her eyes, she looks beautiful with her short blonde curly hair, and exciting smile. She looks at Jakes face. "Before I ask you your name, why are your eyes slightly black and nose swelled?". Jake smiles on one side of his face, she melts, he's so handsome. "It just seems that wherever I go, people want to hit me". She touches Jake gently on the side of his mouth, with her right index finger. "It's the cheeky smile, it will always get you into trouble". She moves forward and puts her arms around his waist. "What's your name?". Jake brushes his hair back with his hand. "Jake, what's yours?". "I'm called Dawn ". She can't help but look deeply into his eyes. Jake puts his arms around her shoulders, as she holds his waist, they slowly move towards each other, as they kiss, they fall in young love together. The sound of Bad Moon Rising playing at the concert becomes distant, as they hold each other tight.

Pete's having a fag and is stood at the fire exit door looking out onto the car park. He sees three white transit vans coming up the main road. Two slowly drive up into the car park and one stops at the fire exit doors in front of him, the third blocks the entrance. Pete looks back into the concert, Dan and Russ see him, he waves them over.

They walk over and stand next to Pete, and see Johnny and another rough looking man sat in the passenger seat, with a large young man driving. Five men walk over from the second van, four walk straight past, and one, Jem Ward stops and stands quietly next to the fire exit door, it's obvious he will be keeping watch, while the other four make their way to the entrance. Wade Barrett stands at the entrance to the pub, while Barney, Aaron and Owen stand in the entrance lobby, office and kiosk, making sure no one uses the phone to alert the police. Pete's a little nervous, “Looks like we've got trouble lads”, Johnny's sat in the van smiling. As he climbs out, he tells his mates to keep watch and stay in the van, he's joined by eight other men who have been walking across the car park. Johnny walks cockily towards Pete, Dan and Russ, as they stand watching their scared, they don't want another youth club experience. Johnny stops in the front of them, a mean smile comes onto his face. “I've had a phone call telling me you were all here today, I thought it would be a good time to finish some business. Where's Sam and Jake?”. The bands and audience have noticed and quietly stand and watch.

Sam's seen Johnny and his fighters stood at the door and walks over, he's been waiting for this day, he knows what it's about. Sam pushes between his friends and looks up at Johnny. “Looks like our day as come, I like your friends, have they come to sing and dance for us, they look that type?”. Jem hears what Sam as said and quickly becomes angry. “Listen hear you little fucker, we'll see how clever you are when we start to fight “. Jem laughs out loud, he knows how good the bare-knuckle fighters are. The hall as gone quiet, some of the audience have walked outside through the main entrance door, past the other gangsters. Johnny and his eight bare knuckle fighters push past Sam and his friends. As they walk in, Johnny walks into the middle of the dance floor and takes the microphone from Angella, she walks away and stands near the stage closely followed by Steve.

Johnny's bare-knuckle fighters make a large circle around him as he shouts into the microphone.” Good evening ladies and gentlemen, I have an extra show for you tonight. A tag team fighting event, between eight of my best bare-knuckle fighters from Nottinghamshire and Yorkshire, who are here to fight Jake and Sam. The prize for the winner will be Cock of the Manor”. Sam looks around for his friend. “Dan, Russ where's Jake?”. They scurry quickly around the hall as the fighter’s pair up. They rush back to Sam who's stood next to the fire door. Dan’s out of breath, he’s panicking, “Jakes not here”. Sam gives a big sigh, “Oh well, a fight is a fight, let's get on with it”. He takes off his shirt and walks over to the middle of the dance floor which has now become a ring. He stands defiantly in the front of Johnny, Sam looks up at him with determination and bravery in his eyes, Johnny looks down at him, he smiles, he’s not seen any fighter look like that before. Sam walks back over to his friends, slim, fit, proud and ready for trouble. Most of the audience have left the club leaving the Skinheads, Rockers, Angella, Steve, Pink ladies and Irish Heather behind. The Blue Tops are walking around the hall, enjoying the excitement and masculinity. Johnny makes the announcement.

“Right everyone, there are four bouts of two-man tag teams, Jake and Sam will fight each team in turn, there are no rules or rounds, each decision is through a complete knockout”. Johnny shouts over, “Hey Sam where's your mate? as he run off”, and laughs. Sam smiles, he knows his friend will not be far. Pete, Dan, Russ and Jan are stood in Sam's corner, Pete’s got a bottle of water for him and a towel they have for cleaning their guitars, Dan doesn't want Sam to get hurt. “Sam, you don't have to do this, these lads fight to kill, just walk away, the Manor will still respect you”. Jan screams at Sam, she’s frightened for his safety, “Don’t fight Sam, it's not worth it”.

Sam's only got two words to say. “FUCK EM”. Pete as found a first aid box and puts some bandages around Sam's hands to protect his knuckles in the fight. Johnny walks around the remaining audience who are now stood in a circle around the fighters. “Ok everyone, I can see that Jake as shit out, he's got no bottle, so Sam will have to fight the contest on his own. My team, first up are the bantamweights, don't forget, each team can tag their partner, but that will be difficult for Sam “.

Johnny laughs, “First bout is Billy Madden and Caleb Baldwin verses Sam”, the pair stand at the edge of the open ring next to their fighting friends. Billy is the first to fight, he's tall, slim, bold and middle aged. He stands in the middle of the ring looking confidently at Sam. Sam stands up and walks over to him, he’s not in the youth club now, he’s trained hard and he’s going to make these boxers suffer. Billy throws a left jab, right hook, Sam ducks and weaves. Billy throws another left hook to Sam's head. As Sam ducks he steps in, puts his left forearm under Billy's left shoulder and elbow, quickly lifting his arm, throws a right hook to his exposed left ribs. Billy drops his guard as he feels a rib break, Sam follows up with a left hook to the side of the head, with a straight right to Billy's nose. Sam spins round with a flying back fist, hitting Billy on his right ear, he crumples and falls to the ground. The crowd cheer, Caleb Baldwin runs over and kicks Sam on his right knee. Sam screams out in pain and finds it difficult to stand on his right leg. Caleb throws a roundhouse kick to Sam's head, Sam blocks it with his left arm, and steps forward on his left leg, with a flying headbutt, hits Caleb on the temple of his right eye, knocking him down to the ground, Caleb and Billy slowly limp out of the ring together.

Johnny walks into the ring smiling, Sam lifts up his right leg, he is in tremendous pain with his knee. Pete and Dan run over to help him onto a chair he as in his corner. Two of the fighters help their friends from the ring. Johnny walks over to Sam," Well done Sam, you're putting on a great display, but the contest will get harder as you go". He puts his hand on Sam's injured knee and squeezes it, Sam cries out in pain, Johnny walks off and makes an announcement.

"Our second fight for the evening is, Jim Hall and Dick Curtis verses Sam". The crowd are tense, Jan's stood in Sam's corner and knows he can't give in. She kneels in the front of him and holds his hands. "Sam, just give it your best, I love you ". She kisses Sam and he smiles. Jim Hall walks forwards, Sam stands up and limps towards him. Jim drops to the ground and spins around with his right leg, sweeping Sam's legs from underneath him. Sam hits the ground hard and the fall takes his breath. Jim jumps on the top of him, pinning Sam's arms down by his side, he brings his elbow down hitting Sam below his right eye, splitting it immediately, blood pours out, Jim hits Sam on the left eye, Sam turns the palm of his hands round, which are now facing upwards, just below Jim's knees. Jim brings his four head down towards Sam's face, leaving him slightly off balance. Sam arches his back off the floor, lifts his hands under the knees of Jim, takes a deep hard breath, and with a ferocious push, throws him up into the air, and over his head. Jim's laid flat out, Sam quickly rolls over and grabs Jim's right foot, he twists and his ankle snaps, Jim cries out in pain.

Sam's still laid on the floor as Dick Curtis runs over, he starts to stamp on Sam's chest. Sam's helpless and lays still for a moment from the pain in his body. Dick drops down with an elbow towards Sam's throat, Sam's already pulled up his arms to protect his face. Dicks elbow comes down, but it is deflected by Sam's forearms. Dick rolls away and stands up, "Come on you wanker, let's see what you're made of".
Sam slowly stands up, his face is badly swollen and covered in blood, his right knee is swelled, and he can't stand on it, the blood from his eyes prevent him from seeing his opponent, Johnny doesn't want the fight to end yet. "Take your time with him Dick, punish him slowly".

Pete runs into the car park in a last desperate chance to find Jake, he hears giggling from behind his van, he runs over and finds Jake and Dawn kissing. "Jake, Johnny's here, Sam's fighting, you've got to come". Pete rushes back to Jan and his friends, who are stood near Sam. "Dan, Jan, I've found Jake, he's coming now". Angella's getting angry, she snatches the microphone from Johnny. He stops the fight, he's heard that Jake is coming. "Wait Dick, don't knock Sam out, I want him to watch as you all punish Jake". Dan and Russ run over to Sam and carry him to his chair. He sits there and is so badly concussed he's not sure what is happening, Jan's crying. "Sam we've found Jake, Pete's going to bandage his hands, and then he's coming in". Angella waves Irish Heather over and they walk up onto the stage. “Come on lads, were going to play and sing for Jake”.

Jakes stood outside as Pete wraps bandages around his knuckles. “Wait until Johnny shouts you”, Jakes smiling, Dawn stands next to him, she wants to know what's going on. “Hey mate, why are they fighting?”. Pete points over at Johnny. “You see that bloke there, he’s a gangster, Sam and Jake have got to fight him for the pride of the Manor, if they lose, Johnny will be the cock, and everyone will have to respect him”. The Pink Ladies are stood near, and have heard what is happening.

Dawn goes into the club and walks towards Johnny, the Pink Ladies follow her, they are interested in what is happening. She stands in the front of Johnny, looks up at his face, and she starts to sing, *My Boyfriend's Back*. The Pink Ladies join in, Irish Heather start to play, Dawn begins to dance in the front of Johnny, the fighters look on, not knowing what to make of Dawn. He waits until she finishes her song. “Well lady, you're a clever fucker, Jake is going to get even more fist now”. Dawn runs back over to Jake, laughing and skipping, no one bothers her.

Johnny walks into the middle of the ring, “Come on Jake, where are you? are you fucking frightened?”. Dick is stood waiting, he really wants this fight. Pete walks into the hall. “Jakes here Johnny, is your lad ready to fight?”.

Irish Heathers know the perfect song and start to sing, *The Boys Are Back*. Pete walks back to Jake. Jake, starts to throw kicks and shadow box, he's getting warmed up, It's time for battle. He walks up to the fire exit door, everyone's jumping up and down singing to the music. Duke, Brady and Kenny walk over to Jake to give him their support. As Jake walks towards the ring, the skinheads follow, the audience part and tap him on the shoulders and they cheer as he walks past. Jake as a big stupid grin on his face, covered in scratches and bruises from previous fights. He walks over to Sam, Duke, Kenny and Brady stand next to him, he looks down at his friend. "Well Sam, it's time to show them what us Yorkshire miners are made of". Jake feels his left and right shoulder go cold, he looks behind and he sees shadow man and shadow woman stood either side of him, their figures are blocking out the shapes of his friends. They smile and give him an agreeing nod, then disappear. Sam slowly stands to his feet, puts his arms around Jake. "Thanks, my friend, I knew you wouldn't let us down". Jake looks at Sam's injuries, a look of revenge comes to his face. "Sam, they aren't fucking with my friend".

Johnny makes an announcement. "Come on Jake, about time you were here, you've done a good job of getting your friend beat up". Dicks stood next to Johnny looking cocky and confident, shouting Jake over. "Come on, you fucking wanker". Dick walks toward Jake, his guard up, cautious from previous fights. Jake walks toward Dick, guard down. As they meet, Jake, throws a furious right punch, breaking Dicks guard and hitting him on the chin. Dick falls back unconscious, Johnny steps in he's not very happy, as Bob Travers pulls Dick to the side of the ring. "Ok everyone, next contest is Tom Paddock and Nedd Painter, my two middle weights verses Jake.

Dawn walks to the top of the hall as Johnny speaks, she runs through the crowd, across the ring, jumps up into the air and punches Johnny in the left ear, as she drops down she runs back into the crowd. Jake laughs, Johnny's not amused. "Who's that Jake?". He smiles at Johnny, he's proud of her. "She's my girlfriend". "Well Jake, when we are done with you, we'll see how much you like her". Johnny feels another blow to his right ear, Dawns punched him again, she's heard what he has said and runs off. Johnny shakes his head. "Fuck it, we'll just kill her". A bottle of coke goes spinning through the air, from the back off the audience, hitting Johnny at the back of the head, breaking, covering him in coke. Johnny looks around, he can see Dawn stood on a chair waving to him, she blows him a kiss, he shouts. "You little bastard".

There's four fighters left, Johnny means to put an end to the fight. "Right lads, it's two on one, nut the bastard, Jake's girlfriend won't think she's so funny now".
Jake stands in the middle of the ring, Tom stands behind Jake and Nedd stands in the front of him. Jake knows what Tom is going to do, it's happened many times when he's played football. Tom runs and pushes Jake from

behind as expected, but Jake uses the momentum to turn into a cartwheel, and as he rolls forward, he brings his right foot down onto the top of Nedd's right shoulder, shattering it. Nedd groans in pain as his right arm hangs down by his side, he turns around and walks away.
Tom runs up to Jake and jumps forward with a drop kick, hitting him on the chest, Jake falls backwards and his knocked onto the floor. Tom starts to kick Jake in the ribs and stamps on his right ear cutting it open. Jake rolls away and Tom lets him slowly stand up. He steps forward and throws two left jabs and a right, hitting Jake above both eyes, causing deep gashes across his eyebrows, his face swells immediately around his eyes, and Jake's vision becomes blurred. Tom steps in and headbutts Jake on the bridge of his nose, Jake falls to the ground, Tom steps over him and looks down. Jake wipes his eyes, he sees Tom bringing up his right foot, Jake quickly rolls to his left, puts his arm around the back of Tom's left heel. He pulls himself forward and strikes Toms left knee, with the palm of his right hand, dislocating the joint and probably tearing both cartilages. Tom falls onto the top of Jake and then rolls to the side. Jake stands up and looks down at Tom holding his left knee. Johnny's stood watching feeling angry. Jake's badly injured, he looks over at Johnny. "Johnny where's your men now?". Sam, skinheads, rockers all cheer for Jake. Jake limps back over to Sam and stands next to him, his face covered in blood and badly swelled, holding his ribs.
Johnny walks into the ring, he's not smiling anymore, things aren't going to plan, but he knows Jake's got his

work cut out. “My last two heavyweight fighters are area champions, Johnny Walker who’s well known for his boxing skills, and Bob Travis, an all-round street fighter”. Johnny takes their arms and holds them in the air. Jake looks over at the fighters, their covered in scars and tattoos, muscles bulge out all over their bodies through training, the knuckles on their hands, swelled, through bare knuckle fighting.

Jakes corner goes quiet, how can Jake beat these two men. He feels a warm glow on both of his shoulders, he looks around and sees Dawn with a lovely glowing, kind smile, he turns around and they hold each other tight and kiss. Johnny and his fighters want to get on with the fight. “Jake, you fucking puppy, I'm going to fuck her when I've finished with you”. Jake pulls away from Dawn's kiss, he looks at her and smiles, she puts her hands by her side. Jake turns around and looks at the fighters, he’s fell in love with Dawn and no one threatens her. Dawn whispers into Jake's ear, “Jake, this is the last time you will fight in this world, be brave, bold and wise, enjoy the battle”.

The two fighters slowly walk towards Jake's corner, Jake's friends all step back, Sam’s sits injured in his chair. Jake closes his eyes and thinks how old Terry Moore as taught him to fight. Jake opens his eyes, as they draw close. He somersaults between them and stands up, people shout, “Come on Jake”, Sam’s watching through his swollen eyes, feeling guilty he can't help his friend. Jake steps forward with a front kick,

Johnny Walker pushes it away, steps forwards and kicks Jakes legs from underneath him. Jake hits the ground hard, and it takes his breath. Johnny stands back as they let Jake stand up. Jake knows he's not strong enough to hurt their bodies, he must go for their joints or throat. Bob steps forward and hits Jake with a forearm smash in the head, splitting it wide open. Johnny throws a roundhouse kick, hitting Jake in the ribs, he goes down on one knee, but remembers what his old trainer taught him. When you look vulnerable, the opposition let their guard down. Both fighters are stood over him, they are going to slowly punish Jake. He suddenly pushes himself up into the air and onto his feet, pulls the palm of his right hand back, and hits Johnny under the nose. He's temporarily paralysed and crumples to the ground. Bob jumps into the air and brings his knee round and hits Jake on the shoulder dislocating it. Jakes falls to the ground, and lucky for him, pushes his shoulder back into place, but it is extremely weak and painful. He stands back up, Bob's furious. He throws a barrage of left jabs and right hooks to Jake's face and body, Jake puts up his arms to defend himself, but most of the blows get through. He staggers back, Bob throws a left and right. Jake blocks them, in a last determined effort, overcoming all the pain, he steps forwards with a right jab, hitting Bob in the throat. Bob steps back as he finds it difficult to breath and goes down on his right knee. Jake steps around the back of Bob, he puts its left forearm around Bobs throat, grabs it with his right, applying the choke hold. His left arm is in agony, he's weak, but he must hold on. Bob tries to pull Jakes arm away, but Jake's determined not to let go. Jake throws himself backwards, to take the fight to the floor. As they fall back, the back of Bobs head, hits Jake in the face, breaking his nose and chipping his two front teeth leaving a small V shape. Jake clings on with the choke hold, as Bob grows weaker he wraps his legs around Bobs waist and squeezes tight. Bob falls unconscious and Jake slowly stands up, Bob quickly comes around and makes his way dizzily from the ring.

Johnny walks over to Jake, they stand in the front of each other, Jakes weak and can hardly see or breath, he's in tremendous pain.
Johnny calls out to the audience. "This is what I do to your friends". He steps forwards and kicks Jake in the stomach, he drops down on both knees, Jakes so exhausted he can't move. Johnny stands over Jake and puts both hands around his throat, he smiles as he squeezes slowly, Jakes face starts to go blue. The audience start to swear at Johnny, "You bastard". Johnny looks over at Sam." Watch Sam, how I'm slowly putting your friend to sleep", Angella starts to sing, Bad *Boy.*

Johnny suddenly feels his right arm being kicked away from Jakes throat, Jake gasps for breath. Johnny looks to his right and sees Dawn stood with both hands on her hips, looking both contemptuous and cheeky. Johnny doesn't know she's had a bad childhood, nothing he could ever do would frighten Dawn. Her days of gymnastics, ballet, tap dancing, netball, volleyball, being a lifeguard and street fighting would all now come into play. Johnny pushes Jake away, Duke runs over and helps him back to Sam's corner. Johnny stands upright like a giant, the crowd all cheer for Dawn. She slowly circles him, her beautiful blonde curly hair hangs down, she smiles as she looks forward to this fight. "Well Johnny, it's time to meet a Langold lass".

Dawn runs forward stepping quickly from side to side, Johnny throws a left jab as she jumps up into the air, she blocks his punch with her right knee, as she comes back down she brings her elbow squarely onto the top of Johnny's head. He wobbles, she steps back, then forward, to the right, left and to the right. She jumps up and throws a forearm smash to Johnny's chin, as his head goes back, she stands still, then ducks to her right, her left-hand strikes Johnny's solar plex, leaving him gasping for breath. Dawn steps back and starts to circle Johnny, he holds up his guard, she slowly stares him up and down, as she steps forward, and then back. Johnny throws a left and right, but it doesn't reach her. "Come on you fucking bitch". But before he can finish his sentence, she kicks him on the right shin, he lifts his right leg, and she kicks him on the left. Dawns kicks are so fast he can't see them coming. She steps in with a right hook to Johnny's ribs, but Johnny grabs her around the head with his right arm, locking it with his left, he laughs. "Now what are you going to do?". Dawn simply brings up the heel of her right foot, and stamps on Johnny's left foot above the toes. He weakens his grip, she strikes again stamping on Johnny's right foot. She grabs hold of his right wrist, twists it round, steps forward pulling his arm straight, his elbow resting just over her shoulder. He rolls towards her, she drops down on her knees, Johnny as to follow his arm or it will break, she bends down towards the floor, throwing Johnny through the air, she's practiced this many time's as a kid. Dawn, keeps hold of Johnny's hand, and twists his wrist as he lays on his left side. She puts her left leg over his right elbow, pulls his arm back, snapping it on the joint, she rolls away, and watches Johnny slowly stand up.

Dawn's on a mission as she walks over to Sam. "Sam, I need that chair". Jan helps Sam stand up, she picks up the old wooden chair and breaks it on the floor, picks up two of the chair legs and walks over to Johnny. He's groggy, but not going to give in. "Well Johnny, this fight is for the Cock of the Manor". He throws a left jab, she steps back and hits his arm with a chair leg. He pulls his right arm back to guard his body, but can't hold it up. Dawn looks at Johnny, he's weak, bruised, arms hanging down by his side, she gives him time to feel, and experience the pain, he had so brutally given to others. She looks over at Jake and Sam, their badly injured. Dawn looks back at Johnny, she slowly steps forward with caution, and reigns down a barrage of blows with the chair legs, hitting Johnny all over his arms, face and body, he's covered in blood, as he struggles to stand. She quickly crouches down and hits him on the right and left knee, his defence his useless, and he slowly falls face down to the ground.

Dawn stops, stands up, draws back her chair legs, holds them over her shoulder and looks at Johnny on the floor. He looks up at her, wondering who this girl could be. Dawns got a warning for Johnny. "If I ever hear about you coming to the Manor again Johnny, I'm coming for you". She hits him on the forehead and he fall's unconscious.

Dawn stands in the middle of the ring, covered in Johnny's blood, looking like she's just been in a major bar brawl. She looks over at Johnny's bare-knuckle fighters, walks over to them, she stops. "Boo", they all jump back. Dawn walks back over to Jake smiling, they hold each other tight. Everyone cheers as the fighter's stagger away, while carrying Johnny back to their vans. They've fought and lost, a deal is a deal, they're not coming back.

Chester takes the stage, "Well everyone what a fantastic day, we've both sung and fought. Let's have a final cheer for Dawn, Jake and Sam". They stand in the middle of the dance floor, Jake and Sam hold Dawn's arms in the air, Jake shouts Chester over and gives Jake the microphone. "Thanks everyone, but it's time for me and Dawn to say goodbye". The audience grow sad, Jake

hugs Sam. “Sam, it's time for me and Dawn to make our way, look after yourself my friend”. Jake turns around, take’s Dawn's hand, and they walk out of the club together, the audience walk out to see them off. Jake and Dawn walk over to his pink Honda 50, Jake holds the handlebars and tries to kick it up, but it won’t start. Duke walks over.
“Come on Jake, you and Dawn sit on your bike and I'll push you”.

Jake sits on the bike, Dawn sits on the back and holds his waist. Duke gives them a great push, the bike starts up and they slowly ride out of the carpark. Jake and Dawn hold up one arm and wave, but don't look back, Duke salutes Jake. “Good luck, you cheeky bastard”. A sad tear comes to his eye as they slowly ride away.

Jake and Dawn ride down the road, the full moon starts to go blood red, the sky begins to darken, the earth shakes. As they look to their right, they see shadow man on a Triumph Bonneville 650 cc T126, to their left is shadow woman, riding a Royal Star 500cc BSA A50.
Lighting strikes, people and places become hazy, fire suddenly lights up the sky, and then there is a sudden blackness. Jakes not frightened, and Dawn looks around enjoying the new excitement. “Hold tight Dawn, looks like we are going on a new adventure”, they laugh as the world goes silent.